Free Bird

Free Bird

GREG GARRETT

KENSINGTON BOOKS
http://www.kensingtonbooks.com

KENSINGTON BOOKS are published by

Kensington Publishing Corp.
850 Third Avenue
New York, NY 10022

All Kensington titles, imprints and distributed lines are available at special quantity discounts for bulk purchases for sales promotion, premiums, fund-raising, educational or institutional use.

Special book excerpts or customized printings can also be created to fit specific needs. For details, write or phone the office of the Kensington Special Sales Manager: Kensington Publishing Corp., 850 Third Avenue, New York, NY 10022, Attn: Special Sales Department. Phone: 1-800-221-2647.

Library of Congress Card Catalogue Number: 2001091611
ISBN: 0-7582-0139-7

First Printing: March 2002
10 9 8 7 6 5 4 3 2 1

Printed in the United States of America

TINA MARIE

Love loves what it loves.
What else can it do, being love?

Free
Bird

Prologue

"Ramblings around the River," by Sister Euless
—From *The Graham Star*, April 22, 1991

It has been a sad week along the river. Our family is so grateful to all of you for your outpouring of sympathy and support following the horrible accident that took the lives of my nephew Clay's wife, Anna Lynn, and son, Ray, in Washington, D.C. Your calls and visits have been a bright spot in this dark time. Ellen says, please, no more food. The freezers are full, and Clay isn't eating just now.

Clay has taken leave from his law practice and returned to Robbinsville to spend some time in the bosom of his family. Pray for us all, for him especially. As you can imagine, he is— we are, all of us—heartbroken. Ashes to ashes, dust to dust. But the Good Book also says that we will rise again to be with Him in glory. There will be a new heaven and a new earth and all our pain and sorrow will fade like darkness at dawn. You all know my favorite song, "I'll Fly Away," how some bright morning we'll all fly away home to God's celestial shore.

I'll return to happier news next week, God willing.

"Ramblings around the River," by Sister Euless
—From *The Graham Star*, June 7, 2000

Well, it's been a busy week down along the river. Alma Jean Shepherd came home from the hospital in Asheville Tuesday. She and Clarence say thanks for all the nice casseroles and desserts neighbors and church have brought. The freezer is full, Clarence says, but he's hard at work making more room.

Charlotte and Glennis McDowell put up sweet pickles last week. Over fifty jars between them. This hot weather has sure been good for cucumbers and okra. Brother Carl Robinson says his tomatoes are the biggest and sweetest he's ever seen. Drop by the parsonage and take a look over the back fence.

Little League baseball is taking up a lot of time for the Al Hartley family, since Tim, Tommy, and Al Jr. are all playing this year. Al says he and Nan need to hire some extra parents just to get the boys to practice.

David and Joanne Carver returned from a trip to Europe, the honeymoon trip they have been putting off for years. Good for them! I guess you'd call it a second honeymoon, since they spent a week in Myrtle Beach the first time they got married. Joanne says people in France were much nicer than she expected, and David says he saw Prince Charles outside Westminster Abbey. Drop by to see pictures, they say.

My nephew Clay Forester and Otis Miller took their act on the road last week to Greenville, South Carolina. The band played four shows and sang for a lot of our men and women in uniform. They're a regular USO, I guess you might say. Next week finds them in Charlotte. Do pray for them as they return late at night.

The azaleas are so beautiful this year. God shows his love for us in every season and in every passing day:

> *Wherever you go and whatever you do,*
> *Always remember that Jesus loves you.*

See you next week.

1

Here is how I woke on that Monday morning, the way in fact I always woke up in those days: by nine A.M., never later, someone started banging on the old upright piano downstairs in the parlor. There was no soothing prelude, none of that tuning you might get with an orchestra or two guys with guitars. Just thundering chords, then one, two, or three aging voices aimed my direction in gospel song. On that morning, it was Aunt Sister playing, and the song was "The Old Rugged Cross." I knew it was Aunt Sister by the rolling boogie-woogie left hand. She had not knowingly played boogie-woogie in fifty years, it being one of the bygone pleasures of her sinful youth, but nonetheless it got into her blood and still sneaked out where you might least expect it. Consequently, I liked her play better than the more formal chording of my mother and Aunt Ellen, although gospel piano is no humane way to wake up a man no matter who is doing it.

My name is Clay Forester, and in those days you did not have to know me very long or very well to see that I was a mess in just about every way a man could aspire to those depths. Even my stepfather, Ray Fontenot, who loved me as his own, used to drape an arm over my shoulder, draw me close, and tell me confidentially, "You know, son, you are a sorry excuse for a human being." I understand that this was his gruff way of expressing his love; I also know he was serious as a heart attack.

I used to be a lawyer like Ray, a pretty good one, in fact. But that was in the past. At the time I am telling you of, I played guitar and sang in a four-piece bar band called Briar

Patch that played all over the Carolinas. The name came from the B'rer Rabbit story, I think. None of us could remember. Briar Patch was not even a very good band, which I had to admit to myself so that I didn't get delusions, as apparently I am genetically predisposed to do. We covered other people's tunes, mostly, things we all liked and I could sing: Springsteen, Roy Orbison, John Mellencamp, Tom Petty, the usual classic rock stuff. Some Stone Temple Pilots, Semi-Sonic, Vertical Horizon, Goo Goo Dolls for the youngsters. We aspired to ska, reggae, and our own songs, but hell, we'd been known to break out Elvis and Carl Perkins in venues where the crowd threw bottles, which happened more often than I'd like to admit. It's hard to be faithful to your art when you play in the kind of places where chairs break over men's skulls and women throw beer on each other and it's a virtual lock that one or more drunken hillbillies will start screaming "Free Bird, Free Bird" until you break down and play some Skynyrd. Christ Almighty, I hate that song.

So that was my life. I once had larger aspirations, but about ten years before the time of which I speak, I suffered what I guess you'd call a personal setback, and I did not rebound from it. Or rather, I did rebound from it, but in wholly unexpected and unhealthy ways: back to my childhood home, to my old room, to a bizarre existence surrounded by old women who thought somehow that everyday life was a fitting excuse to sing praise.

Aunt Sister—Eula Mae was her given, but being she's the youngest, she grew up being called "Sister," and so there she was, sixty-some years old without a proper name to call her own—anyway, Aunt Sister switched over now to a rollicking "Onward Christian Soldiers," so I rolled out of bed, planting my feet on the floor with a reverberating thud so that the women could relax a little. They seemed to take the project of my continuing salvation seriously. Besides Aunt Sister, the women were my mother and Miss Ellen, the oldest and the scariest of the three. She was over seventy, but she still played piano at the Grace Tabernacle in Robbinsville. My mother played organ across from her most Sundays, except when she felt her life was being threatened by some new ailment, and on those occasions one of those Adams women from out Yellow Creek Road—not the ones on Talluah Road—would do their best to fill her heels. The week before, she had in fact been bedridden with colon cancer, although by Monday it was apparently far enough along into remission that she could join her sisters on the back porch to rock and shell peas and sip moisture-beaded Coca-Colas and act scandalized by my backsliding ways.

Don't misunderstand me. They were lovely Christian women, kind to children, generous to the poor and colored. But it is also true that they were capable of drawing and quartering a man with the silken strands of their words. My stepfather, Ray, in fact had moved out fourteen years before the time of which I speak, an act of sanity for which I admired him greatly, although he and my mother were still married and maintained a better relationship than most couples that I had known, my late wife and me included. He escaped; I stayed on in that household of women because I did not know where else to go, or how to live, or what to do with myself, because as I'm sure you recall, I was a sorry excuse for a human being.

I pulled on a Springsteen tour T-shirt, a pair of ratty Levi's, and my Birkenstocks, splashed some water on my face, then tramped clown-footed down the stairs so they couldn't pretend they didn't hear me and look up with badly acted surprise from some innocent conversation about my shortcomings.

"Morning," I called out as I entered the kitchen. I opened the fridge and spent a few minutes looking through it and ignoring the food already sitting at my place at the table.

"I made you some hotcakes," my mother said from the doorway to the parlor, her voice as soft as room-temperature butter. "I don't suppose they're any good now."

"Thanks, Momma," I managed to say, and I sat down to a lukewarm stack of buttermilk pancakes. She—Evvie Forester Fontenot— sat down across from me, and my eyes confirmed what my nose already knowed—that she had been to the beauty shop that morning for frost and curls. I cut and speared my first bite, poured a little more Aunt Jemima, and

took another as Aunt Sister started up with "In the Garden."
Miss Ellen was probably knitting: I heard her humming dis-
tractedly, then singing the end of each line before the two of
them struck up the chorus in harmony, something like this:
    "Hmmmmm Hmmmmm alone
    Hmmmmm Hmmmmm roses."
    I chewed my aging pancakes reflectively. That was what my
mother's love tasted like: sweet, sticky, and stale. Hard to
swallow. It clogged my chest and sometimes made me gasp for
air. I took a long glug of orange juice, sour now after the
syrup, and then my mother cleared her throat, her opening to
edged conversation.
    "What time did you get in, Clay?" Momma asked without
looking up from her hands—she had gotten her nails done
too, but I could see she was not crazy about the color, peach
or coral or some such thing.
    "Late," I said. "We played our first night at a club in
Charlotte, had to drive half the night to get back."
    "What'd you make? I suppose it was enough to justify
playing the Devil's music on the Lord's Day?"
    "Five hundred. Split five ways, less gas, less stitches for Otis."
    "Sweet Jesus preserve us," she said, although it was strictly
pro forma alarm, since she did not bring her hand to her chest
as she would for moments of genuine distress. "Where at this
time?"
    "Right smack in the middle of his forehead." I drew a line
over my eyebrows with my finger. "Twelve stitches. He closes
his eyes, he looks like a cyclops."
    She couldn't help laughing, and she hated herself for it. She
did not approve of my life, but she was ever a sucker for a
punch line. That must have been how my father won her; I
heard that he was a funny man, even if he wasn't worth a
damn in any other respect.
    "You ought not to keep a drummer around that can't stay
clear of those kinds of things," she said, trying to stop laughing and be solemn and motherly. "That Otis is trouble. I've
been telling you for years."
    "Yes, ma'am." Twenty-five years, at least. I used to go over
to Otis's house in fifth grade to spin records, the beginning of

her long train of rock-and-roll resentment against Otis, although after his mother died when we were in seventh grade—and to her eternal credit, since my mother is a closet racist, and Otis is the blackest of my friends, from the top of his modified 'Fro to the bottom of his Lenny Kravitz conquistador boots—my mom used to take food over and take Otis out shopping every August for school clothes.

From the time we were fifteen Otis and I put together garage bands that played pizza parlors and private parties. And when we were seventeen we put together a band that played "Stairway to Heaven" and "Layla" at a church talent show in Asheville, a band that in fact was chased off the stage and all the way to the boys' restroom by a throng of shrieking junior high girls, like something out of *Hard Day's Night* or something. What they would have done if they had caught us I will never know; all the same, I looked around daily for something that could compare to the surreal adrenaline rush of that moment.

Momma was waiting for my response, though, so I picked up in the present. "A good drummer is hard to come by. If he was just a bass player, now . . ."

She gave me an acidulous look of disapproval, but if she really knew me, she'd know that I didn't need to be lectured about alcohol and self-destruction. Since my personal setback, I hadn't so much as taken a swig of beer. When we were on stage, I sipped at a Dr. Pepper, and if I happened to see a fight brewing in front of us, I unplugged my guitar and just walked away.

There's enough pain and heartache in this life without having to go looking for it.

When I said earlier that Ray Fontenot was my daddy in all but name, I was alluding to some of that heartache, which starts early and, I suppose, doesn't let up until you die. Here it is, for what it's worth: My real father, Steve Forester, a.k.a. Steve Forrest, left us when I was still in diapers to try his luck in Hollywood. He couldn't get his car to start—it was a 1961 Triumph that Momma said he spent near as much time pushing as driving—and Momma was screaming at him and throwing things, so he abandoned it, boarded the bus to

Asheville, and then headed west from there. The car was about all he left behind, and it was about as worthless as he was: Ray and I had been trying to get that car to run for nigh on ten years and nary a peep did we hear.

He never came back, but he did write us three letters, coinciding with his three major speaking parts. In the first, he wrote about how he thought he'd be able to bring us out there shortly. In the second, he said things were harder then he ever imagined. In the third, he didn't say much beyond he wished he'd never come. There wasn't a fourth letter that I know of. No one knew what happened to him after that, and after Momma had people look for him without any luck, she had to have him declared legally dead eight years later to marry Ray. He dropped out of sight, and sometimes even out of mind, if a missing father can ever truly be called missing. And then late one night I was watching that cable show, you know the one where the guy and his little robots make fun of bad movies, and lo, there it was: *Mission to Mercury,* his starring role, in all its B-movie glory. And there he was: my dad, the so-called Steve Forrest, a dimple-jawed Rock Hudson lite done up in cheap spaceman duds. The pounding in my chest was a strange mixture of awe and embarrassment, something like Hamlet at last tracking down his daddy's ghost and finding him in a pair of Goodwill overalls.

"Momma," I called back into the house when he came on screen. "Momma, come quick."

Within seconds, she ran down the hall toward me, slippers flopping, clutching her robe about her throat. "Is the house on fire?"

"It's Daddy," I said, and I pointed to the TV. "Isn't it?"

She squinted at the screen, padded right up to the set, dropped her hands to her sides, and shook her head like she couldn't believe it. "Yes, that is your daddy." She stood for a moment more before letting out a long breath. "My God, he looks silly. And what are those things at the bottom of the screen?"

"They're robots," I said. "They're making fun of Daddy. Apparently he was one of the worst actors in the history of . . . history, I guess."

"Clay Forester," she said, and she whirled on me, "if you can't say something nice about somebody I'd thank you to keep your mouth shut." She watched my father for another moment as he piloted his cardboard spacecraft toward strange and unknown lands. Then she started bawling, which brought the rest of the house to life just as the show went to commercial.

Miss Ellen, of course, was first to arrive and take stock of the situation. "Young man," she said, exhaling frost at me, "you should be ashamed."

"I am," I told her. "Pretty near all the time."

But then the show came back on and some order was restored, explanations tendered and accepted. We settled back to watch as my father made contact with the surprisingly shapely female inhabitants of Mercury, and on one of the commercial breaks, I heated up some microwave popcorn and passed it around. It seemed to be an occasion of some sort.

"He was a handsome man," Aunt Sister offered at length.

"He always was that," Miss Ellen said. "Although it's clear now he couldn't act his way out of a paper bag. *Carousel* gave him the big head, I suppose, he was awful good in that, but whatever made him think people would love him just as much in Hollywood, I will never know."

"I do not like those robots," my mother said, and that was the last I knew about my father until Ray called while I was sitting there that Monday morning eating pancakes.

"Your mother wants me to talk to you about something," he said, his voice apologetic. "Come for lunch?"

"Gladly," I said. "But Ray, my mother is less than four feet away from me." I put my hand over the receiver and leaned forward. "Momma, what do you want Ray to tell me?"

"Oh," she said, looking her nails over again, "this and that."

I stifled the urge to blaspheme, and instead released my most piteous sigh. Two could play that game. "All right, Ray. Barbecue?"

"You bet," he said. "See you in a few, son."

I hung up and tried without success to get my mother to meet my gaze. I never realized that fingernails could be of such all-consuming interest. My aunts were singing "I'll Fly Away," the second hand on the stove clock was moving in distinct and separate clicks, and at last she got up to clear my plate.

"Well," I said. "I guess I'll get around. Go see what the old man wants. I'm sure it's important."

She paused with her hands in the dishwater, looked over her shoulder, and delivered her usual parting: "Clay, you really ought to get married again. Settle down. Take up your work. Make a real life for yourself." There was a new urgency in her voice that morning, almost a tremble for some reason I couldn't fathom; I didn't perceive that I was noticeably more distressing or distressed that morning than in weeks, months, years past. Still, I'd reached the point where I just nodded my head in agreement when she said it—nodded because it was true, all true, everything she said, and I knew it the way I knew I ought to love my country, worship my God, support my local sheriff.

"Yes ma'am," I said softly. "I surely should." And I went off to find some clothes that a man could wear without embarrassing his stepfather.

Ray and I were always the only white customers in Dolly's, which was as it ought to be. The fewer white people the better; we'd just ruin it with Elvis knickknacks and combo platters and plastic sporks, the most useless utensil on God's green earth. Bobby Blue Bland and Muddy Waters were playing on the jukebox, and barbecue here was brisket so tender it fell apart in your mouth, served on wax paper with Wonder bread, onions, and sliced dill pickles. The sauce came in plastic cups, and it was as hot and sweet and musty as love in a backseat.

I'd eaten most of my food. We'd been making small talk on North Carolina basketball and other such essential topics, and I was beginning to eye the cherry cobbler when Ray cleared his throat. Unlike my mother, Ray never cleared his throat for pleasure, so I knew that either he was choking or this was truly serious business.

"Son, your mama got a telephone call last night from Santa

Fe, New Mexico," he said, and he looked up from the table to watch how I would receive his news. "It's about your daddy."

All the meat I'd ingested became an iron lump in my stomach. "I hope to hell he doesn't think he's coming home after all this time," I said. "That train has left the station."

"No, son. He's dead. Died yesterday. The funeral's in New Mexico Friday."

Etta, our waitress, came over to see if we wanted cobbler, and I have to tell you, even with that bombshell dropped we nodded our heads at her. It was that kind of cobbler.

"So I thought since you'd need to go to the funeral—"

"Like hell, Ray," I said, then caught myself. "That man in Santa Fe was no more my father than Etta here."

"And I sho ain't no man's father," she said, slapping our bowls of cherry cobbler down in front of us. And that's for certain; her bosom weighed more than my entire body.

"You're my father, Ray, the only one I've ever had. You took me in; you raised me; you did your best to make me a good man. I don't have a father in New Mexico. Case closed."

He smiled sadly in appreciation. "Still, son, the last thing that man did was ask for you. He made a mistake, sure, and it was a big one, but—"

"He should have thought of that a long time ago." I took a bite of that crust, golden and buttery and coated with the cherry filling. "He left his family. And he never cared what happened to us after he left. No Christmas cards. No birthday cards. No hey I'm still alive cards. Good riddance, I say. Tell me that he burned to a crisp in those wildfires around Los Alamos and I'll be a happy man."

B.B. King and Lucille took up "The Thrill Is Gone," and I closed my eyes and shook my head in time to the music. I didn't want to talk about it anymore.

"Damn, son, " Ray said after a verse and a chorus. "I can't believe you're making me say this."

I opened my eyes. His face was red as his cobbler. "Well, spit it out, old-timer," I said. "I'm a busy man."

He took a good look down at the table, rubbed at a spot of

barbecue sauce there, cleared his throat. "Son, I don't believe in signs. You know that. It's a bone of contention between me and your momma, if you don't mind my saying so. Unlike some folks, God does not deign to speak to me in an audible voice and remind me to take out the trash. But yesterday, something happened."

I spooned my last bite, pushed my bowl away from me, arched an eyebrow, and waited. He looked up at me, his gaze dropped immediately, and he went on.

"I had some time on my hands last night, so I went out and put that head gasket on your daddy's car."

I nodded. "The one that came in last week. I still need to pay you for that."

"Yes, you do. But that's not what I want to tell you. I put the gasket on. I got everything tightened down. I hooked up the battery. And then I turned the key and she started."

I swallowed my last bite of cobbler and sat up straight. "You got the Triumph started?"

"I did. And she kept running. And started up again when I turned her off." He shook his head and pursed his lips, like he didn't know what to think. "We've been working on that car for ten years." He looked around, maybe to see if there was some way he didn't have to say this. "Son, don't you think it means something that last night of all nights, his car comes back to life?"

"You're scaring me now," I said. "Not with your haunted car story. But you are scaring me."

"It's got to mean something, son. Don't you think?"

I sat up straight and looked him in the eyes. "Ray, I don't care if that man's ghost walks in the door over there and starts singing 'Fever.' " Ray was a big fan of Peggy Lee. "He was not my father. You are. I'm not going to Santa Fe tonight, tomorrow, or ever. That whole damn state is on fire, anyway. Plus I've got a show tonight. And tomorrow night. And the next night. I couldn't go if I wanted to. Plus I don't want to. Can I be any more explicit?"

Ray sighed and shook his head. "No, son. I said what I came here to say. What you do with it is up to you."

"Thank you, Ray," I said, leaning across the table. "I know

you mean well. And I know the Christian thing to do would be to forgive the bastard. But I'm not interested in doing the Christian thing."

He sighed, for this was a bone of contention between us. Ray was a good Christian and devout Southern Baptist, although not so devout that he felt personally led to boycott Disney, convert the Christ-killing Jews, or shove women out of the pulpit and make sure they were at home cooking for their husbands where they belonged. I felt bad, and I hung my head a little. "Listen, I gotta go. Otis is expecting me at two."

"All right, son. When do you want to pick up that car?"

I stood there for a second and then I shrugged. "Hell, Ray, I don't know. We can talk about it later, okay? Thanks for lunch."

"Always a pleasure," he said. He got up and hugged me, and damned if there wasn't just as much love in his eyes as before we sat down to talk. I guess fatherhood suits some.

He patted me three times on the shoulders when he hugged me, like he had since I was old enough to remember being hugged; then he sat back down, and as I walked out, he waved his good-bye, one finger raised like he still had one more thing to say.

He didn't think I saw him gesture to Etta for more cobbler as I shut the door.

But I did.

2

There's a line in one of my favorite old movies where some dried-up bird of a contract actress tells Cary Grant that their life together must involve no domestic entanglements of any kind. He's a bit chagrined by the idea, even though he eventually gets rid of her and falls for Katharine Hepburn, and I think he was right to be chagrined. A man needs some domestic entanglement, and even if you tallied my mother in that category—which gets us into some spooky psychosexual territory I'd just as soon not traverse—there was otherwise so little entanglement to my life that most of the time I felt I might just slip free of the planet and disappear.

That included my current girlfriend, if you'd care to call her that. I guess it was only appropriate, seeing how I'd otherwise regressed in my life, that I took up with my high school girlfriend Tracy York when she came back on the market a couple of years ago. She had just divorced her pathetic drunk of a husband, Mark, after thirteen years of marriage. He beat her when he was drunk, and finally when he put her in the hospital, her dad, Alvin, called the cops and Ray, not in that order, and together they got her to see the light. Since wife-beating was not one of my own particular vices and drunkenness was a thing of the past for me, naturally I found his behavior loathsome, but in truth, I think my vices were just as large as Mark's, if not as lethal. Tracy just seemed to be one of those women drawn to men who are no damn good—like most women, since most men are no damn good, I feared—and maybe she just traded Mark in for a different model.

But that's a lot more analysis than we engaged in out loud.

In truth, I saw her at the Fourth of July picnic when she first came back to Robbinsville, and we got to talking, and then to holding hands while skyrockets arced over our heads, and then to some unspoken understanding that we would try to help each other in some way if we could. Ah, but that last phrase was the ticklish one, for truth to tell, neither of us really had much to offer anymore.

When two people who have lost everything come together, a strange dance ensues. If you could watch them, they might look like a couple so concerned about stepping on each other's feet—and wary of being stepped on—that they're hardly even moving to the music. Maybe only their proximity would indicate to you that they were dancing at all. And that was where we had been, and where we were.

She was not the girl I remembered. I know that I had no leg to stand on in that department, but before she married Mark she was smart, opinionated, perky, and so open that you felt like you could step into her life as through an open window. Now she resembled me in some respects—closed off, fearful, and furtive—but she was unlike me in that she was a thinker, she relived her past, she tried to figure out what went wrong. Since what Mark did wasn't her fault, maybe it was even a comfort, but since what happened to me was, and since I already knew all too well what went wrong, I tried not to think so much.

Our griefs were so different that truly it was hard to relate to each other. She lost herself, tiny pieces of self beaten loose by the fists of her brute of a husband, until there was nothing left of her and someone else had to step in to save what remained of her life. I lost everything but myself, all at once and by my own hand, and no one could step in to give back to me what I had lost, not even the God who gave Job new children, the God who told Joel that He could restore the years that the locusts had eaten.

Because I didn't want new children, and I didn't want the years.

I just wanted my wife back.

I wanted my son.

I wanted another chance, and that could never happen.

So there were, at last, only two things we had in common: both of us were damaged, maybe beyond repair; but we shared memories of an innocent time before the locusts came, a time when we cared about each other. And maybe, somehow, that could be a comfort, although I'd yet to see how we do much more for each other than help each other take another step forward toward we know not what.

Tracy used to be a dancer. I used to look down and find her spinning in front of the stage, her laughing face shining up at me, her long blond hair flung every which way by the shaking of her head. She still came to hear us play sometimes, if it was nearby, but she didn't like it the way she used to. Noisy drunks naturally didn't hold much attraction for her these days, so she didn't like most of the clubs we played, and when she did come to one of the nicer joints, she sat in a back booth and listened intently and wanted nothing more than to leave as soon as the last set was through.

Well, we'd all changed.

All of us, I guess, except for Otis. Whatever my mom might have said about him—and justly so, because sometimes his behavior was more than borderline moronic—there was something reassuring about his refusal to face the intrusion of maturity.

I went over to wake him up after my little talk with Ray about my genealogy, and found him on the floor of his living room wrapped only in a blanket. He was playing Super Mario, listening to vintage Aerosmith, and happily munching on Froot Loops straight from the box.

With a name like Otis, and the way I've described him, I know the temptation might be to expect him to be one step up the evolutionary scale from Arnold Ziffel, but truth to tell, there's more to most people than we give them credit for, even if—like Otis—they take their sartorial inspiration from Sly Stone, Jimi Hendrix, and Elton John. Otis went to Warren Wilson, a good liberal arts college in Asheville, for three years before his dad had the first of three heart attacks and he had to come back and run the Texaco station for him. He did that for nine years, until the third heart attack left him an orphan, so maybe he deserved a second childhood. At any rate, he was taking it.

He paused the game for a second to nod a greeting when I came in, and to chase his Loops with a swig of warm Budweiser.

"How you feeling?" I asked before throwing some clothes against the far wall to make a place for myself on the couch.

"Okay," he said. "My head hurts like a son of a bitch. Or it would if they hadn't given me that Percodan. Man, I love Percodan."

He was ready to drink again and I grabbed the beer out of his hand. "Do not be drinking while you're taking painkillers. We've got a show tonight. Not to mention I'd like to keep your sorry ass alive."

He looked up at me with his sad puppy eyes. "Now who ever got hurt by introducing a few innocent chemicals into their bodies?"

"Mama Cass. Jimi Hendrix. Jim Morrison. Me. I could go on."

He rolled his eyes in a "whatever" and started the next round of his game: what looked to me like Mario fighting a bunch of wild strawberries and chocolate bars, although I could have been less than lucid from my gospel-induced lack of sleep.

"Listen," I told him. "I got some news. It's kind of—I don't know—bad. Freaky bad."

"You look a little freaky," he said. How he could tell that with the attention he was giving to the game I do not know; maybe he felt something about my presence when I came in. Otis was the kind of person who talked about vibes and auras. He got in with a bad crowd of New Agers when he was in college, and once he kicked this guy's ass because his astral self shot Otis the finger. But anyway:

"Ray told me my dad was alive."

"I could have told you that," he said. "Your presence in my living room makes it an established fact."

"No," I said. "He *was* alive. Once. But now he's dead. He died yesterday. In New Mexico. Some woman called the house last night while we were in Charlotte. But maybe it's all bullshit. I mean, Aunt Sister took the message. Maybe she thinks the woman said my dad was dead in New Mexico when what she really said was, Would you like to change your long-distance provider?"

Otis put down his controller, leaving Mario to be flattened by what appeared to be a giant marshmallow. "You're shitting me," he said.

"About which part? About Aunt Sister, yes. About Ray, no. Ray said they're burying him up there on Friday."

Otis made a mournful sound and shook his head. "I'm sorry, man. Really I am. Did he burn up in those fires around Los Alamos? Did he get radiation poisoning? I have a friend at Sierra Club that says that when the Los Alamos labs burned they let loose all kinds of toxic shit. It's too bad, man. Whatever happened. But if the government killed your dad, then dude, I think you need to take up the gavel again or whatever it is lawyers have. Don't let the government get away with it. Stand up for him."

I blinked rapidly a couple of times, a pretty normal response to Otis. I'm not the only one who has it. Then I found my voice. "Otis, are you mental? I have no feelings for him. The man walked out on us thirty-five years ago. I never knew him. If they don't bury him in that space suit I won't even recognize him."

"But he was your father, man. You've got to go to his fucking funeral."

I shook my head. "The man was not a father. He was a sperm donor. And I'm a little rusty, but if I remember how that particular procedure works, he was probably happy as punch to donate."

Otis reached for the six-pack next to the couch, saw my disapproving look and interposing foot, and instead lifted a half-full glass of milk up off the table. At least I think it was milk; I did not want to investigate more closely. He chugged it down, wiped his mouth with the back of his hand, and shook his head. "Dude, you should definitely go. You should be the bigger man."

"This is not about who is the bigger man. I could be the

biggest man you ever saw. I could be so big I scare women and children and crush cars with my feet. Bigness is a moot issue here. We've got shows every night this week. I don't even have time to fly up, and Ray has this crackpot idea that since he finally got my dad's Triumph running I ought to drive it to the funeral."

Otis's eyes got big, and I could see he was getting all spacey on me. "He's right, man. It's like your dad is making amends. It makes all kinds of cosmic sense."

"Maybe so. Ray thinks it's a sign from God."

The CD player flipped to the next disk, Fleetwood Mac. Now there was a dysfunctional family for you.

"You should definitely go," he said, "as long as the radiation has died down." He looked intently at me, saw that I was in no mood to listen to more persuasion, and shrugged just like Ray. "Well, we can tell the guys about it tonight. But if you decide you want to go, don't make the band an excuse. We can put together a show that doesn't need two guitars. Or we could get one of my buddies from Asheville to sit in for you for a few gigs."

"Otis, I know I can be replaced. I don't want to go."

He shrugged. "Okay, man. Your choice. Have you talked to Tracy?"

"Not yet." I picked up something from under the heap of clothes that I thought might be a pillow. It was, and I squeezed it a few times. I liked the feel of it between my fingers. "Maybe I'll go by and see her after I leave here. I'm ready to roll."

"You sure you don't want to hang for a while? I've got more cereal. Hey, I've got Cap'n Crunch." He motioned vaguely toward the kitchen, although knowing him, it could have been in any room of the house. "You used to eat Cap'n Crunch by the boxful. Remember? It made my mom so happy. She couldn't cook for shit, but that was one thing she could give you that you liked. We'd eat cereal for dinner sometimes. She just used to stand right at that counter there and smile and smile." He stopped, bit his lip, turned his head away from me.

I sighed. Fleetwood Mac played "Never Goin' Back Again." When it became unavoidable, I spoke into the silence.

"You miss them," I said. "I know."

"I know you do," he said without turning around.

I set the pillow back on the heap and stood. "Well, on that upbeat note I'll take off," I said, and I raised a cautioning finger. Otis was someone who really needed a mother; maybe I could give him mine. "One controlled dangerous substance at a time. Do you hear me?" I picked up the six-pack and tucked it under my arm for safekeeping.

"I hear you," he said.

"You have any more in the house?"

"Nope," he said. He wouldn't lie to me, so at least I knew he'd just be flying on painkillers all day, not the worst thing he could be doing.

We did our special handshake—regular shake, soul shake, then fists top and bottom—and I stood up. "What time you picking me up?" Otis drove the equipment van and I usually rode with him.

He checked his watch, which apparently didn't work—he shook his wrist, then listened to it—then looked at the clock on the VCR, which was a line of blinking dashes.

"I'll call you when it's time," I said and opened the door. "Later."

"Later," he said and went back to his game.

I decided I wasn't up to a serious talk with Tracy, and I certainly wasn't up to going back to the house, so what to do for my next few hours was a quandary. As I passed the Dairy Queen, I decided to start by wasting a half hour over a soft-serve sundae, and as I was pulling into a space, I recognized Tracy sitting at a window booth. She saw me, her sad face broke into a smile, and I was caught. And I smiled back, because now that I was there, I discovered that I was genuinely glad to see her.

"Brownie sundae," I called to the little Hendricks girl behind the counter, and I slid in next to Tracy. She was dressed for work—since she came back to Robbinsville she did the books for her dad's hardware store, something less than a full time job, really—and she looked good: black slacks, a sheer black silk blouse with a black camisole beneath, sensible black flats that she had propped up on the plastic bench opposite.

"I felt a Blizzard calling me," she said, giving me a hug. "Oreo." I took a look. She was about half finished with it and it had gone all gooey, so I guess she'd been sitting there for quite a while.

I took a deep breath and scanned my hands on the table in front of me. When I realized my mother's influence, I put my hands under the table out of sight. "Can I tell you something, Trace?"

She nodded gravely. Her blue eyes, which used to sparkle, were now limpid. Still beautiful, but I could see that she had pulled back behind them, as though that were any solution.

"I just came from lunch with Ray. My real dad finally turned up after all this time. Or his corpse did. He died yesterday in New Mexico, and everybody apparently thinks I should go to the funeral. He asked for me."

"Wow," she said and reached for her cup. "What are you going to do?"

"What would you do?"

She slurped, then put the cup down, then sat quietly, thinking. I asked a good question, and now she was imagining how it might feel to be me just now. We waited until she was ready. "I don't know," she said at last. "I'll bet you can't see any reason for going. I could understand if you're too mad to go. It's quite a shock. But Clay, aren't you the least bit curious? I would be."

"Well, okay," I admitted. "I guess I am. But anyway, I can't go." I made a too-bad face. "We've got gigs all week."

She made a face too, but it was not such a pleasant one. "Don't give me that. You've chosen to live a life without real responsibilities. So don't try to act like an upstanding citizen now to get out of something you just don't want to do."

"Whoa, Betsy," I said. "I haven't chosen anything about this life," for that seemed to be true, although I guess even the act of not choosing is a choice of sorts. "And I do have responsibilities. Lots of them." At the moment, I couldn't think of one to save my life.

"You've got to sing somebody else's shitty songs for stinking drunks in dives across the great state of North Carolina." Bad sign. She only cussed when she was furious, and since that much was still true of her, I unconsciously drew my head and shoulders in like a box turtle confronted with violence. She softened when she saw my reaction, and her voice lowered. "You really should go, Clay. Find out why he asked you to. Find out who he was. Who knows? Maybe it could be important to you in some way." She moved her lips together like she was spreading lipstick; it was what she did when she wanted to choose her words carefully. "Maybe—maybe it could be a healing thing for you."

"Healing? I'm not sick," I said. She dropped her eyes to the table. "I don't need healing, really. Do I?"

She took my hand. Hers was cool and a little clammy from her drink, but I squeezed it and eventually she squeezed back. "We're survivors, Clay, you and me. That's something, I guess. But surviving isn't enough after a while. Do you know what I mean?"

I moistened my lips. "I begin to fear that I do."

"In three years, we haven't talked once about a future. Maybe that's my fault too. But both of us are halfway through our three score and ten and we're living with our parents, for Christ's sake. I want a life of my own again someday. I want to have kids. Don't you think at some point we have to pick up and move on down the road a bit?"

"I don't know," I said quietly. "I don't think I know how." I barely got it out. I couldn't believe I had said it, but she just nodded her head. It was not news to her, and she smiled sadly and took both my hands.

"Go to New Mexico. I'm asking you to. For you, first and most important. For me, maybe just a little. Maybe you'll find out that the past really is past and you won't be haunted by it any more. Maybe you'll learn something from it and move on."

"Like you've done?" I said and instantly regretted it.

"I want to move on," she said. "Maybe one day you can help me do that."

I was filled with a dangerous feeling that made me kiss her upturned lips. "Come with me," I said. "Maybe we'll make this discovery together."

She thought about it, but I could see by her pursed lips that ultimately it was going to be a no. "I'll always remember that you asked me," she said. "But you know as well as I do that Luke has to face Darth Vader alone. Yoda said so."

Well, that was true. He did.

We got up out of the booth, and I walked her to her dad's Olds, which I now saw was parked right next to my old truck. I took her in my arms and was about to kiss her when, over my shoulder, she saw Otis's six-pack of Bud in my truck bed.

"Beer?" she asked. Not in an accusing way, but a curious one.

"Huh?" I turned, followed her eyes, and explained.

It touched her for some reason, and she kissed me gently on the lips before opening her door.

"You're a good man, Clay Forester," she said. "I love you, you know."

"I know," I said.

"And you're going to New Mexico?"

I sighed and shrugged. Like Ray, I too had a problem with signs and symbols, but sometimes when they gang up on you and clang you in the head like the lid of a garbage can, only a fool can deny there's something going on. There was something out there for me to learn, or to finish. Or something. "Yeah, I guess so. I mean, if Yoda says I must. I can leave in the morning as soon as the gospel piano sounds. Hell, maybe I'll even take the old Triumph; if it breaks down before I reach Asheville I'll take it as a sign I was never really supposed to go."

"Be safe," she said. "Come back."

"Don't be ridiculous," I said. "How could I desert all my responsibilities here?"

"Uh-huh," she laughed, a ghost of the old Tracy peeking through for a moment, and she closed the door, started the car, and blew me a kiss as she drove away.

I realized, strangely, that I was going to miss her. It was an odd feeling, after all that time, to miss one of the living.

Very odd.

I got into the truck to head over to Ray's to see if that car really would start.

Because of course, as always, I had my doubts.

3

They were all waiting for me on the porch when I pulled up in the Triumph—rocking, sipping, cackling, fanning their faces with *Good Housekeeping* and *Inner Room*.

"Here he is, here he is," Aunt Sister squealed as I shut off the engine, and I swear to you, every one of those elderly ladies got to their feet and started clapping.

I felt like Engelbert Humperdinck.

But I get ahead of myself, and I've committed to putting down on paper everything you need to know, so a word or two on my so-called father Steve Forester's car. It was a Triumph TR-3, yellow, black leather interior and convertible top. The body was good, and the interior was perfect since the car had sat covered for a good twenty years before Ray strong-armed me into helping him wrestle with it, an epic struggle that I imagined then as being like Jacob and the angel, maybe, and sure to hamstring us financially if not actually pop our hips out of socket.

It was a tiny car. I could even push it up a slight incline. The backseat was slapped flush up against the front seats, and was really more of a cargo space if the truth be known. There was also a luggage rack on the back big enough to lash down a carry-on bag and not much more.

It was odd to slide into it, to fire up the engine, to listen to it idle, *putt-putt-putt* like an oversized go-cart. My father had driven this car, had washed it and waxed it, had wooed my mother in it and, for all I knew, conceived me in it. And now he was dead.

I drove off down Ray's long driveway, past towering pines

on one side and the Cheoah River on the other, and out onto Highway 129.

My father was dead.

I would never meet him, know him. Never. Of course, he would never know me, never meet my wife, see his grandson. But maybe he was better off. He had missed out on a whole lot of heartache, hadn't had to climb down in the pit with me and wallow around for the past ten years.

Son of a bitch. Who needed him? I was glad he was dead. I was so angry that I shut my eyes for a moment and had a fleeting image of myself accelerating and ramming his car into a tree, a familiar impulse, I'm afraid, but one I set aside just as quickly. Everyone would still be dead, everything would still be an unredeemable mess, and I probably wouldn't harm a hair on my unlucky head.

It was a steamy afternoon even with the top down, and I thought for a bit about driving out to the lake for a quick dip before I went home, but I had to get back and get ready for the show, which is how I found myself pulling up to the house during what I knew to be prime old-lady loitering hours.

"Otis is coming by for me at four," I said, a conversational attempt at the flying wedge I would need to get past them and inside the house.

"Plenty of time," Miss Ellen said. "Plenty of time. Sit a spell. Have a Coke Cola."

"I'd rather not," I said, as they pulled me down into an empty rocker and then settled back themselves, watching me expectantly.

I'll confess: I broke under the strain.

"What?" I asked, looking around at them. "What are you three old women staring at?"

"Ray told us," Momma said. "Told us that you're taking the Triumph out to New Mexico for your daddy's funeral. When are you leaving?"

"Tonight after the show," I said. "Which I've got to go get cleaned up for—" I rose up out of my chair.

"In a minute, Clay, in a minute," Miss Ellen said, raising a hand to magically seat me again. "We were just wondering. What made you decide to go?"

"Yes," Aunt Sister said. "Evvie said Ray said that when Ray told you about your daddy you didn't want to go."

"I don't want to go," I said. "And I didn't decide to go. I don't ever decide to do anything." Which was a lot more than I meant to say, and a lot angrier than I intended to be to these good women who were looking at me with a trace of alarm leavened by the usual superior amusement. It must be really something to be a woman and be so superior. "Everyone seems to think it's a good idea for me to go. Do I understand that right?"

"Well," Aunt Sister began, then shut her mouth, since Miss Ellen would probably want to answer and did.

"Your mother and I think it would be good for you," she said. "Close the door on the man, I say," as though it was that simple, as though, for example, recognizing that you are a wreck is all it takes to make you suddenly whole and healthy.

But what I said was, "Yes, ma'am. Maybe you're right."

"I wish you'd start while it's still daylight," Momma said. "I worry about you, driving in the middle of the night—"

"I don't think the band can do without me tonight," I said. "And I'll be fine. You know I can never go to sleep right after I play. I'll be good for a long stretch of road."

They sighed, almost in harmony. I could almost hear them thinking: Why did I have to do everything my own way?

"I've got to grab a shower," I said, rising. "Otis'll be here any minute."

"Otis will be here exactly twenty-five minutes after he's supposed to be," my mother said. "But you go on in if you've a mind to. We'll just sit out here and talk about you behind your back." And then they all gave me those gleaming beatific smiles, as if to make that truth more bearable: Yes, we're going to sit out here and talk about you. And yes, we love you dearly.

God save us from such love, I thought, but all the same I smiled back and raised a hand in a departing wave.

All my gear was already in the van, so really I just had to pick some stage clothes, which wasn't some sort of Judy Garland outfitting decision. I had on clean jeans that fit pretty well, so I pulled out a clean navy T-shirt and my red Converse high-tops. I was set. I also threw a couple of days' underwear and socks into my old road warrior carry-on bag, plus one of my dark lawyer suits, a white button-down shirt, and black shoes for the funeral, assuming I ever got that far. I'd lash that on the back of the car with some bungie cords and be ready to head out as soon as we got back from Charlotte.

After I got out of the shower, I got dressed, then noodled around a little on my acoustic guitar with some old Fleetwood Mac and Eagles, then went downstairs for a sandwich before we left.

Otis came up and rang the doorbell at 4:27. My mother let him in, kissed him on the stitches to make his head feel better, and then asked him if he felt sleepy, if he had any dizziness, and if he'd see a brain doctor about an EKG.

"Yes'm," he said, ducking his head and smiling, his standard response to my mother. "But right now I feel just fine."

"Otis, Otis, Otis," she said sadly.

"You'll have to keep an eye on him while I'm gone," I told her, to which she rolled her eyes. As though I needed to give her mothering lectures.

"What time will you boys be home?" she asked, putting her hands on her hips like we were in fact still teenagers on a curfew.

"Four," I said, looking to Otis, who nodded. "Maybe four-thirty."

"Merciful God," she said, shaking her head and turning her eyes skyward. "Send your angels to watch over them."

"Thanks, Momma," I said, bussing her on the cheek. "I'll call you from the road."

"You boys be careful," she said. "And Otis, you steer clear of trouble tonight. For me, y'hear?"

"Yes'm," he said solemnly. "I will do that."

She blinked rapidly a few times, then wiped her hands on her apron and stepped back.

"Bye, Momma," I said. "I'll call you from the road."

"Bye," Otis said.

"Bye," she said, and then we walked out to the van and headed for Charlotte. Otis had been listening to Creed, which

I liked well enough, but after two songs I asked him to change the music to something a little quieter, more contemplative.

"We can do pregame music in a bit," I said. We always liked to play upbeat stuff—Def Leppard, Aerosmith, Van Halen, UFO, Ian Hunter—to put our game faces on so we could hit the stage feeling pumped up and not a hundred years old, which was what we were becoming and what I often felt these days.

"Okay, how about some Hornsby?" he asked, flipping through his CDs.

"Pop Hornsby or jazz Hornsby?" I asked. "Because I know you like the old pop stuff better."

"Yeah, that's good stuff," he said. " 'The Way It Is,' 'Mandolin Rain' . . ." He drifted a little, then corrected his steering.

"Sure," I said. "But the new stuff kicks ass. The chord modulations, the complexity. Pat Metheny and Branford Marsalis . . ."

Otis stuck in "The Way It Is" and posed like a smiling Buddha. "There is also perfection in simplicity, my son," he said.

"Those songs are three-chord wonders," I said.

"No, man. They're simple, but the solos are lightning in a bottle."

We drove for a while, Bruce Hornsby's clear tenor flying over his piano chords.

"What the hell does that mean?" I said after we'd been driving for a while. "Lightning in a bottle?"

"It's a figure of speech," he said, looking over from his driving. "You know, like a metaphor?"

"I know what a metaphor is," I said. "Sure. Comparison of two things. You are a jackass."

He laughed, but I had to admit, the music was just right. "So," I said after a bit, "what shall we do tonight?" The crowd the night before had been mostly a rowdy rock crowd, with the usual screamed requests for Southern rock. "They didn't go for Orbison last night at all. Except for 'Pretty Woman,' which they probably thought was a Van Halen song anyway."

"Hell, let's just add some more Aerosmith and then do a twenty-minute version of 'Cocaine.' "

"Christ no," I said. "I hate that song."

"Hold the morning edition for that news flash," he said. I looked up and he was drifting over into the other lane again, so I gave a little tug of the wheel to correct it. "How about some Skynyrd or Molly Hatchet early? Kind of a preemptive strike, get it over with?"

"Hell, no. You toss in 'Flirting with Disaster' and it's not some kind of vaccination. It tells them 'Squeal for more.' "

"Point taken," he said. He was driving on the shoulder now, and I yelled at him.

"Pull over, dumbass," I said. "You can't drive for shit."

"It's just the pain pills," he whined. "I'm not doing that bad."

"Pull over," I said. "This is one disaster I can stop from happening."

He gave me a look, like he was trying to figure out if he wanted to call me on something, but what he wanted to call me on, he didn't say. He did turn on the blinker, ease onto the shoulder, and stop.

"Okay," he said. "You've got the con." He sat there, waiting. It certainly didn't look to me like I had the con.

"Well, get your ass up out of the captain's seat," I said.

"Come around," he said. "I'll climb over."

I grunted with exasperation and got out. Cars whooshed by, and a semi let out a long honk that almost startled me directly into its path.

"Jesus," I said. My heart was pounding, my hands shaking. I spread them across on the steering wheel for Otis to see. "Like I couldn't hear him already."

He looked at me again, keenly, under his brows, but I turned away from him, got my breathing under control, and shifted into drive. "Mandolin Rain" was playing, and I turned it up until I heard the words—I didn't want any songs about heartbreak just then—and then turned it clean off, and we drove in silence for a bit, if you can call the whir of out-of-balance tires and the sniveling of an overstressed Ford engine silent.

I was glad to be back behind the wheel. I'm really a good driver. I'm almost always right on top of things, alert to details, seeing the road in all directions.

Of course, it's the *almost* that always gets you.

We were low on gas—the light had actually come on shortly after we traded places—so we pulled off U.S. 74 at the Forest City exit and eased up to the pump.

"I'll pump," I said and handed him a twenty.

"You want anything?"

"Get me a Dr. Pepper. No—make it two. One for now, one for later." I came around to the pump and pulled the nozzle loose. Otis called back from halfway to the door, "Do you want some chicken? I'll buy."

"Not from this rattrap," I said. The chicken in this dive had been sitting under the infrared lamps since Hoover was president.

As I took off the gas cap and turned on the pump, a green Plymouth minivan pulled up on the other side of the island, a harried mom with several kids. The ones who got out were about three and five, boys both, and I watched them walk in, each hanging from a hand as if it were the only thing anchoring them to this world. I stood there seeing them long after the door had closed behind them.

That's when I felt the eyes on me, and I looked up and saw the boy who had stayed in the car. He was maybe nine or ten, and he had his finger stuck in one of those Harry Potter books to mark the place, but had stopped reading for a moment to watch me. He had longish hair, not a fashion statement, but simply hair creeping over his ears and eyes that needed cutting.

He saw I was looking up and blinked, but his eyes stayed on me, so I smiled a little—a tentative smile instead of a big grin, because there are some scary men in this world, and probably most of them have big smiles plastered across their faces—and then inclined my head in a nod, single, simple.

He didn't smile, just sat looking at me for a bit out of his big, serious eyes. Then he opened his book again, dropped his head, and began reading.

The mother half dragged, half carried her other two back

to the car. "We're going to be late," I heard her tell them, and after she had the three-year-old in his car seat, she came around and climbed in without even a look at me.

I was putting the nozzle back in the pump, which was how I happened to see the oldest boy one last time. He had looked up from his book again, and his face was solemn, like he was full of deep thoughts, and he just raised his fingers in a sort of good-bye.

They were long gone when Otis found me standing out there, my head down, my hand on the pump for a little extra support.

"Clay," he said, and I didn't answer him.

"Clay. If it's a heart attack, nod once."

I didn't nod, but still I couldn't answer. There was a hard lump in my chest, like my mom's pancakes had solidified: cold, heavy, cancerous, deadly.

He took my shoulder and pushed me upright, although I didn't meet his eyes. "Was it the little boys?"

I still couldn't nod. Sometimes it just hit me harder than others.

My son Ray would have been nine years old that year.

Otis took my arm, opened the passenger door, put me inside. He came around and started the van, and we got back on the highway. He looked over at me a couple of times, but I didn't say anything, and at last I could feel him getting ready to blow. The third time he looked across at me, his eyes were full of tears.

"How long, man?" He didn't expect an answer, so he forged ahead. "How long are you going to blame yourself?"

I looked out the window at the darkening woods. "How long is there?"

He pounded the steering wheel for emphasis. "You ought to give yourself a break. There was nothing you could do for them. It's a blessing that you're alive."

I looked across at him, earnest and upset, and back out into the trees. "Not for me, it isn't."

He looked away from me and took a deep breath, and it was a long time before he felt he had enough control over himself to talk. "Well, it is for me, Clay. What would I do without you? And it is for your folks. And for Tracy." I reached over and turned the Hornsby back on, loud. A root canal without anesthesia was less painful than listening to this. The music rang, rattled, and when Otis reached over to switch it off again, the silence echoed as well.

"I miss them too, Clay," he said, and there was an edge to his voice. "Ray was my godson, for Christ's sake. Do you think you're the only one who hurts?"

"I know," I croaked. "But I was the one driving."

He shook his head, and the van careened a little bit while he did it. "You had a few glasses of wine and then you went to the airport. I know you feel like you could have done something, that things could have been different, that if there's not a reason things happen, then how do we go on in this fucked-up world? But Clay"—and here he raised his right hand from the wheel and pointed at me—"if you'd been as sober then as you are at this moment, that garbage truck would still have run the red light. And they'd still be dead."

Ah, good friends. They always think the best of you. Of course, they have to, to protect their investment. "I would have seen him coming," I insisted. "I could have gotten out of the way."

He shook his head again. "I don't think so, man. But I know nothing I say makes any difference. They're still dead."

I nodded and looked back out the window. "Anybody ever tell you that you talk too much?"

"Nobody's ever gotten a word in," he said. "You know what?"

I sighed. "I'm sure you're going to tell me."

"Damn right I am. That's my job. So hear this: You think you have a handle on this. I know you, man. You see the years passing, you think you're piling so much shit on top of the trapdoor that there's no way the alligators can get out. Only it's not alligators down there, Clay. It's plutonium."

"Isn't that a mixed metaphor?"

He waved his hand dismissively and went on. "It's not alligators, it's radioactive waste, and there's no safe place in the house while it's down there."

"What's the half-life of plutonium?"

"A lot longer than your sorry ass is going to be here, believe me. Why can't you be even the tiniest little bit like me? I say anything that comes into my head, I talk about things, I try and move on. Why can't you just talk about it?"

"Thanks, man," I said.

"Which means, 'Yes, Otis, you're right,' or 'Okay, Otis, shut up and drive'?"

I just gave a narrow smile. It could mean either.

Or it could mean both.

Our gig in Charlotte was at Checker's, a hundred-seat club that had a small dance floor, a bunch of booths, and a long bar on our left that came uncomfortably close to the riser and had in fact been a contributing factor in Otis's painful evening the night before. Our equipment was already set up, but, suspicious or superstitious musicians that we were, we all took our personal gear home each night, except of course for Otis's drums—too big and bulky for casual lugging. After we got inside the club, which was cool, dark, and musty and smelled like smoke and spilled beer, I pulled out my guitars. My electric was a 1976 Gibson Les Paul, a beautiful and heavy ax with a cherry sunburst pattern. I also played an acoustic Martin on a couple of songs. I set both of them up on their stands, then started switching on amps and the sound system for a sound check, which we'd do as soon as the others arrived, and listened to Otis hitting his bass drums, *thump-thump-thump,* to check the action on his pedals.

You always knew when Rusty and Brian arrived; first you heard vague murmurings of discontent, like maybe the Children of Israel were wandering through the Wilderness somewhere nearby, murmurs that grew distinct as they approached. Anytime you walked up to them you would find them in mid-argument. I had this idea that if you went up to the living room window of their house in the middle of the night you'd find them poking each other in the chest and taking sides on Courtney Love, or mustard potato salad versus mayonnaise.

"I told you not to take that exit," Brian Gentry was saying as they cleared the back door, their guitar cases dangling from each hand. Brian, our bass player, looked like a wrestler—the actual kind, not the show-business variant. He was short, a bundle of muscles, and he bounded all over the stage like he was bouncing across the wrestling mat. He was also our second lead vocalist, a guy who was good enough to carry his own band if he wanted. "You always think I don't know where we're going. I know where we're going."

The object of this harangue, Rusty Hamilton, was tall and gangly, with red hair in a long ponytail. Sometimes he had a neatly trimmed goatee and mustache; just now, he had only a little blues mustache on his bottom lip. He had the stage presence of a totem pole, but he could throw the notes around; he was one of the best lead guitarists I'd ever worked with. When he talked, which was seldom, it was quietly, in measured tones. "You were asleep yesterday. You slept the whole way down. I woke you up when we got here."

"Hey," Brian said as they saw us. "What's on the agenda for tonight?"

"Not a damn thing," Otis said. "Let's do this damn check and go over the set at the Colonel's."

"We ate at KFC last night," Rusty said, squatting next to his case to open it. "I want pizza."

"The world does not revolve around you," Brian said, to which Rusty replied phlegmatically, "I didn't suggest that it did," to which Otis and I just looked at each other and shook our heads.

After Momma had been in their company for about five minutes, she pulled me into the kitchen to say, "Those boys. They act like they're"—and here she did her trademark lordy-lordy laugh, ha ha—"queer or something." And then she looked at me past the feigned amusement for a response.

"First, Momma," I said, "that's not a nice word. It's like saying 'nigger,' which I know you would never do." She shifted uncomfortably. "Second—and you'll pardon me, I know, for my lack of curiosity—it's none of my business what anybody does with his own penis."

"Well, I'm sure—" she began with a giggle, but couldn't think what she was sure about. The word *penis* flustered her, and so she just sort of oozed back into the living room.

What I knew about Rusty and Brian was that somehow,

despite all appearances, they were inseparable. Brian was a social studies teacher and coach in his day life; Rusty worked at a music store in Asheville giving guitar lessons. They lived in an old frame farmhouse in the foothills of the Smokies that used to be part of a pig farm, and they liked to sit around on our off nights and drink beer and watch Warner Brothers cartoons or Three Stooges. Rusty was a closeted intellectual, but he was quiet enough—and his sardonic asides funny enough—to mostly escape censure.

"There's a Pizza Hut down the street," I said. "That's what I want."

"Amen, brother," Rusty said, pulling forth his vintage Fender Stratocaster and gently setting it on its stand. Then he unpacked his Takamine acoustic and did likewise. We plugged everything in, put the microphones on the stands, made sure we were still tuned—light strings especially have a way of stretching out of whack—and then we were ready for our sound check. We yelled for Bobby Ray, the guy who owned Checker's, and he came out from the back room and slid into a booth.

Rusty and I conferred for a second about a song.

"You want to do 'Paperback Writer'?" he asked. We were still working on the backing vocals, so I shook my head. I don't like to rehearse at sound check. I like to nail a song we know backwards and forwards and leave the stage feeling like a rock god.

"Walk This Way," I suggested, and he nodded, so we shouted it back to the others. We did the old Aerosmith song straight through. I played rhythm on that one and Rusty took all the lead runs. We didn't do any of the stage business—the poses, the choreography. We just played and I sang. We all nodded our heads when we finished, and Bobby Ray gave us a thumbs-up.

"Bass is a little light," he said. "Everything else is fine. Drums sound good."

"Drums sound good," Otis said. "Give me some more of that Percodan."

"Is Brian too soft or is it the system?" Rusty called out. "Brian."

"Damn," Brian said, adjusting the volume on his amp. "Who's trying to silence my distinctive voice?"

"If only it were that easy," Rusty muttered just loud enough to hear.

"Let's get some pizza," Otis said, balancing his sticks atop his snare and pushing back from his set. "I can hear those pepperoni calling my name."

The restaurant was crowded, but we got the circle booth back in the corner, and after we ordered two big meat-lover's pizzas, a pitcher of Bud, and a pitcher of Dr. Pepper, we looked over the set list from the night before.

"Anything y'all want to try different tonight?" Brian asked as our waitress, a little girl named Debbie, set down our pitchers. Otis was giving her his best meat-lover's smile, and I elbowed him in the ribs. "I thought things went pretty good last night except for when Otis threw his sticks at that big lumberjack-looking son of a bitch."

"Don't remind me," Otis said, smarting from the twin blows.

"I want to try a little more acoustic stuff tonight," Rusty said, looking at me. "Monday night crowd might be a little more reflective."

"Might be," I said, although I had my doubts. "Let's put it in and change it up on the fly if they're throwing beer and pretzels at us for being sensitive girlie-men." We hid a couple of softer songs in the middle of each set, pursed our lips, nodded approvingly, and hoped for the best.

As our pizza came, Brian looked over at me and said, "Hey, man, Otis told us about your phone call. I'm sorry. That's fucked up."

Rusty nodded, his mouth full. "I called Peter Bushnell this afternoon. He said he could sit in with us for a few nights. I told him if it was okay with you, we'd do it." They all looked at me.

"We can do trio stuff for a few nights if you'd rather not bring someone in," Brian said.

I waved a hand dismissively. "Peter is always great," I said. "And you can play some of that stuff I won't do."

"The penis songs," Otis chortled, almost expelling his Dr.

Pepper though his nostrils. I was infamous among my rock peers for refusing to sing songs that were too explicitly about sex or sexual prowess, which is a whole lot of songs if you think about it; I figured that a guy on the road to forty has no business pretending he's a teenager, although there are plenty of rock stars older than me doing it. Just a personal preference, that's all. Sex is a whole lot more trouble than it's worth, if you ask me.

"Yeah," I said. "The penis songs. Knock your smutty little selves out."

We ate for a bit, but I could feel them looking at me, and I knew I was going to actually have to talk about it.

"How are you feeling about this dead dad shit?" Brian asked. "This has got to be a weird thing to come up after all these years."

"It'll do till something weirder comes along," I said. I was remembering Ray sitting across from me at Dolly's, remembering his embarrassment and my hot anger. "I don't really know what to think. I'm just going to go and see what's what. Maybe there's something that'll explain . . ." Here I raised my hands vaguely. What could explain a lifetime of absence? My father left me. He went away. I never saw him again.

I shook my head. "I don't know. I just know I'm going to New Mexico."

"That'll be a nice drive," Rusty said. "It's beautiful out there."

"Beautiful?" Brian said. "You're living smack in the middle of God's country and you think desert and sagebrush—"

"One doesn't have to replace the other," Rusty said, and I breathed an inward sigh of relief. They were off again, and I was off the hook.

We sat in the booth closest to the stage as it got toward eight o'clock. We saw some faces from Sunday night—regulars or neighborhood people, I guessed. Otis was scoping out a table-full of women a few booths back, but since they were behind me I couldn't get a look at them. There were a half-dozen people sitting at the bar, probably twenty in the club when we got up to go on. Bobby Ray was going to lose some money unless they did a lot of drinking. Somehow, though, even though it was just a handful of people, there was already enough smoke in the club to choke a heifer. It smelled like the morning after at Hiroshima.

I slung the strap over my shoulder, took a pick off the mike stand (I had a dozen of them stuck up there) and tore into the seven-note introduction to AC-DC's "Sin City." I let the last note hang out in the air and attract some feedback to get their attention, and Brian yelled out over it, "Ladies and gentlemen. Children of all ages. We are Briar Patch, and we are going to rock your world."

And I know it sounds pretty ridiculous on the face of it, but then Rusty and I threw down some hard chords and the bass and drums came in and I started singing and damn, if we didn't rock the house.

4

"Man, that was a great fucking show," Otis said later when we were packed up and headed back home. It was a great show, which I guess shouldn't have surprised me, but it always did.

"It went pretty well," I said, which got Otis to hooting.

"Dude, you had them eating out of your hand. What about that pretty little thing at the front table?"

A group of UNC-Charlotte girls had come out to dance, and one of them in particular—a slender blonde in black with her hair cut like Rachel on "Friends" used to wear it a couple of years back—was dancing next to the stage and smiling and giving me the big eye.

"She must have liked the way I smelled," I said. The way I smelled right now was like barbecue ribs smoked over a bonfire of Winston Longs.

But this show had been a good one, all right. Our first set was pretty straightforward rock and roll, with some John Mellencamp and acoustic Goo Goo Dolls that let me stretch my voice a little. After we finished the set with Stone Temple Pilots' "Sour Girl," the UNC-Charlotte girl sidled over to the edge of the stage where I was kneeling to retune my guitar, and said, "You've got a great voice. Can I buy you a beer?"

I looked up at her and smiled, not my big smile, since just about nobody got my big smile in those days, just the hey, how you doing smile. Giving too big a smile is like leaving too big a tip. "So you wouldn't want to buy me a beer if I didn't have a great voice?"

She pursed her lips and turned her head slightly to one side. "That sounds like somebody sidestepping a question."

"Guilty," I said.

"And that sounds like somebody refusing to answer a question."

She was pretty sharp for a twenty-something. "Guilty again. Thanks. I don't drink."

"How about a Coke?"

I shook my head. "Thanks, though."

"Damn," she said. She raised her arm and smelled beneath it.

"It's not you, believe me," I said, and it wasn't. She was something special. "I've been standing in the pool of saliva coming from our drummer since he first saw you get up to dance."

She leaned forward so we could be all confidential. "So, then if you don't mind my asking—"

"Ask away," my outstretched palm said.

"You're a nice-looking guy, a great singer, and I'm an appreciative fan, and you're not interested in me at all." I shrugged. It was an unfortunate truth. "Are you married? Gay? Going steady?"

"Nope," I said. "Ascetic." She shrugged and gave a sad little smile, and I guess I thought that would end the conversation, but right before we started up our next set, a befuddled waitress brought me a glass of water and some crackers, "Compliments of the young lady," and I saluted her before I drank.

We talked more during the second break. Her name was Denise; she was interested in design or finance, she didn't know yet; her daddy was a Charlotte lawyer I knew by reputation as a dirty fighter on behalf of big corporations, a real bastard like I had once been, and her momma was a country club alcoholic having an affair with their maid.

"Isn't life interesting?" I said.

"That's one way to think of it," she said, and if we had both been drinking we would have shared a cynical "Cheers."

Between sets, the jukebox blared, and right now it was blaring old Police "Roxanne," which we had been getting ready to do and now would need to replace, and "Can't Stand Losing You." She toyed with the straw in her drink, which was one of those icy fruity things, margarita or daiquiri, I couldn't tell which. "So what about you, Clay? What's your interesting story?"

I was just getting ready to make up something when Otis leaned over us and said, "Pardon my barging in on your conversation. Clay, Bobby Ray wants some Skynyrd."

"God help us," I said. "I'm not playing 'Free Bird,' not unless someone holds a gun to my head. And maybe not then."

"He seems kind of ticked off. He says he asked for some Skynyrd last night. I don't remember that."

"You don't remember because he asked me last night."

Otis settled heavily into the chair next to me, trying simultaneously to smile at Denise and glower at me. It was not a pretty sight. "Dude, this is not just a fling for some of us. This is my job. Let's make him happy, okay?"

Denise leaned forward, giving Otis a good view of cleavage. I was happy for him—Otis loves cleavage—and happy for her, too. Here was some backstage intrigue. Not to disappoint, I struck my best petulant artist pose, like Norma Desmond, maybe, in *Sunset Boulevard*. Upon reflection, it was a little over the top. "I will consent to 'Saturday Night Special' or 'I Know a Little.' Maybe 'You Got That Right.' But I will not play 'Free Bird,' 'Sweet Home Alabama,' or "Tuesday's Gone' under any circumstances. That is my final word." I threw the back of my hand up to my forehead, threw my head back like an emoting silent-film actress.

"Cool," Otis said, and he rose to go consult with Brian and Rusty. "Mademoiselle," he said to Denise, tipping a imaginary hat.

"He's funny," Denise said. "And he'd be cute, but those stitches across his forehead are a disaster, design-wise."

"Finance-wise too," I said.

"What's his name?"

"That's Otis. He's my oldest friend," I said, for so he was. "From Mrs. Ferguson's first grade class on through . . . everything."

"Everything?" She arched an eyebrow and I hastened to defend my sexual preference.

"Okay. Almost everything. In fourth grade, he kicked Tommy Brando's ass because he knew Tommy scared the shit out of me. He was a big old boy. In high school we double-dated. And later . . ."

Later, other things happened.

I stood up. "Always a pleasure," I said, and I took her hand for a second. "I have to go back on."

Our last set was my favorite, but at the same time I was nervous about it. Randy had decided I was ready to play my solo version of Fleetwood Mac's "Big Love," the pluckity-pluck classical guitar version that Lindsay Buckingham plays on the Mac live album, and my fingers were not feeling up to the task. It went pretty well, though I flubbed a couple of changes here and there. My picking and plucking were not up to the standards of Rusty, who taught me to play the song in the first place, but my voice got me through it. What followed was our lone Orbison song of the night, "In Dreams," and I started playing the opening chords and singing by myself. And for whatever reason—because the people out there were drunk, or tired, or because we truly were playing well—the audience was listening. We weren't playing at them, like we had been much of the night, but for them, with them, through them.

And the recognition made me listen as I sang, and damned if I didn't start to choke up, me, of all people. I came to the point where my voice had to sail out clear and high, and I let the words float atop the notes, almost like Roy used to, singing about lost love that only comes back in dreams.

When we strummed the last chords and let them fade, it was silent. There was a long pause, and then the applause, and I was breathing again and Rusty was getting out his man-dolin, and we started John Mellencamp's "Check It Out," and we were almost through for the evening.

We were in fact packing up for the evening when Denise came up to the stage again. She'd been sitting reflectively dur-ing the last songs, hadn't even gotten up to dance when we turned up the juice at the end of the set. And even as her friends were moving toward the exits, she waited for a bit, until no one was standing nearby and she could talk to me without anyone overhearing.

"You're a tremendous singer, Clay," she said, and when she got close, I could see her mascara had run. "That one song was the prettiest thing I've ever heard."

"It's by Roy Orbison," I said, because even though she hadn't identified it I thought I knew what she meant. "He was one of the great pop singers."

"What was her name?" she asked, and I suppose I could have blinked or said "Whose name?" or made a joke and avoided the question entirely, because I was an expert at all of those. But, again, I knew what she meant, and her recognition of the emotion behind the song was a forged connection between us now that I could not dishonor with dishonesty.

"Her name was Anna Lynn," I said quietly. "She was my wife."

"You must have loved her very much," she said, and then she turned away and ran for the john because she was crying and she was too old and too sophisticated to be caught with raccoon eyes.

"Dude, that's not how you're supposed to pick up girls," Otis said from behind his drum kit.

"It's how I pick up girls," I said, and of course he couldn't argue with that.

"She was sure pretty, though," he said later in the van. "You could have steered her in my direction."

We were way outside Charlotte, the highway was dark, dark, and we were the only vehicle to be seen in either direction. "Tried to, man," I said. "She said the stitches destroyed your symmetry or something like that."

"I'm symmetrical everywhere that counts," he said.

"Uh-huh." I was looking down the road; all I could see was the area right in front of the headlights. I did a lot of driving at night, and I was always amazed that no more than I could see I always ended up where I meant to be going. "Do you believe in miracles?" I asked.

"There's one right there," he said. "You asking that question right when I was thinking about it. I was just thinking that you're setting off on a great adventure. It's kind of a miracle, don't you think?"

I glanced over at him and could barely see him in the light from the dashboard. I could just see his lips move as he went on. "I mean, here I've been thinking if you don't get out of here you're never going to change. You'll die in that house. And then, out of the blue, a bolt from above, a blast from the past—"

"I get your drift, Casey Kasem. So my dad dying is a miracle? Seems pretty ordinary to me. Everybody does it these days."

He shook his head, and I could see he was preparing to get all zen on me. "You've got to learn to see the miraculous in the ordinary. Everything that happens is miraculous. That you and I are driving in this van down Highway 74 listening to Steely Dan is miraculous."

Again, even with the Steely Dan—we were listening to "Aja," which is a great song—it seemed pretty much part of the everyday to me. It's what we did just about every night, on one highway or another, with some music or other. There was a word, though, that still echoed from earlier, and first it made me laugh and then it made me wonder.

"Okay," Otis said after a bit. "I'll bite. What's eating your cereal over there?"

"Change." I shook my head and laughed again. "I'm as free as a bird now. And this bird you'll never change."

He did his Yiddish father act. " 'Free Bird'? You're drawing your philosophy from Lynyrd Skynyrd now instead of your best friend?"

"Since when do I draw my philosophy from you? Unless it's 'Hope I die before I get old.' That seems to make sense."

He laughed. Then he said, "All right, you devious bastard. You started to say something and I made the fatal mistake of letting you off the hook. Go on. Say it."

"I just felt . . . shit, Otis, I don't know. What does it mean?

I am as free as a bird. I am. I have no responsibilities, no schedules, nobody to be accountable to. Why do I need to change?"

I didn't have to turn to feel his withering glance. "Dude. That is self-evident."

And it was. I turned my attention back to the road. "Steely Dan. Man, can you believe those guys are still putting out records?"

"Nobody is putting out records any more. You're showing your age."

"Well, if I can't show you, who can I show?"

"True. Although I hope you know that there are some things I do not want you to show me."

I laughed. "And vice versa." We settled back smiling, and then the smiles faded slowly, and then we just sat, the night rushing by outside, the engine whining like an overtaxed lawnmower, before I gathered the cojones to return to what was still on my mind.

"Otis," I said.

"Here and here," he said.

"Do you think people can change?"

"Yes," he said. "Yes I do. I most surely do. But it's not easy."

"Don't I know it."

Again, the glance. "Dude, you haven't even tried to change. This trip will be the first step you've taken outside the rut you've worn for yourself in ten years."

I took a deep breath. "This is absolutely the last thing I'm going to say about this."

"Okay."

"It's a scary thing, man," I said. "I like the rut. I mean, I don't like it, but I'm content. I mean, I'm not content—"

"But you're safe. Or you think you are."

"Maybe. When I think about going back out in the world, it's like I get one of those panic attacks or something. I can feel my heart pound in my temples."

I felt his hand on my arm for a moment, and then he leaned back into his seat. "Call me anytime. Day or night. I'll take my cell phone onstage if you want me to. I'll take your call in the middle of a set. Hell, I'll take it in the middle of my solo."

"It might be an improvement," I said, glad he didn't have his sticks at hand to throw at me. But I also knew he would do it. I was that important to him. And again I was ashamed for the way I'd once treated him, the way I'd thought of myself as somehow better than he was because I was better-educated and a little higher up the social ladder. Because I wasn't better. He was stronger and gentler and sometimes even wiser than me. Always had been. "Hey," I said. "Do you remember when we used to drink a case of Budweiser of a Saturday night out at Cheoah Bend and sit on the picnic tables and watch the moon float up over the lake? How when we got toasted we'd drink a toast—"

"To eternal friendship," he said softly. "I remember it like it was yesterday."

"Was this what you imagined?"

There was a long silence then, nothing but road noise and the tape flipping to the other side, and after this uncharacteristic silence, when he spoke it was with uncharacteristic seriousness. "I couldn't have imagined that my family would be gone. That your family would be gone." He shook his head. "No, man. The only thing I got right was this. Us."

Us. This from the man I had all but written out of my life after Anna Lynn and I took up our sparkling lives as bigtime lawyers. Otis had just been an embarrassment to me when we moved to D.C. On his first visit, he had jumped into the Reflecting Pool on the Mall with all his clothes on, had attached himself one afternoon to a tour group of high schoolers because he wanted to hit on one of their teachers, and at a cocktail party at our townhouse in Georgetown, over a fine dry Merlot I had paid thirty-eight bucks a bottle for, he had engaged one of the senior partners in my new firm in an earnest discussion of the role of music in the quality of life, had in fact argued to this patron of Lincoln Center that one song by Led Zeppelin—during their seminal early blues period, of course—was worth a hundred Mozart symphonies.

It's a terrible thing to be ashamed of your past, and more terrible still to be ashamed of someone you love.

I think he knew things had changed between us. His visits dropped off in the last years we were in D.C. even though he had sold his dad's service station and had no real commitments to keep him from coming. He was up for little Ray's birth, and came back to stand godfather when we christened him in the National Cathedral—we were Episcopalians in those days. He wrote often, sending quotes and weekly wisdom for Ray to learn from when he got big enough to read, which of course, he never did.

We didn't talk about how I was feeling about the change in our relationship, and I never thought to think about how he felt. The closest we got was one time about two months before the end, when I was back from Alaska for a week and we were all walking down Wisconsin toward M Street, where there was an Ethiopian restaurant Anna Lynn really liked. Otis looked around at the shops, at the busy streets, at the clothes people were wearing, and just shook his head.

"What is it?" I asked.

He smiled a little sadly and shook his head again. "Nothing, man. I'm really proud of you. You know that?"

I nodded. I didn't get it then. I was counting the hours until he left for Carolina. But I got it later.

Otis was the first person to reach the hospital after it happened. I don't know to this day how he did it; if you want to talk about miracles, his almost instantaneous appearance at my side was nothing short of it. He was there with me, in fact, when the doctor came out the second time. Dr. Jordan, her nameplate said, and she was black, with wiry hair graying at her temples. I was sitting there with my head in my hands, and it was Otis who got up to meet her, who first saw her shake her head no. It was Otis to whom she said, her voice low and musical and tragic, "His heart stopped on the table. I tried open heart massage. His internal injuries—they were too severe." She stopped, and I could feel her eyes on me. She was measuring me to see if I had a noose around my neck and she was getting ready to pop the trapdoor beneath me. "I'm sorry. Believe me, we did everything we could."

"We know you did," Otis told her, and what I had long thought was country simpleton in him had suddenly been transmuted to a grace and gentleness I had forgotten, had never myself possessed. "Thank you for trying. Please tell your team that we appreciate them. They'll be in our prayers."

"And you'll be in ours," she said.

I looked up at her as she turned to go. She was blinking back tears, and then she walked slowly back toward the operating room. I thought doctors got used to seeing people die, but maybe you never do. Maybe sometimes you can just hide it better than others.

"Can I see them?" I called after her, and she stopped as though she had run into some barrier.

"Mr. Forester, I wouldn't," she said, turning to face me, and she bit her lip. "They're—they're not the way you want to remember them."

I nodded. I knew what she meant. And coward that I was, I didn't go to them. I didn't go, even though every atom of my body was screaming at me that there was where I needed to be, there howling like a beast over them.

But howling was never my style. I wish it were. Otis howled; when I woke in the night to find him watching over me in Anna Lynn's old rocking chair, his eyes were bloodshot from weeping.

Her parents wanted her buried in Grand Rapids, and some folks expected I'd want to bury her in D.C., but none of that felt right. I brought them back home to Robbinsville, buried them in a mountainside cemetery above Ray's place that is surrounded by azaleas, and I moved back in with my mama until I could get my shit together, a milestone I never quite achieved.

But at least Otis got me through that first night, and he and Ray and Momma got me through the next, and somehow I continued to make it through night after night without howling, without climbing inside a bottle, without driving myself into a bridge abutment at ninety miles per.

But God help me, the joys in my life were tiny ones: a good song and home cooking and a decent movie on cable TV in the middle of the night.

Maybe that's how it is for lots of people. But it never feels like enough.

It never feels like enough.

"You'll look in on Momma for me while I'm gone?" I asked.

"Dude. Like that woman needs looking in on." But he smiled. "But you know I'll do it."

"Thanks, man. I owe you."

"It doesn't work that way," he said. We were heading through Asheville on I-40 now, the lifeline I'd be following all the way to New Mexico after I picked up the car in Robbinsville.

"Man, I wish I'd thought to leave the car in Asheville. I'd be on the road now."

"You should go in the morning."

I shook my head. "I don't want to."

"You fit to drive?"

I did a quick internal check: fine; rolled my shoulders to check the tension: lots; and blew into my hand to check my breath: musty. "I feel good. I'll be awake for a while yet no matter what. You know that. I'd like to get started before I decide not to do it at all."

When we pulled up in front of my house and saw all the lights blazing, my first thought was that in a twenty four-hour span I'd lost my mother and father both. That's when Otis pointed to the parlor window, where the sisters now gathered, waving. "Those are some good women. They got up to see you off."

"God help me," I said, but all the same it gave me a warm feeling in the pit of my stomach. They were good women, even if they drove me completely batshit. "Want to come in?"

He laughed very hard at that. "Not for a million dollars.

Hey, do call, okay? Not because you're in trouble or anything. Just to tell me what's going on."

"I'll do it," I said. Otis leaned across, and although we were not huggers, he put his arms around me and gave me a bear hug. It felt good, and I realized that although my dad had left before he could give me a brother, I'd managed to find one anyway.

It was the first time I'd ever felt glad my father left when he did. Were there other things I'd gotten out of the deal, other undisclosed and unexpected gifts? I guess I was going to find out.

"Later," he said, giving me a good slap on the back and pushing me away as though the whole hug thing had been my idea.

"Later," I said, and I climbed out and headed toward the house and inside. It smelled amazing, smelled of cooking and baking, crispy and buttery, and again I was happy I'd decided against the convenience-store chicken under the heat lamps. My mother and aunts, roused from sleep and attired in the matching monogrammed dressing robes I'd gotten them the previous Christmas, had also been thinking about miracles.

"Now," my mother said, picking nonexistent lint from my sleeve, "we couldn't let you go off without some food. You don't eat well."

"He forgets to eat," Aunt Sister said, finding lint on my other sleeve. "I worry so for him."

"Well," sniffed Miss Ellen, who liked to act as though she had no more interest in feelings than in extraterrestrials, "we've packed a picnic for you. Everything will fit in that backseat, if you can call it that."

"Everything" was three fried chickens with extra livers and gizzards, fresh baked loaves of bread, and a chocolate layer cake. Sister had made her famous cheese straws, and Miss Ellen presented me with an insulated jug of her coffee, so strong that you could walk on it. I liked to say that in another life, Ellen had either been a lumberjack or cooked for them.

"Well," I said, and it was all I could think of to say. "I'm overwhelmed." They beamed; even Miss Ellen's face cracked momentarily with something that might charitably be called a smile.

Sister and Ellen gave me quick hugs and a chorus of drive safe, don't forget to call, we'll be praying for you, and left me with my jug of coffee and my mother.

"Well," she said. Now it was her turn.

"Is this a good idea?" I asked her, not speaking of Ellen's coffee, which probably was a good idea, although no long-term health studies had been done on it.

She nodded and smiled a little, sadly. "I believe so. I didn't do right by you where your father was concerned. I hated him so for so long."

"Momma," I said in mock consternation, but she raised her hand.

"It's true, son. I know it's un-Christian. But I was so angry. So I never told you any of the good things about the man. There were a lot of them, you know."

I honestly didn't. "What do you mean?"

She sighed. "Lord, Lord. There wasn't anything he couldn't do, seemed like. He was so artistic and creative. He could act. Sing. You got your voice from him. I used to pretend otherwise—there's another sin, pride. Lord, I've piled them up over the years. You've seen the picture he drew in high school, the one on the stairway. I couldn't bring myself to take it down. And he was so funny. Even when he was leaving and he couldn't get that little car to start, he said something that had me laughing at the same time I was crying and throwing plates at him."

"I wish I'd seen it. Do you remember what he said?"

She shook her head. "No. I don't remember most of what he said, or did. I don't really even remember what he looked like when he left. That's why it was such a shock to see him on TV that time. It's been more than half a lifetime, after all." She put her hands up on my shoulders and turned me to her. "But I want you to know something. I married your father because I loved him, because I believed he was a good man. And maybe he was, in his own way." She blinked and picked out a corner of the kitchen ceiling to look at. "I'm sorry I made you hate him too."

I set my coffee on the counter and pulled her close. She fit under my chin now, was in fact shrinking year by year. Someday she wouldn't be there at all. "So you did love him after all?"

I could feel her nod against my chest, felt her body-waved hair bristly against my chin stubble. "Those first years after he left, I was a wreck. Just a genuine wreck. I don't know what I'd have done without Ellen and Sister. I was sleepwalking through the days, let me tell you."

I knew all about that, the sleepwalking, but I couldn't remember anything of those days she was talking about. "Is that when they came to live with you?"

She nodded again. "They had to. I mean, Sister or Ellen had to put you to my breast when you squalled." She sniffed. "I was that far gone."

"I didn't know that."

"Well, Lord." She sniffed again. She was getting her control back. "How could you? You weren't any bigger than this." And she spread her hands apart like she was telling a fish story, and not a very satisfying one at that.

"I'm going to get going," I said, and I gave her a big hug. "Will you check on Otis while I'm gone? Make sure he doesn't overdose or have a concussion?"

"I suppose," she said.

"Make sure he's eating something besides cereal."

"We'll take him some of this leftover chicken tomorrow."

"Thank you," I said, a thanks that tried to encompass the food, the truth, and in some sense, the years she'd put me in the center of her life. "You're a good mother."

"Well, I try," she said briskly. "Are you sure you won't get some rest and get started in the morning?"

I shook my head and picked up my coffee. "It is morning, Momma."

"Well," she said, checking the clock and showing surprise, although I know perfectly well that she hadn't ever been up at 4:00 A.M. before in recorded history. "So it is."

"I'll be careful," I said. "I'll see you soon."

I walked out to the car, which started right up again, so I guess I was committed. I looked back at the house. Sister and Ellen waved and left the window, but Momma waved as long as I was in sight.

I reached the end of the driveway, looked both ways down State Highway 129, made the spur-of-the-moment decision to turn left—the roundabout way toward Tennessee, rather than right, toward Asheville and the interstate—and, wonder of wonders, I was on the road.

5

It was a beautiful night, the temperature just right with the top down, and I sped around Lake Santeetlah and farther into the Smokies on the winding highway. It had been a snap decision forsaking the interstate, and I couldn't account for it. I couldn't drive fast because of the curves and the darkness, and I had thought I wanted to get there as quickly as I could. But it also seemed right somehow, as though something or someone other than me had decided to turn the wheel and drive west.

My one regret, as I deliberated between chicken and Aunt Sister's cheese straws, was that for some reason, when I turned on the lights, the radio conked out, and while it was only AM radio, I coveted the noise. I pulled over on the way out of Robbinsville to confirm that yes, I could have one or the other, and resigned myself to a long night's silence.

But it was too quiet. Even with the purring engine—damn, Ray had done a good job with this machine!—there was too much nothing. I started to think, and I don't like to think.

So for a while, I sang. Orbison songs like "Crying" and "Only the Lonely." When I got across the Tennessee state line and was reduced to "Ooby Dooby" I knew it was time to move on. I sang Sinatra. I sang my favorites off *Songs for Swinging Lovers* and then slowed it down with some sad songs: "What's New?" and "Guess I'll Hang My Tears Out to Dry" and "One for My Baby," all the songs I used to do in the karaoke bar in Alaska. But my voice was starting to go, even with the soothing warmth of a couple of cups of coffee, and so by the time I was approaching Tellico Lake I started whistling hymns—a measure of my desperation—in between nibbling at the food so I could at least enjoy some of it while it was still warm.

I had one hand in the backseat feeling around for a leg when I began to feel the call of nature. I clamped my legs together, hoping I could ignore it for a while, but it was insistent. I'd had a big Dr. Pepper on the way back from Charlotte and a lot of coffee of late, and I was going to have to pull over, even though the road was two-lane again and narrow and with not much in the way of a shoulder. I did happen to be on the inside part of the hill instead of out on a ledge, for which I gave thanks, and I pulled over as far as I could, almost into a clump of vegetation, and climbed out carefully.

I unzipped and let loose a laser beam of a stream and felt relief almost immediately.

And then I saw the eyes in the bushes, gleaming golden in my headlights, and no more than five feet away. A mountain lion. Maybe a bear. And although I couldn't have stopped pissing in the event of a nuclear attack, I did start backing away, peeing my way back to the car.

"Oh shit, oh shit, oh shit," I said under my breath, a sort of mantra. Then I remembered that the convertible top was down even if I reached it, and realized that I was doomed.

There was a crackle as the brush parted, and the eyes moved down the slope and into the road—and when they reached the road, they were about five inches off the ground.

And although I couldn't have stopped pissing if God had commanded it, I started laughing.

What emerged from the bushes was a dog—a small, gaunt dog at that—who stepped forward onto the shoulder and sniffed tentatively at the air.

"Chicken," I explained. "My mother makes the best fried chicken in seven counties." I leaned in and took out the chicken leg I'd planned to consume before the crisis of micturition. "Here," I said, holding it out for him. "Take it."

The dog made no move to come closer. In fact, he seemed to regard me with some suspicion and actually took a giant step backward as I knelt to get closer to his level.

"Here," I said. "Doesn't it smell good? I know you must be hungry. You look like you haven't eaten in a while."

No doing. So I raised up, shrugged, took a bite of chicken, and for the second time in twenty-four hours, almost got run over by a semi—some overweight bastard sneaking around the weigh stations on the Interstate, maybe—who went whooshing by at breakneck speed.

"Jesus Christ!" I shouted, jumping out of the road, and the dog turned to flee, which was when I saw that he was missing his right rear leg. I cartwheeled my arms crazily for balance, which at least kept me from joining the foliage. When I could step back, looking and listening in both directions and hearing only the departing truck, I found the dog's eyes again, partway up the slope.

"Hey," I said as soothingly as I could with angry blood rushing through my veins. "Everything's okay here. No harm, no foul. Do you want to try this chicken thing again?"

No movement, so I got one of Aunt Sister's cheese straws and held it out. "How about trying some of this? Cheese makes it taste better."

He shuffled down the slope and the closest to me he'd been since I first saw him—about five feet away. He turned his head sideways, appraising me, and sniffed at the food. His ears flopped as he turned his head, and I saw that one of them had almost been torn off and had healed jaggedly.

"You've been taking a walk on the wild side, haven't you?" I said. "My mama would say it looks like life has just chewed you up and spit you out." I tossed him the food and he sniffed at it, then wolfed it down. Then I held out my hand, and he gave a tentative wag of what was left of his tail. His head was down, submissive, and with upraised eyes he sniffed at my hand.

"It's okay," I repeated. "I'm a pretty decent human being, as human beings go. Listen, you want to come with me a ways down the road? You stay around here, you're going to get run over or starve to death."

He turned his head again in appraisal.

"I'm not talking marriage. But there's got to be a better place for you than here. What do you think?"

He was weighing it.

"I have a whole tub of Aunt Sister's cheese straws. And it would be better if somebody else ate them. They give me gas, I'm sorry to say."

Clearly, even those on the fringes of the animal kingdom—which was obviously the place where this wretched puppy had spent most of his time recently—had heard about Aunt Sister's cheese straws, the staple of every church picnic, youth lock-in, and choir fellowship. He let me pick him up, and I put him in the passenger seat, where, after a moment's start when I put the car in gear, he began to watch the road ahead happily, his tongue lolling to one side of his mouth. He was a little unsteady as a sitter—missing such essential sitting equipment as he was, he sort of leaned a bit against the door—but all seemed to be working out.

I put the roof up until such time as I was convinced he wouldn't try to leap out, and we drove along happily for about forty-five minutes. I was starting to get tired, and my eyes were feeling tight and dry, but I thought that maybe my recent frights had added a couple of adrenaline-fueled hours to my driving capability. We crossed over the lake and finally got onto Interstate 40 about twenty miles west of Knoxville. The sky to the east was starting to gray, and I was feeling like I could make it at least as far as Nashville and maybe as far as Memphis when suddenly I took in a smell—if you can describe what I initially thought must be a truckload of festering human cadavers overturned in the road in front of us as a mere smell; I actually looked for a semi jackknifed in the ditch—that turned me into a mouth breather, for what little good it did me.

There was no such truck, of course. The road was clear of carcasses of any kind. No roadkill. No contiguous swamp exuding swamp gas.

Only then, still gasping for air, did it occur to me to look to my canine companion.

He sneaked a cross look at me then looked nonchalantly out the window.

"Was that you?" I asked, and he ducked his head and

began whimpering. It was clear that I was not the first person to ever ask this question.

"Okay," I said when I felt I was capable of rational thought again. "That was pretty bad. I've smelled less noxious things in feedlots. But you've probably been out on your own for awhile, right?" He didn't need to nod; each of his ribs was obvious. "So you've been eating roadkill and stuff for a long time, right? Of course you're going to grease the air once or twice on a diet like that."

He looked up at me hopefully, anxious to agree. I raised my hand to pronounce a papal dispensation, think no more of it, my friend, and he cringed down against the door and whimpered at the sight of it.

"Hey," I said. "Oh, hey." I lowered my hand slowly and felt around behind the seat.

"Here," I said. "Have a cheese straw." That perked him up right nice, as my aunts would say, and I was able to turn back to the road.

I love sunsets and sunrises—sunrises particularly, because there's the sense that you could be the only human being watching it. Many's the time I've lain awake for an hour or two after getting home and seen the sky go gray then red then orange and watched that ball float over the horizon and gone to sleep with a smile on my face.

This was not, apparently, my canine companion's reaction, for he took a good look at the full-blown sunset, yawned, and lowered himself onto his front paws to sleep.

It was about six o'clock when I had crossed over the Tennessee River, and the road started to feel a little bothersome when I heard the phone ring. I did not of course bring a cell phone or own such a phone, but it was unmistakably the chirping of such a phone, and since there weren't many places in my cramped environs it might hide, it took me only two rings to find it beneath my seat, and two more to figure out which one was the talk button.

"Hello?" I said into it.

"That you, Clay?" the voice of my stepfather asked.

"Is that you, Ray?"

"Hell, son, I must have left my cell phone in that car the other night while I was working on it." I could almost hear his mouth spreading with a smile as he generated this tale. "Well, since I've got you on the line, how are you doing? Where are you?"

"I'm on I-40, an hour west of Knoxville with a car full of goodies and a flatulent dog."

"Come again?"

"A dog who farts. He is in fact a three-legged farting dog, if you want the whole story, and he looks like hell. He's been out on his three-legged farting own for a long, long time."

I could hear Ray absorbing this information. "What's his name?"

"I don't have the slightest idea. Nothing much seems to suit him." I slowed down a tiny bit without thinking about it as a Tennessee trooper appeared of a sudden in my rearview, although I wasn't speeding.

"I had a three-legged bird dog once named Buster. Of course, he had to retire from bird-dogging when he lost the leg."

"Of course."

"But that was a good old dog. Does he look a'tall like a Buster?"

I appraised my canine copilot, and he looked up at me with interest. "Now you mention it," I told Ray, and so it was decided.

The trooper swooped past me doing at least ninety, and since he had no lights flashing, I wondered what the scoop was. Emergency, hunger, bladder distention?

"What does the country look like thereabouts?"

"Well," I said, taking a look around, "about like the ground around Winston-Salem. Hilly, lots of trees. Very green."

"Your mama was wondering if you'd care to call her once or twice a day to let her know you're safe. I said I believed you would not want to do that."

I flicked off the lights; it was getting light enough I didn't need them. "You believed correctly, sir. But if, for example, you and I were to talk every now and then, you could report my safety and pass on my love."

"Well, maybe I could at that," he said. "So it sounds like all is good so far. How far you going today?"

"I'm tired. I'll probably stop in Nashville for the day and sleep. Maybe I'll drive some more tonight. Maybe not."

"Well, make sure you're rested. How's the car?"

"Running okay. The generator's not charging too well. I think the belt's slipping a bit, so I guess I could try soaping it. But probably I'll just have to put on a new one."

"Don't forget to do that, son. Have fun. I'll talk to you soon."

We hung up and I smiled and smiled. Ray had never left something in a car he was working on in his entire life; I've never seen such a paragon of organization, of everything-in-its-placeness. But it was typical. That was my favorite kind of love, what I got, I realized, from Ray and Otis and Tracy even, expressive yet somehow not oppressive.

Now that the lights were off, I tried the radio, but still nothing, which was a little disconcerting; it presaged some serious further electrical problems.

"Well, Buster," I said, "I guess it'll just be some stimulating conversation today." Which was where we were when we saw that—and I admit this seems too much to believe, but I assure you it's true—leaning against the Crossville exit sign was one of those life-size crosses toted around by freaks and fanatics, and beneath it, sprawled out on the shoulder of the highway, not more than five feet from the rushing traffic, some sort of recumbent human being.

Buster started barking and I shook my head. "I don't get involved in things like this," I told him. "It's my secret of how to get through life."

Buster barked some more, which is to say he could have been protesting or arguing or just venting some steam.

"All right," I said. "We'll take a look. That's all. If he's dead, we're moving on. You may not have a taste."

I took the exit, then backed down the access road until we were just across the culvert from the cross, and there I got out.

"Stay here," I told the yapping Buster, who wanted to hop out too. "I do not have a leash for you and I didn't rescue you from a fate worse than death just to have you get bulldozed on the interstate."

Speaking of which, a car-carrying semi swooshed by just then honking its horn, and the shape on the ground didn't so much as flinch.

"Shit," I said. I approached at right angles, taking in as much as I could: a skinny white ankle seeing unaccustomed sunlight; tan coveralls like retirees might wear to putter around the house; a small plastic Safeway bag of possessions; a gray and unruly crown of hair like a tonsure. His cross had small casters underneath the long crosspiece to make the thing roll, which some people might think of as cheating, but I could see that this was one heavy mother of a cross, made from solid four-by-fours and about eight feet tall. It also had red reflectors on the back so traffic could see him better, and some foam shoulder padding to make long days of cross-carrying a tad more comfortable.

"Hey," I said, kneeling down beside him. "Hey, old-timer." I gave him a little nudge with my hand, and he stirred, rolled onto his back, and the most brilliant blue eyes I've ever seen opened and took me in with a glance.

"What is it, son?" he said, as though there were nothing out of the ordinary in lying down next to a highway, or in being awakened by somebody in that state.

"I was just checking on you," I said. "I thought you might be dead."

He sat up blinking at the morning light and chuckled, and his laugh was low and musical, like water burbling over rocks. "No, son, this isn't where that happens."

"Ah," I said, and I got to my feet so I could put some distance between us if I needed to. "Okay."

"The Lord told me I'll at least get back to Sacramento," he said, and it sounded so eminently reasonable that I just said, again, "Okay."

"My wife is in the hospital out there." He sighed. "It doesn't look good. So I'm headed that way. The Lord told me

I'll get to see her again. I just don't know what's going to happen."

"Listen," I said, before my exhausted brain could catch up
to my mouth. "I can take you as far as Nashville, at least."

He smiled at the little Triumph. "In that thing?"

"Maybe we could hook your cross up like a fifth wheel
trailer or something."

He got to his feet and stretched. "Ah, these wheels aren't
much better than for show. I had one fall off t'other day, and
believe me, I wasn't moving too fast."

"Okay," I said. "We can lash it on the back."

"All right, then. I'm obliged to you."

When he stood up I could see that he was thin and wiry,
somewhere around sixty or seventy, and when he shouldered
his cross and I helped him carry it across the culvert and up
the slight rise to the access road, I could tell that he was a man
still of immense strength. That thing must have weighed two
hundred pounds.

"I see you've got a friend," he said as Buster yapped excit-
edly, his tail wagging.

"I met him on the road," I said. "You've certainly made a
hit with him. He didn't react this way to me when I first ran
into him last night."

We pushed the top of the cross up so it stuck between our
seats and all the way to the dashboard, and somehow we
fixed the back end high enough, propped as it was on my
overnight bag and picnic basket, not to drag.

He settled in across from me, his bundle in his lap, Buster
nestled down between his feet like a friendly cat.

"Again, I'm much obliged," he said, only the top part of
his head visible over the cross. "My name is Matthew.
Matthew Simons. I'm a sinner."

"Well, sir," I said, extending my hand under the cross, "my
name is Clay Forester, and I'm sure I'd have to say the same if
I were to give it much thought."

And why don't you give it much thought? It is a danger to
give a Bible-believing cross-carrier that kind of opening, and
if I'd been a little less tired I'd not have done it. But he didn't

ask the question, didn't pull out the path-to-salvation gospel tracts. He just settled back in his seat a bit after shaking my hand with a firm grip and looked straight ahead.

"I need to warn you," I called over as we prepared to pull back on the highway. "Buster down there has a little problem with gas. I picked him up last night, and I fear he's been eating some things that aren't so good for his digestion."

"Now how bad could it possibly be," he called back, "a tiny little dog like this?" and about that time Buster again demonstrated conclusively how bad it could be and I was thankful we'd had to take the top down to accommodate the cross. Although Matthew didn't speak, I could see his eyes water, and then he began to laugh, harder and harder, and I had to join him.

"Never look a gift horse in the mouth, my daddy always used to say," he said at last. "And I suppose the same principle goes here with a free ride."

"It is pretty bad. I'm sorry."

"You can't choose your family," he said, "but you can choose your friends. Given that, there must be a reason you two found each other, although I'm hard-pressed to imagine what that might be. Lordy." And he laughed until I chimed in again, because truly it was the most god-awful thing this human nose had ever experienced, and having it come from that forlorn little package was really something. I didn't know what, but it was something.

The sun was already shining bright and warm, and I noticed that Matthew's bald crown was red and balding from days uncounted under the summer sun.

"You should use some sunscreen, sir," I said. "I believe I could pick up some at a convenience store if you'd use it."

He shook his head and brought his lips together. "The Lord'll do what the Lord'll do."

"What the Lord is going to do is give you skin cancer," I said.

He looked across at me and smiled. "Maybe so." And he settled back into his seat as best he could, which was his way of saying, so be it.

I was ever a so-be-it person too, if for different reasons, so

I didn't push. Instead I said something I'd always wanted to say: "So, old-timer, what's your story?"

"Ah," he yelled back, "just the usual. Man of God. On the road. Traveling town to town."

"On foot?"

"Mostly. If He tells me to, or if time's a-wastin' I'll catch a ride. You can mostly tell when it's His will. Not so many people stop once they see the cross."

"It's a little intimidating," I admitted. "Not to mention hard to fit."

"So there you go. I've been carrying this cross or one like it for nigh on thirty years. My wife left me some time back, took our daughters off to California."

"Where was your home?"

"Birmingham, Alabama. I used to be in the steel mills. But God spoke to me out of the fire and slag one morning and told me to get up out of there, take up my cross, and proclaim his word. I told my wife, and she said I was crazy." He smiled again, sadly this time. "Maybe I was."

"So she's your ex-wife? Is this the one in the hospital?"

"Yes. I suppose she is. My ex-wife, that is. I don't feel that way about her, but she was married two more times after me. Although she's not married a'tall just at the present time."

We passed over the Caney Fork of the Cumberland, then up a long hill. It was beautiful country, farmland and trees, and we drove for some time uninterrupted by anything other than the occasional whiff of pure phosgene from the right floorboard, and a good spell of holding the breath took care of the worst of that. I was feeling slow and sluggish and knew that I ought to be looking for a place to light and get some rest. I didn't feel right stopping just yet, especially since I'd promised Nashville when I stopped to pluck Matthew and his cross off the highway. But I kept yawning and jerking upright as I was falling asleep, and I guess I also didn't feel right about propelling Matthew and his cross off a bridge. And finally we were getting to the outskirts of town, which was as good a place to stop as any.

"Matthew," I called across to him, then said, "Sir," and put my hand on his forearm when he didn't appear to hear me.

He turned and nodded. "I've been driving all night, and I think when we get up to Nashville I'm going to have to stop and rest."

"I can catch another ride whenever you're of a mind to stop," he said. "I thought you looked a mite tired."

"Will you have some breakfast with me?" I asked, and yawned a big jaw-stretcher that threatened to break my head in half.

"If you feel up to it," he said. I saw a Cracker Barrel up ahead, thought it would do me some good to pump some additional fat into my veins, and took the exit. There was a Motel 6 just down from it, and it would do me just fine. I thought I remembered that they took pets as well, although the thought of Buster asphyxiating me in that tiny room decided me then that the car was a fine option for him. I pulled around to the back of the restaurant and parked next to a tour bus, leaving plenty of space for the cross.

Our waitress seated us and handed us menus and we commenced to browse. "Anything you want," I told Matthew. "It's my treat."

"Thank you, son. The Lord'll bless you for it."

"He's blessed me plenty for one lifetime, believe me. I'm not doing this for eternal reward. I'm doing it for you."

He closed up his menu with satisfaction and looked across the table at me. I was playing with the golf-tee puzzle on the table, trying to see if I could leave less than seven of the damn things in the holes.

"It's all the same to Him, you know. 'Verily I say unto you, inasmuch as ye have done it unto one of the least of these my brethren—' "

" 'Ye have done it unto me,' " I concluded. "25 Matthew."

Another smile creased his leathered old face. "So you had some schoolin' in the Good Book before you became a heathen."

"Had and have," I said.

"What'll you boys have this morning?" asked Carlene, our waitress.

"Boys," Matthew smiled. "Ma'am, you just made my day. I believe I can feel justified now in ordering the Old Timer's

Breakfast. Could I have hash browns and fried apples both with that?"

"Why sure, hon. Bacon or sausage?"

"Bacon."

"And how'd you like the eggs?"

"Sunny side up and soft as a woman's heart."

He was a charmer; Carlene touched at her bangs and smiled before turning to me. "All righty, then. You, sir?"

"Momma's Pancake Breakfast. I'd like the eggs scrambled, and bacon." We also ordered milk and juice, and then Carlene padded off to put in our orders.

"You haven't told me your story yet, son," Matthew said.

"I don't suppose I have," I said, piddling with the golf tees some more and actually dropping one or two on the ground so as to be able to bend over and retrieve them.

"What I'm wondering is, what brings you driving all night across the great state of Tennessee? What prompts you to stop and pick up a three-legged dog and an old man with a life-sized cross?" He fixed me with his steel blue eyes and wouldn't let me go until I spoke.

"Well, sir," I said, "it's a tale that's just as odd as anything you could want to hear." And so I told him the most recent particulars, dwelling only a little on my father's desertion and not at all on my recent life. "So off I went across the hills and hollers. And here I am now, on my way to Santa Fe, New Mexico."

He fixed me with those eyes again, measuring me, it seemed, to see what he could tell me that wouldn't overwhelm me. Then he placed both his palms flat on the table and leaned over toward me, and he spoke.

"You are on a spiritual quest, Clay," he said. "Nothing will ever be the same for you again." Then he leaned back in his chair as Carlene returned with our biscuits, and he applied butter and apple butter with practiced precision while I tilted my head and studied him for a change.

"Is that prophecy?" I asked at last, and he shrugged, his mouth full of buttermilk biscuit.

"Son, let's not talk shop over this wondrous breakfast. Although, do you mind if I stop chewing and turn thanks?"

"Be my guest," I said.

"Great Lord God," he said, "bless this place and all in it. And bless this food. Amen."

Carlene showed up with plates stacked up and down her forearms, all of which we were apparently intended to eat. And so we did, in silence for a bit, mouths too happy to speak. As our bellies began to distend, though, so did my curiosity, and so I ventured, "Did you say you've been carrying this cross for thirty years?"

He nodded. "Not this cross, of course. I go through crosses like some folks go through underwear and socks. But one cross or another. It's been a long, hard stretch. Still, I suppose the Lord knows what he's doing."

"How long since you saw your family?"

"A couple years," he said. "The girls, they backslid. Turned their backs on the Lord. I can't blame 'em really. What did He ever do for them but take away their daddy?"

"Yes sir. How old are they now?"

He reckoned for a moment. "Your age, or closeabouts. I can remember their birthdays and all, but I don't have much truck with the passage of time."

Thirty years.

"Do you miss them?" I asked.

"What I want in this life isn't important," he gruffed out, although the lump in his throat told me different.

I nodded. We all try and save our sanity somehow.

After we had finished up as much of our breakfasts as we were going to, I wrapped up some bacon for Buster, and Matthew wrapped up his for the road, biscuits and such.

"You want anything for the road?" I asked as we passed through the country store section on the way to the register.

"Some of these stick candies would be nice," he said, and he picked out a few while I paid.

"Thank you, son," he said again. We went out and extricated his cross from my cheese straws, and he shouldered it in his best cross-bearing manner. "Press on toward the prize. God'll bless you."

I believed that about as much as I believed that Haley's comet had crashed into the earth unbeknownst to us, but I just stifled a yawn with one hand and shook his strong, skinny hand with the other. "Take care of yourself, sir. I hope your trip is a good one."

"The trip home is always good," he said. "It's once I get there that was always my problem."

"Well maybe this time you'll know what to do."

He stood for a second, a sad, slow smile growing on his face, and he nodded. "I hope and pray, son. I surely do. Now you go get you some rest."

And he smiled and inclined his head, then turned laboriously and made his way up the entrance ramp and onto the highway. The last time I saw him before I turned into the motel parking lot, he had his head down, his load shouldered, and he was carrying his cross to California.

6

I dreamed of crosses spread across the landscape of what I imagined to be New Mexico: yucca plants and tumbleweeds and tufts of brown grass sprouting from white sand around me. Smoke from some unseen forest fire somewhere made me choke like a tubercular chain-smoker. I myself was carrying a cross, dragging that unwieldy wooden son of a bitch through the sand—wheels or no wheels, this was no fit terrain for such a thing—and when I reached a likely spot, I said something like "This is the place, I think," at which point I stuck my cross into the ground like a flagpole on the moon, shimmied up it, and stuck there watching the world go. I awoke groggy and confused in my cell-like room. It was late on Tuesday, near dark, to be sure. I had slept for eleven hours and I still felt tired, bone-tired as my mother would say. And why not? I was operating on a ten-year gospel-induced sleep deprivation. And so I dozed a little longer before I got up, splashed some water on my face, realized it was going to take much more than that to get me going, and took a complete shower and shave.

When I returned to the car, Buster was nowhere to be found, which was what I'd half expected. I strapped my bag onto the luggage rack and wandered around behind the motel. He was scrounging around the dumpster, licking up some kind of gray-green liquid oozing out of the bottom of it.

"Jesus, Buster, get away from that thing," I said. "Come on over here."

He walked over to me sort of sidelong, shaking his tail and ducking his head in case I wasn't the benign presence I had been up to this point. I scooped him up and rubbed his tummy, but did not accept his proffered kisses. "Thanks. I think I'll just eat my garbage firsthand."

I filled up on gas and got a newspaper to read, and then I dipped into the food packed for me. If I didn't eat it shortly, it was well on its way toward becoming dumpster material. After feeding some chicken to Buster—he needed a bowl or some such thing; no wonder he was drinking goo—I decided to toss the rest, and then had a piece of the slightly cross-squashed but still luscious sour-cream chocolate cake while I read the paper. The king of Syria dead; New Mexico wildfires mostly out but Colorado's fires raging; the Tennessee lieutenant governor's wife and young son still missing after four weeks; a committee on race in Tennessee releasing an optimistic report on future relations between blacks and whites, surprise, surprise; war in the former Yugoslavia, the former Soviet Union, and the former Congo. Why even read about it? As Molly Ivins once wrote, it was just one more thing I couldn't do anything about. I closed the paper and set it down.

Then I opened up the sports pages: Tiger Woods expected to win U.S. Open; Shaquille O'Neal expected to blow foul shots in the NBA Finals. I could at least while away a few pleasant moments reading the baseball box scores. Ray taught me how to read a box score, and I remember once he told me, "This is one thing that'll never change. My grandfather taught me how to do this; you can teach your grandchildren. Shoeless Joe Jackson or Junior Griffey, you measure them all the same way. In the box score." I was never going to have grandchildren, of course, but I did still have Ray. Thinking about it got me missing him, and so I called the house to see if he was home.

"Leave a message," was the terse reply from Ray's answering machine—he was probably out tinkering in the garage again—so I did.

"Hey, old-timer. See what you can find out about the funeral arrangements up in Santa Fe and call me back. I'm fine. Talk to you later."

Then I decided to call Otis and see where he was.

"Otis," he said after the second ring.

"Hey," I said. "You'd never guess what I'm doing."

"Clay," he said. "Damn, it's good to hear your voice, dude. Where are you?"

"On the road just outside of Nashville," I said. "So far I've picked up a three-legged farting dog and an old guy carrying a cross. I expect a fat lady and a pig-faced man at any time."

There was nothing but laughter for a second, then a whoop. "Dude, you almost made me run off the road," he said. "You must be tripping with Ken Kesey or something. Did you say a three-legged dog?"

"I said three-legged farting dog," I corrected. "Ray told me to name him Buster, which I did, although it didn't stop him from farting. Nothing could stop him from farting. He's better than a car alarm, though. Anybody had half a mind to steal this car, he'd drive them off screaming."

"I'm on the way to Charlotte," Otis said. "It's so weird to be on the road at the same time, going in different directions. The universe is really playing some changes on us."

The universe. If Otis isn't one with the universe, he at least claims to be on a first-name basis. Me, whenever he talks about the universe, I see distant stars and a whole lot of black space. I've got a perfectly good god I used to believe in, back when I still believed in things. Why get all transcendental about quarks and quasars?

"Hey," he said, remembering something. "You should call Tracy if you get the chance. She called me this afternoon to see if you got away okay. I told her I'd tell you if I talked to you."

"Okay," I said. "You've told me."

"So what're your plans, my man?"

I finished up my cake—which is to say that I ate until I knew that if I took another bite I'd be violently ill—and checked the map. "I guess I'll get around and drive for a while tonight. I want to get as far as Fort Smith, maybe Oklahoma City. I'll see how I feel. Then I'd like to get on a daytime driving schedule. I'm going to have to be on a daytime schedule in Santa Fe for this farce."

"Screw that daytime bullshit, man," Otis said. "We are creatures of the night."

"Uh-huh." I had a sudden vision of Gene Simmons of KISS, tongue extended. "Listen, say hi to the guys. And remember, you promised to stay out of trouble."

"Done and done. I've been out of trouble all day long."

"You've probably been asleep all day."

"Well, yeah, that too."

"It's a good start. Hey, I'll talk to you later."

I checked my watch. 7:30. Tracy would be at her folks'. "Let's go," I said. Buster seemed willing. I pulled onto the access road, then onto the highway, then accelerated up to a good humming seventy-five. Traffic had thinned out and I was back in the country in what felt like no time. Buster punctuated the silence with three lethal farts, spaced about twenty minutes apart. I was beginning to see that if you could get the pattern down, Buster was something like Old Faithful. You could set your watch on him.

"I think we can get to Memphis in time for dinner," I said. "I would dearly love to have some barbecue."

Buster seemed to have no opinion about it.

I picked up the cell phone and dialed, clamped it to my ear so I could hear.

"Hello," came the gruff male voice, a little put-out at having to answer the phone. It was Alvin York, who still scared the crap out of me. I'd been calling his house since I was in eighth grade. I guess some things you never grow out of. He was in his late fifties or sixties now, certainly past the prime of intimidation, but I still felt myself sit up straighter as I heard his voice.

"Yes sir," I called into the phone. "It's Clay Forester, sir. May I speak to your daughter?"

"Clay, she's already gone to bed, I think," he said, then called off to his wife Martha to confirm. "She said if you called—" and then I lost the rest to a cell glitch.

"What's that?" I shouted into the phone.

"Said to leave a number, if you could." After a moment's hesitation, I gave him Ray's cell number and hung up.

There was a lot of dark highway before we got anywhere. I smiled, then stopped smiling; it was like the universe: a sprinkling of lights, and an awful lot of dark, dark space.

It's in the dark space that dark thoughts emerge. I think it was Hemingway who wrote about how it was easy to be hard-boiled in the daytime, but at night it was a different matter, and nothing truer did he ever write. I sang for a while, but it didn't seem to work as well as the night before; I was getting farther away from my shelter and I was starting to feel the elements.

Sublimate, I told myself. Happy thoughts.

Otis and that spring break trip to Myrtle Beach, bodysurfing and drinking Busch and talking up the snooty Jewish girls from Brandeis. Otis climbing over the barriers at the Air and Space museum to climb into the ME-262 jet fighter, the docent screaming, him fleeing from security out onto the Mall.

Otis sitting beside my bed after my family was dead, watching over me to make sure that I didn't do some violence to myself.

No, you idiot. Happy thoughts.

Ray teaching me to fish. Bait fishing first: worms and stink bait at Lake Santeetlah, bass and crappie and catfish in rivers and ponds. Then, when I was older and worthy of it, fly fishing. Strict rules about how to use the wrist, about how to tie a leader, how to wade a stream. The plop of the leader and fly onto the water.

Plop. Plop.

But that brought back one of the days after Ray and Momma and Otis arrived in D.C.: Ray and I walking around the Tidal Basin.

The trees were so full of cherry blossoms that the branches couldn't hold them. As we walked, clusters of blossoms plopped into the water. The gutters and streets were full of blossoms, pink and white turning gray and black with dirt and soot.

We walked on around toward the Jefferson Memorial. I did a report on Jefferson when I was in eighth grade. For years he was one of my heroes, and the monument was one of my favorite public spaces in D.C., so without really thinking about it, I wandered in and stood in front of the bronze statue, twenty feet tall on a six-foot pedestal.

"What's that in his hand?" Ray asked. "Document of some kind. Declaration of Independence, maybe?"

I said nothing, just stood, hands in my pockets.

"A great man," Ray said.

"A dead man," I said. "Nothing left of him but words."

"Ah, but what words," he said gently. We were standing next to the southeast wall, and Ray read:

I am not an advocate for frequent changes in laws and constitutions, but laws and institutions must go hand in hand with the progress of the human mind. As that becomes more developed, more enlightened, as new discoveries are made, new truths discovered and manners and opinions change, with the change of circumstances, institutions must advance also to keep pace with the times. We might as well require a man to wear still the coat which fitted him when a boy as civilized society to remain ever under the regimen of their barbarous ancestors.

"Isn't that beautiful?" Ray had asked. He was a man who could find beauty in many places: the sun glinting on water, a spray of azaleas, a perfectly written neoclassical sentence.

I grunted and walked back outside. Ray got us some hot dogs and Diet Cokes from a vendor next to the Tidal Basin, and we took a seat. Ducks paddled out on the water. I could hear some sort of dinging, perhaps a railroad crossing, way off in the distance. A jet soared along the Potomac on its way to Washington National. Thomas Jefferson was still standing behind us, tall, free, and defiant, but I could no longer see him, could no longer even imagine him. I saw other faces.

"I can't stay here, Ray," I had said, and I was further panicked by the panic I heard in my voice. I stood up and Ray stood with me.

"It's all right, son. We can go someplace else. Memories hit you?"

Oh, yeah, memories. Anna Lynn and I had walked drunk around the basin late one spring night a couple of years before, celebrating her winning her first big class-action suit against a major polluter. Back in those days we thought one person could make a difference. We thought we were alive for a reason.

We thought we were going to be together forever.

"No, Ray," I said, shoving that thought out of my head as I always did. "It's not this place." I nodded at the ducks, the cherry blossoms pushed across the sidewalk and under the wheels of cars by the breeze. "It's this place." I spread my hand in a sweeping half circle: the Potomac, the Washington Monument, the Capitol, Georgetown off unseen in the distance to the northwest. "I can't stay here. I'm coming home."

He looked me in the eyes and nodded, but he asked, "What are you going to do there, son?"

I took a deep breath, let it out. "I'm going to try to stay alive," I said. But that wasn't fair. Ray was scared; I could see it in his eyes, glistening. I took another breath, let it out. "I don't know what I'm going to do, Ray, and honestly, I don't care. It doesn't feel like I'm ever going to care again. But—"

"But maybe you will, son," Ray said. "Maybe you'll grow strong and mend and learn how to go on." He put his hand on my shoulder, then moved it to the middle of my back. That hand felt strong, secure, massive—a wall to hide behind or a lifeline back to the world, whichever was needed. "I'm so sorry, son," he said, and he was weeping, and I felt a catch in my throat and thought that I might cry, too.

But I didn't, and I don't, not because I have some hang-up about men crying—I'd kick somebody's ass if they made fun of Ray's tears that day—but because it felt like an indulgence I had no right to, that I didn't deserve.

I was in fact dry-eyed as I looked over at Buster, who had brought me back to the present, to Tennessee and Interstate 40, with his singular gift.

"Happy thoughts," I said to him, and he wagged his tail, lost his balance, and fell into the front floorboard. I laughed before he gave me a withering stare and scrabbled with what dignity he could muster back onto the seat.

"I'm sorry," I said, and I was. He was now my only friend.

It was headed toward ten o'clock, and I was past the Tennessee River, through Jacksonville, but still a ways out of Memphis. "Damn it," I said. "No barbecue tonight." I stifled a yawn and Buster settled in to go to sleep. The inner man was speaking. Barbecue, he said. I must have barbecue.

"Tomorrow," I told him. I took an exit to get gas and consult the AAA map Ray had put in the dash: sixteen hours and twenty minutes of drive time to Santa Fe at fifty-five miles an hour. I had two more driving days to do that, plus I was going a lot faster than fifty-five. Barbecue, the inner man said. Stay in Memphis. Get barbecue. Drive on tomorrow.

"You keep quiet," I said. And then the universe opened up for me. I saw a billboard for Corky's Barbecue, the legendary rib place, and saw that they had a location on Germantown Parkway, not far off the interstate.

"Ribs to go," I muttered, to myself and the inner man, both of us now happy. We'd have Memphis barbecue and I'd still make Fort Smith.

Except, of course, that the universe and I weren't on a first-name basis, our mutual friendship with Otis notwithstanding.

Oh, the barbecue was wonderful. I made a mess the likes of which that little car had probably never seen before. I went through ribs like a chainsaw goes through saplings, and God saw that it was good. I got wet and dry—that is, ribs with sauce and also with the special dry seasoning—because I couldn't decide which I liked better, and even after eating them I couldn't, except to note that the wet were more of a challenge to cleanliness.

I had driven all the way through Memphis and had just crossed the Mississippi into Arkansas. The lights of the downtown skyscrapers had disappeared behind me. West Memphis, Arkansas, was an altogether seedier proposition than Memphis, Tennessee, and I was happy to be moving through it mostly in the dark. The kind folks at Corky's had given me a bunch of lemon-scented moist towelettes, and I was in the process of cleaning my face when the night began to grow darker. It wasn't an eclipse or freak atmospheric condition, I figured out pretty quickly. The Triumph's headlights were fading.

"Not a good sign," I told my canine friend. "I don't want you to go all gaseous on me, but it looks like we're going to be sidelined for a bit."

The lights went out completely, and then the engine went within seconds, the electrical system completely dead, no spark left to fire the controlled explosions of an internal combustion engine. I shifted into neutral and was near enough an exit that I could get off the highway at a pretty good clip. I was heartened to see a couple of buildings on my side of the highway, all of them lit up even this late.

Going up the off-ramp ate up a lot of our momentum, but I was able to coast into the nearest parking lot, which turned out to be Curly's Place GIRLS GIRLS GIRLS Topless if the multitude of badly lettered signs was any indication. A truck stop with an all-night diner sat the next parking lot over, but I saw a bright halogen streetlight around the back of the strip bar and thought it would be a decent place to look the car over—lots of light, and nobody around to watch. For me, having a car break down or needing help in general has always been something of an embarrassment.

So when I ran out of coast, I got out and began pushing. It wasn't much of an effort until I had to turn the wheel—no power steering—and get it around the back corner of the building. I grunted with the strain, and the steering wheel gave a bit with the effort, but we made it, me raising my hands and feeling exultant as Rocky on the steps of the Philadelphia Museum of Art, Buster with his head cocked sideways and looking at me like I was a strange new form of life.

I popped the hood and immediately saw the problem. I'd thought it was alternator-related, and it was; the smell of singed rubber coming to my nose was my first clue that the belt that had worried me some hours earlier had broken and lay tangled across the hot engine block.

"Well," I told Buster, who had his paws up on the top of the door and was balancing on his lone hind leg, "how hard can that be to fix? Get a new belt on, get the battery charged, and we're on our way again." I could check the truck stop for belts, at worst get the number of a parts store I could call in the morning. "Get ready, I'm closing the hood." Which I did, gently, so as not to startle him too much; he was a startlesome creature.

"I used to talk to my dog," came a still small voice from behind me that frankly scared the shit out of me. I jumped and whirled simultaneously—I wish I could see the replay—to find a little boy sitting on the back steps of Curly's Place GIRLS GIRLS GIRLS Topless.

He was maybe six or seven, but he was small for his age, dressed immaculately in khaki shorts and a navy Ralph Lauren polo shirt; his shoes were a little scuffed, as kids' nice shoes almost always are, but they were tiny Cole Haans, and his crew socks were an immaculate white.

"Hey," I said, trying not to use my you-scared-the-shit-out-of-me voice and failing miserably. "I didn't see you back there."

"I'm not very big," he said. "I wasn't hiding, though."

"No," I said. "I'm sure you weren't."

"You don't know my name," he said.

I nodded. "That's true. What is your name?"

His lips began to fidget back and forth and then he shook his head, his hair falling back and forth over his face, and he said "Mommy says not to tell people my name."

"Okay," I said. "Your mama is probably right."

"I like Cocoa Puffs for breakfast," he said.

"Really," I said. "I have a friend who likes Cocoa Pebbles."

"Does he like Fruity Pebbles?"

"Not as much as Froot Loops." I sat down on the steps, leaving a good distance between us so he wouldn't feel threatened. "Have you ever had Froot Loops?"

"Oh, sure," he said. "I used to eat breakfast cereal all the time when we lived with my dad. Now I have to drink barley green for breakfast." He scrunched up his face.

"Barley what?"

"It's this green stuff. Powder. You mix it with water. Mom says it's good for me. I don't like it."

"I'm big on Cap'n Crunch myself," I said. "I'll bet you didn't know that."

"I like it too."

He was a good kid. I looked into the sky and saw the

moon, almost down. "Where's your mom?" I asked, hoping maybe I didn't already know the answer. "You really shouldn't be out here by yourself."

"She's inside," he said. "I can't come in because she says it's a toxic environment."

It probably was that. "Do you sit out here all night?"

"No," he said, hanging his head. "Sometimes I sit at the restaurant. Sometimes I wait in the hotel if there's something on TV I can watch. But TV preachers were on, and they make my head hurt. And I don't want to sit in the restaurant any more. Flo smells. She makes me cough when she hugs me."

I was getting more and more angry the more he talked in his accepting way about the world as he knew it. This was a good kid, a bright kid. What kind of life was this? What kind of mother would do such a thing to her son?

Not my problem. I don't get involved in things like this, I had told Buster, just prior, admittedly, to picking up the cross guy back in Tennessee, and although all told that hadn't turned out badly, my way still seemed the best way to go through life; if you get involved you could get to caring too much, and bad things always seem to come of that.

But this was just a little boy, and it was his life we were talking about. It wouldn't hurt to call Child Protective Services or whatever they called it here in Arkansas, let them know about this little boy sitting on the back steps of a strip club in the middle of the night. And who knows? Maybe they could help his mom too, help her get a steady day job, help her get out of the life.

"I'm going in to use the phone," I said. "I wish you'd go back over to the restaurant."

"Mom is coming out soon," he said. "She gave me her watch to hold." He held it up and pointed to the eleven. "See? When the hands are on the eleven and the twelve she comes out to eat with me."

It was a cheap watch with a faux leather band, in sharp contrast to his nice clothes. On the dial face was a stick-figure drawing of a boy, and across the bottom of the face was a name: Michael.

It was the wristwatch of a proud mother.

"She'll be out in about five minutes," I said, trying to reconcile this data. "Good for you." I held myself back from tousling his hair, which clearly called out for such treatment, as I got up and stuck out my hand. "It was really nice to meet you."

He shook my hand solemnly—he had been brought up well, certainly in better society than this biker bar—and then waved at Buster, who yipped.

"Will you watch out for Buster while I'm inside?"

"Can I pick him up?"

"Sure, if he'll let you. See you later, okay?"

But he was down the steps and lifting the frantically wiggling and wagging Buster into his arms, who for a moment wasn't a battered, farting three-legged dog. He was just a puppy with a little boy, and something about the scene made me want to cry.

I haven't been in many strip clubs in my life, but this was certainly by far the seediest and the rowdiest. I heard AC-DC's "Girl's Got Rhythm" well before I opened the front door, and inside it was almost deafening. A gang of Harley riders in black leather sat against the far wall, looking up at the stage, where the feature dancer was swooping around the chrome pole clad in a scanty pair of panties and nothing else.

"What can I get you?" the bartender yelled when I asked for the phone.

"My car broke down out back—" I started to say, then held up a single finger and indicated the beer tap.

"Who's this?" I yelled when he brought the beer, which looked and smelled as good as I remembered. He knew I meant the dancer, not the beer.

"Calls herself Natalie," he said. "Been here a couple of weeks. She's good as hell."

I looked across at the stage and tried to ignore her breasts, which although they weren't big were firm and, like the rest of her, sleek and beautiful. She moved like a real dancer, not a tittie dancer, and her swings around the pole had a grace to them. She wasn't just here to shake her ass in guys' faces, although I was sure that the distinctions were lost on some of the folks here, who were the same yahooing, rebel-yelling-screaming rednecks who would have fought to get me to play "Free Bird."

I put my hand around the beer, felt the beads of moisture cool against my palm, raised it to my lips, and looked back across the room to where Natalie was dancing.

The music had changed: still AC-DC, but now it was "Walk All Over You," which fit her perfectly. She seemed to have a reserve or distance as she danced; I found it really attractive. It was like she chose to dance on her terms, whatever we might be thinking as we watched. Then she looked out across the room and met my eyes and looked away, like I was just another of these beer-swilling yahoos, and I put the beer down and scooted it out of my reach, which is what I should have done all along.

"Hey," I called to the bartender. "She belong to the kid out back?"

The bartender gave me a quick glance, then looked back down to the glasses he was washing. "What kid?"

"Nothing," I said. "Thanks." I left the beer sitting untouched on the counter—would it ever get easier?—and walked out without using the phone. Something I couldn't fathom was going on, and maybe it really was none of my business, like I'd thought all along.

The two of them were playing and laughing when I turned the corner. Michael was down on the ground giggling and Buster was licking his face. "Stop, Buster, stop," Michael was saying, although Buster and I both knew he didn't really mean it.

"Hey," I called to Michael, "I'm going over to the truck stop. Would you mind putting Buster back in the car when your mom comes out?"

"Okay," he managed to get out before Buster was on him again, yapping, tail wagging so hard he couldn't stand upright. I smiled and sighed and got my bag, and then I turned to wheel it across the dark parking lot past the slumbering, lumbering semis—running lights on, engines idling—and then back into the light.

In the store section I could have had my choice of CB radios or antennas, but nothing even remotely fan-beltish.

Sonny, who sat with slicked-back hair behind the counter sur-
reptitiously smoking Luckies, pushed me the Yellow Pages for
the Memphis area, and I wrote down the number of an import parts shop on Jackson Avenue in midtown Memphis I
could call in the morning.

Then I took a seat in the restaurant to get a cup of coffee
and—okay, I will confess—to see if I could get the scoop on
Michael's mother if she came over. Since some children's
books and crayons were piled on a table, I figured that was
probably Michael's hangout, and I grabbed a booth nearby.

"Coffee," I told the waitress, who looked like and was a
Flo: big sprayed hair, ample bosom, red lipstick, Juicy Fruit.

"You want anything to eat?" she asked me. She did smell
like cigarette smoke, although she seemed nice enough.
Maybe Michael was a little too sensitive.

"What's good?" I asked, scanning the menu.

"Best chicken-fry in three counties," she said. "Mashed
potatoes, salad, and rolls with that."

I wasn't really hungry—I could still smell the ribs on my
fingers, which brought flashing back a guilty memory of once
carrying Tracy's most intimate scent into our American government class—but I never turn down the chance to sample a
good chicken-fried steak. "Sounds good," I said. "And coffee,
black."

"All right, hon," she said, giving me a friendly wink. "You
won't be sorry."

I turned toward the window and looked out into the parking lot Michael and his mother would be coming across. It
was about ten minutes later that I saw them. She was dressed
in khakis and a blue oxford shirt, and she held his hand as
they walked. In her other hand she held a plastic grocery bag.

Flo was dropping off my food, and she was close enough
that I could see how she lit up when she saw them. "Isn't he
just the most beautiful little boy?" she asked, and I nodded.
He was certainly way up there.

They took a seat at the table catty-corner from me where
Michael's books were already piled, and Michael's mom put
her bag on the table with a rustling grunt and took out the
menu.

"Flo," she called, and Flo came over a little nervously. "What's vegetables tonight?"

"All we got left is corn, darlin'," Flo said, somehow aware that all hell was going to break loose. "Okra was gone at ten-thirty. I tried to set some back for you but someone ate it."

"Flo," she said, making a stab at calm, "corn is not a vegetable," and she pursed her lips. Then she turned to Michael and said brightly, "How about some salad and tofu?" She produced a package of tofu from her plastic bag and passed it over to Flo, who took it by one corner like she'd been handed a dead cat.

"Okay," Michael said.

Flo went off with her unaccustomed burden of soy curd, and Michael's mother was left murmuring at the menu and shaking her head. "I know better than to expect organic produce," she was saying, partly to Michael but not much. "But would it be too much to expect some things without white flour, processed sugar, or hydrogenated oils?"

"Probably so," I chimed in with what I thought was a good-natured but sympathetic shrug. "Although this is pretty good stuff." I raised a bite of my steak on my fork.

Her face rose slowly to take another look at me. She'd seen me when she came in, but had ignored me. "Would you like to know what that chicken-fried steak is going to do in your digestive system?"

"Not really, no." She looked at me, in fact, as if we'd never seen each other before, and I was doing my best to meet her there, although it's hard to pretend you haven't seen a beautiful woman naked when both of you know you have.

"He likes Cap'n Crunch," Michael said.

"It's true," I told her quizzical face. "It's my lone remaining vice."

And then, when she still sat looking at me quizzically, I said, to try and put her at ease, "Your son and I are old friends."

"Really?" It was not a friendly question. Her claws were out; this mother was poised to pounce.

"That's right," I said. "I know he likes Cocoa Pebbles—"

"Puffs," Michael said.

"Right, sorry, Cocoa Puffs for breakfast," and I ticked things off on my fingers, "that he doesn't like to watch TV preachers because they make his head hurt, that he doesn't like having barley greens for breakfast, that he has a mother who loves him very much, and that his life used to be very different."

She stood up over the table, one arm between me and Michael, and now she wasn't wary or quizzical—she was angry and scared. Very scared.

"Come on, sweetheart," she said, not taking her eyes off me. "We'll eat later. Let's get out of here."

"Hey," I said in my most calming voice. "You don't have anything to worry from me. My name is Clay Forester. I'm a musician from Robbinsville, North Carolina. My car broke down—it's the little convertible with the dog in it behind Curly's Place GIRLS GIRLS GIRLS Topless."

"Buster is his dog," Michael said.

She looked at me for a long moment before she sat again. "So he didn't send you?"

"Not that I'm aware of. He? Unless you're speaking of God, in which case I have to say, who knows? We're not on speaking terms."

With the talk of God, I had unknowingly passed from one realm to another. She lost her fear and seemed to gain some sense of surety. "Are you a Christian, Mr. Forester?"

Oh, Christ. "I never know how to answer that question," I said.

"Then you aren't," she said.

I sniffed laughter. "That's what I would have thought you'd say. Would have thought, that is, if I hadn't seen you recently in another setting."

"Whatever do you mean," she said—not a question—and she met my gaze proudly, and with her son watching the exchange avidly, I couldn't pull the trigger on her.

"My mistake," I said. "I thought maybe I'd seen you somewhere before."

"I get that a lot," she said, and then she shut down like a plant at closing time. "Honey, let's go wash your hands."

And when Michael looked back in my direction, she turned

his head forward like they were Lot and his family escaping Sodom.

"Bitch," I said under my breath. I pulled a ten from my wallet and left it on the table. Then I walked my bag across the overpass and on to the Motel 6 on the other side. I wasn't disappointed at the accommodations, at another night in a Motel 6. Actually, I was beginning to realize that I loved Motel 6. I could afford better, sure, but there was something about the monastic, cell-like nature of the place that appealed to me. It was all I deserved, I thought. Or maybe it was comforting in some sort of womblike way.

I flicked through the channels—nothing good on HBO or ESPN—wished for a good book, and turned to the window. I looked out on I-40: sparse traffic, a few stolid semis rushing commerce to the far reaches of the Empire, vacationers looking to get just a few more miles in before they crashed for the night.

And across the highway, I could see the truck stop, the lighted restaurant, and if my eyes weren't playing tricks on me, a little boy sitting alone in a window booth.

It was a long, sad night.

1

I called the import parts place at eight, got a guy named Troy Felix on the phone who got all excited when I told him what I needed and said he'd deliver the belt just to see the car, put me on hold for a bit, and then came back on with a disappointed groan.

"Mr. Forester, I don't have a belt in stock that'll fit it. And I guar-own-tee you, ain't nobody else does. But they promise to overnight it to me, and I can bring it out there to you first thing in the morning. Will that work for you?"

"Let's do it," I said, and prepared myself for a day of lounging around the Motel 6. "I can catch a few z's, maybe catch up on my correspondence." I gave Troy my number at the hotel and thanked him.

Then I climbed back into the tiny monk's bed shoved into the corner of my tiny abbey room, put the pillow over my head to drown out the road noise, and went back to sleep for a few hours.

It was restless sleep, lots of going up and down through dream states, and I must have had half a dozen garbled dreams about little boys in trouble. In some of them I was the boy; in some of them, Little Ray was in danger. But all of them had that common thread. I woke up wondering about Michael and his mother and if they were in some kind of trouble.

At eleven, I showered, shaved, and dressed to walk across to the truck stop and to check on Buster. On the way, I poked my head in at the motel office and asked Betty, the manager, to extend my stay another day.

"Sure enough," she said to me, her smile bright as a solar flare. She was somebody's grandma if there's any justice in the universe. "We're sure glad to have you another day."

Buster was underneath the dumpster again, but seemed to be there more for comfort than for comestibles. When he saw me coming he squeezed out, his tail waggling wildly.

"I'll bet you saw some interesting things out here last night," I told him. "Hang around for a bit and I'll bring you breakfast."

Flo, of course, wasn't working the morning shift, but I took the same place I'd sat last night, kind of to feel like a regular. Darla was the morning waitress. She was a scrawny girl with caved-in cheeks and a bad bleach job, but she at least didn't smell like smoke. She was probably mainlining heroin instead.

"Pancakes," I said. "Hash browns. Bacon. Two eggs, scrambled. Orange juice. And give me a couple of orders of sausage to go. Crumbled, not patties, if you can."

"I'll ask," she said, as though I was asking for escargot or béchamel sauce.

She left, and I sat looking over at the table where they had sat the night before. And had I really seen Michael over here sitting in one of these booths last night, maybe while his mom was back on stage?

I asked Darla when she came back, all bad-teethed grin because the cook told her he could crumble my sausage. "I met a little boy last night when my car broke down. He was sitting back behind the strip club. Do you know anything about him? Does his mama treat him okay?"

She looked me over real good before she said anything. "Well," she said confidentially, "I'll tell you"—and here she looked around the dining room to make sure nobody was listening in—"I'm not supposed to talk about them. Not so much as a syllable."

"I'm just worried about the boy," I said, trying to put on my nicest face. "It doesn't seem healthy, that's all. It's none of my business."

She cocked her head to one side and said, "No, sir, it isn't. But if it'll make you feel better and maybe put you in a tipping mood, I'll tell you this. That boy is as well loved as any little boy I know, my own two included. And I wouldn't be in that woman's shoes for all the gold in Fort Knox. And that's all I'll say." She zipped her finger across her lip.

"Okay," I said. "I had a little boy once. I just wanted to know he was okay."

"Listen," she said. "He's as okay as he's gonna get. Okay? I'll go check on your order."

I ate my breakfast slowly. I really ought to stop ordering pancakes; they're not good for you, they sit in your stomach like a lump of lead, and anyway, nobody makes them like my momma.

I dropped off some sausage with Buster and gave him the lowdown—we were stranded for the day but would get on the road first thing in the A.M.—and urged him to lay low unless he felt the need to stretch his legs, at least those he had left. Then when I got back to the room, I did something I knew was almost crazy and probably a result of sleep deprivation: I called Momma.

"Forester residence," Miss Ellen said, as she has for more years than I know, even after Momma married Ray and I was the lone remaining Forester.

"Good morning, Miss Ellen," I said. "This is your prodigal nephew speaking."

There was a moment's pause, and then a strange and unaccountable warmth as she announced to the room, "It's Clay. Clay's on the telephone." She seemed her old formal self when she returned. "I suppose you'll be wanting to talk to your mother?"

"Yes, ma'am," I said. "In a minute. How is everything there? How are you feeling?"

"I'm feeling quite well," she said, "and all of us are keeping busy. We've got church tonight, I suppose you know. Will you be able to go somewhere? Is there a good Baptist church nearby?"

"I'm stranded out on the highway west of Memphis," I told her. "I'm waiting for a part for the car. It's coming tomorrow, and then I'll have some driving to make up, but I believe I can do it without too much trouble. The only church hereabouts is one where women dance without all their clothes on. I was thinking about going there for worship tonight. Is that the kind of church that would be good for me do you think?"

I could hear her push the phone away from her and announce, "Ellie, your heathen son wishes to speak to you," and then my mother, breathless, full of questions about my well being.

"I'm fine," I said, "fine," and after the initial gust of wind, she settled down to a strong breeze.

"Are you getting enough rest?"

"Yes, ma'am."

"Are you eating well?"

"Yes, ma'am."

"Is the car running okay?"

"Yes, ma'am. Although it's got a little problem just at the moment, Ray did a bang-up job getting it going. It'll get me there just fine."

"Have you learned anything on your trip yet? Anything at all?"

I had to stop and think about that for a bit. "Yes, ma'am," I said at last. "Although I don't know just yet what it might be, I believe I have."

"Well praise the Lord," she said. "Steve Forester's death is part of a great plan for your life."

"Yes ma'am," I said. Isn't it, though? "Has anyone called Santa Fe to check on the funeral?"

"I believe Ray was going to do that this morning," she said. "The woman who called us was . . . Rosalena, wasn't that right, Sister? Rosalena Fischer. Don't know a thing about her. I suppose she's Mexican. Or Jewish. But she's probably all right nonetheless." Then she said, a little lower, "I have a suspicion that they were lovers. Him and her. Maybe living together all these years."

"Do you, now?"

"I do. I mean, why wouldn't he have found someone after all this time? I don't have any right to complain about that. And why else would she be the one who called us? Who knew your name and asked us to give you the message?"

"I don't know, Momma. Rosalena, you say."

"That's how I understand it. Mexican, like I said."

"Or Jewish."

"Right. Or maybe both."

I made sympathetic noises. Whatever dark forces had induced me to call were wearing off, and now she was just my annoying mother again. "I gotta go, Momma," I said. "Tell Ray to call me later, okay?"

"So soon?" she asked. "Why, we—"

Which was what she was saying when I hung up on her and tossed the phone away from me onto the bed. Jesus.

Take Jesus, even. If my mother understood that Jesus was a Jew, she'd probably give up her faith. I just didn't understand that, never did, and it was one of the things that really tripped me up with the whole God scene—how could you claim to follow somebody who loves everyone and then choose for yourself who you're willing to love?

Well, like the cross guy said, you can choose your friends, but you can't choose your family.

Maybe the truck stop had some reading matter besides the over-the-road magazines and travel guides I'd seen on the trucker side; surely in the convenience store one could glom a Stephen King novel to go with your Corn Nuts and Baby Ruth. A day by the pool reading trashy fiction, maybe looking over my sunglasses at the nonexistent woman who wouldn't be caught dead dipping her toe into the tepid pool of the Motel 6 in East Memphis, Arkansas, on a Wednesday after noon—or any other afternoon, to be honest. Still, it felt like a plan, and the walk down the access road and across the highway, originally so tedious, was starting to seem common to me, like the bus ride that I used to take from Georgetown to the office in D.C., or the Blue Ridge Parkway from Robbinsville to Asheville; after a while you could do the drive without even looking up from the dash.

I fell asleep in a lounge chair next to the pool in a new pair of plenty-of-room-in-the-seat shorts I bought in the store. With a new straw hat on my head, I looked like somebody's goofy father on vacation. There was a Nordic family of four—another goofy dad, a somewhat chunky mom, and two big, chunky Aryan boys—playing loudly in and around the water, so my sleep was a testimonial to the power of hot sun and exhaustion. I had picked up what I thought was a good novel, King's *The Girl Who Loved Tom Gordon*, but I was out by mid-first chapter, and there I remained, sopping up the sun, until I woke up some hours later with a lethal sunburn on stomach, arms, legs, and feet.

I slid into the pool hoping for relief; the soles and tops of my feet felt like I'd stuck them into a toaster oven and closed the door. For a few minutes, the shock of the cool water helped me pretend I wasn't in serious trouble.

It was about six in the evening when I finally got up enough courage to make the long, slow walk back across the highway. I needed some sunburn stuff badly, and if I could just endure the pain until I got there, I thought all would be well. The blue T-shirt I had on was one of my oldest and softest, but the way it was rubbing against my chest and upper arms, it could have been lined with broken glass. Every step was misery, as my poor feet rebelled both above and below.

But then I was in the store for the third time that day, stocking up on Solarcaine and Tylenol, and five minutes later I was sitting in a truckers' shower stall slathering myself head to foot with Solarcaine and choking in a roiling gray cloud of propellant and product. I was going to be high as a kite if this stuff still had any brain-killing inhalants in it.

Once, I would have been happy about that idea, but for some reason, as I was struggling for a breath of air with even the tiniest bit of oxygen in it, it didn't seem so compelling. I would have opened the door if I hadn't suddenly had a vision of myself stepping into the corridor all oiled up like rough trade at the gay truckers' ball.

No, thanks. I figured I'd just stay in there and suffocate.

At last, the air cleared some, or at least my lungs adapted to breathing Solarcaine. I shrugged my shirt back on, pulled on my pants and lightly tied on my shoes, and limped out into the truckers' lounge.

One old boy was sitting near the showers watching *Big Trouble in Little China* on the overhead monitor. His nose wrinkled up as I approached, and he took one look at me and shook his head. "Shoo-oo-ee, boy, I've hauled pigs that didn't smell like you do. You take a bath in that shit?"

"Near enough," I said. "I haven't gotten burned like this since I was a teenager at the beach."

"Well, let's hope you never have another'n like it," he said. "You get on out of here."

"Yes, sir," I said, and I trudged on outside to air out. It was hot in the back parking lot, the heat still rolling up from the asphalt and in the air itself, so as soon as I thought I had dissipated enough toxic gases to make it less likely I'd spark a run for the exits, I went into the restaurant, eased into my booth, and waved at Flo.

"Evening," she said, coming over with a menu. "Why look at you. You're all shiny. You look like a shiny red lobster."

"Which is about what I feel like," I said. "That'll teach me to have a leisurely day by the pool."

She tsked sadly and shook her head. "Grown man like you ought to know how to take care of himself."

"It's true," I said, "it's certainly true."

"What'll you have, darlin'?"

"Start me off with iced tea, a lot of it."

"Check." She went off to pour me a glass.

I took a look outside, and there, far across the parking lot, saw Michael sitting on the steps with Buster. Michael had him sitting in his lap like a kitten and was rubbing his tummy. Buster's tongue was hanging out of his fool head. He probably hadn't had love like that in a long time, maybe not ever.

"Just breaks my heart," Flo said when she looked across the way. "Beautiful little boy like that."

"Why can't they go home?" I asked.

Flo shook her head. "Can't do it," she said. "That woman's between a rock and a hard place."

I shook my head in sympathy. Mostly I felt for the boy. I suppose that must be why after I ate my meatloaf and trudged hot-footedly home, after I lay on my back for hours trying to get comfortable, the noise from the highway bouncing around my head like a pinball, I felt compelled to get to my feet, to cross the narrow room, to pull back the curtains and look outside.

There was Michael across the way, sitting in a booth by himself. It was 1:30 in the morning by my watch, and I started cursing under my breath as I pulled my clothes on, tears of pain springing to my eyes as I dressed. "Christ almighty," I said as I pulled on my shirt. "Damn it to hell," as I pulled my pants over lobster legs. "Piss, shit, fuck, fuck, fuck," as I tied my shoes onto my even more tender feet.

What I wouldn't have given for a car that worked.

I bought a pack of cards in the truck stop store and padded into the restaurant, catching Flo's eye as I entered. It's just me, my wave said, and she relaxed and approached the booth as I sat across from Michael.

"Flo, I believe I'll have some pancakes," I told her, cutting the new deck. "Maybe you could bring some for my friend here as well. On me."

She turned her head sideways a second and made a face—pancakes were not on her instruction list from mama—but then she relented. "Okay. Two orders of hotcakes coming right up."

Michael had been coloring Scrooge McDuck in a coloring book about Donald and his known associates. He was coloring Scrooge green, like his money. I shuffled the deck, cut it, and started laying out a game of Klondike on my side of the table. I dealt out the seven foundation cards, and we worked in silence for a bit.

"You're a good colorer," I said after I felt him looking across at me. With a flourish, I laid a red seven on the one row that was going well.

"I'm okay," he said. "My mommy's really good."

I looked up at him and he dropped his head. "Did you have a good time with Buster today?"

He looked back up at me, and now a smile creased his face. He nodded, then put his head back down and returned to his coloring.

"I'm glad," I said. "Buster's a nice dog."

He looked up at me for a second, thought about what he wanted to say, and decided to say it anyway, even though it was just a whisper. "He's got really bad gas."

I laughed. There was a black eight, and I set it down. "He sure does."

He dropped his voice and leaned confidentially across the table. "Mommy says we shouldn't talk about gas. But Buster's gas is so bad she couldn't help it. He had gas while she was sitting on the steps with me." He started giggling. "Mommy was saying, 'Bad dog. Bad Buster.' And then he had gas again."

I laughed too. "He's a force of nature," I said. "Like hurricanes and earthquakes. Only with Buster, it's dog farts."

Michael was drinking milk at that moment, and he laughed so hard it spouted out his nose. He was coughing and laughing and I had to set down my cards because I was laughing and Flo was charging over to box my ears until she saw how happy he was and she started laughing too.

"Boys," she said, cleaning up the milk sprayed across the table.

"I've never seen anybody shoot milk out of their nose like that," I said when we could both breathe again. "Really. That was pretty good. That could be a marketable skill. You could join a circus and do it every night."

"Gross," he said. "My mommy wouldn't like it."

"Well, then it's a good thing she didn't see it," I said. "I won't tell."

"Promise?" His eyes were suddenly serious, and I couldn't do anything but nod and say, "I promise."

Flo brought out our pancakes and some syrup, and Michael could barely control his glee. He poured a pool of syrup an inch deep. Flo had to bring more. I helped him cut, but he could do everything else all by himself.

I had my mouth full of a too-big bite when he suddenly said something after minutes of food-induced silence.

"My dad is not being nice to my mom," he said. He didn't look up from his plate when he said it.

"I'm sorry to hear that," I said. I picked up the cards at that and slid them around on the table.

We sat there for a while in silence except for chewing and swallowing and the scrape of cards on the table.

"He hasn't been nice to her for a long time," he said.

I nodded. "My dad wasn't very nice to my mom either."

He looked up. "Did he make her cry?"

At the earliest edges of my memory, I could hear my mother weeping late at night for her husband who had gone away for good. "Lots of times," I said.

He bit his lip, looked down, looked back up again.

"Did he make you cry?"

I sighed and shook my head. "No. He wasn't around to make me cry."

"My dad made me cry," he said. "Lots of times. One time he said I was too loud, so he spanked me. He was really mad. I made him too mad. I had to go to the hospital. I cried and cried."

He looked up at me, his eyes liquid and brown. If that father had been in front of me at that moment I would have cut his throat. As it was, I could only sit and look into his eyes, sad and yearning, and distract myself from my anger by leaning my tender sunburned chest into the table and saying, "I'm sorry, Michael. I'm so sorry."

"How'd you know my name?"

"I know lots of things about you, remember?" Then I relented. "It's on your mom's watch."

"Ha. I'll bet you don't know my whole name." He crossed his arms with self-satisfaction.

"You'd be right," I said. "Do you want to tell me?"

"Michael Martin Cartwright," he said.

That name was familiar somehow, and I started to have a bad feeling in my stomach that was totally unconnected with my sunburn and the resulting nausea. I tried to keep things light: "Well, Michael Martin Cartwright, where is your daddy now?"

"In Nashville," he said. "We live at 1128 Fifth Avenue. It's a really big house. Sometimes the governor comes to eat with us."

I jotted down the address on my napkin with his red crayon and put it in my pocket. "Michael," I said, "it sounds to me like your daddy is a really important person."

His mouth fell open and he covered it with his hand. "How did you know that?"

"I'm a good guesser," I said. "A lucky guesser." I put the napkin in my pocket. "Michael," I said, "I want to tell you something. And I want you to remember it. Can you do that? You've got a really good memory for remembering things, don't you? Will you remember what I'm going to tell you?"

He nodded solemnly.

"It isn't right for people to hurt other people. Especially for daddies to hurt people. I was a daddy once, with a little boy like you. I didn't mean to, but I hurt my family too. That wasn't right. And I've never stopped being sorry for it."

He reached over and put his hand on my arm. "It's okay," he said. "Don't be sad."

"Okay," I said, blinking. "I'll try."

"Do you love your little boy even though you hurt him?"

I nodded, and when I thought I could trust my voice, I said, "Every single day."

He took his hand back and picked up his fork. "Where are they? Your family."

"They went away," I said.

"Like my mommy and me?" he asked. "Did they run away from you?"

"No," I said. "They went away in a different way."

He looked at me, and he didn't understand, and I guess maybe I wanted to tell him for some reason, wanted to tell somebody. I was a long way from home.

"They died," I said.

"Oh," he said, and he sat there silently for a bit, turning this over in his head. He took a bite, chewed, and then he asked, "Does that make you sad?"

I blinked and nodded. "Every single day." I pushed my plate away. Grief and pancakes do not mix, as I should know better than anyone. "Michael, let's keep all this our secret, okay? Your momma will worry if she thinks I know—"

"What secret?" she asked, and I jumped and banged my poor sunburned knees against the bottom of the table. I didn't hear her coming. Our conversation had been too involved and involving, I guess, or I would have seen her approach, watched her face grow red and her jaw clench, seen her ball her hands into fists. "What are you doing here? Get away from my son before I call the police. Flo!" she called.

I slid out, wincing. "I'm sorry. I didn't mean to frighten you. I couldn't sleep, and I thought—"

"What you thought is of no interest to me," she said, moving in between me and the table. "Get away from my son."

"He's nice," Michael said, but she whirled on him.

"We never talk to strangers," she said. "Never."

I took a deep breath and tried to put myself in her shoes. But it was hard, particularly hard when she was stepping on mine.

Unintentionally, I'm sure.

"I'm going," I groaned. I threw a wad of bills on the table. Maybe Flo would pass on the extra. "I'm sorry."

"You ought to be," she growled.

"Listen, lady," I growled back, "I've been here babysitting your baby while you've been—"

"It's okay," she said sharply, pulling her boy close and not coincidentally, covering his ears. "This mean man is leaving us alone now."

I opened my mouth to say something else, met Michael's frightened eyes, and decided against it. I nodded sadly to him and turned for the door. Maybe the Tylenol was kicking in, because I felt strangely calm, almost reflective as I stepped into the parking lot and again pronounced my judgement: "Bitch."

Interlude

"Ramblings around the River," by Sister Euless
—From *The Graham Star*, June 14, 2000

This is a time of much sadness as we consider the events of the past week. As many of you know, we heard Sunday that my nephew Clay Forester's father, Steve, Robbinsville High School Class of 1960, remembered for his roles in the high school musical theater productions of South Pacific *and* Carousel, *passed away Sunday night in Santa Fe, New Mexico. It was a double shock for us, as I'm sure you can imagine, since we had no idea he was still alive. Clay left for New Mexico to attend Steve's funeral in New Mexico on Friday. Please pray for him as he travels so far from home.*

Many of you have also heard the sad news that Alma Jean Shepherd came home from her doctor's appointment on Monday and found Clarence lying under the table. That nice young Dr. Modaressi made a point of telling Alma Jean to pass on to all those who brought over desserts and casseroles after her surgery that they are not responsible for the use that Clarence put them to, and truly his heart could have stopped at any time even without the extra weight he put on over the past few weeks.

Today is Flag Day! Remember as you display the Stars and Stripes to reflect on the sacrifices so many people have made over the years so that we could enjoy our freedom.

I hope to return to happier news next week. In the mean-time:

> *Wherever you go and whatever you do,*
> *Always remember that Jesus loves you.*

8

I sat up all night, hurting and totally pissed off. I couldn't lie down; the pain was too great. It felt as though I was being pricked by hot needles. So I sat at the table in my uncomfortable chair and watched the sun come up. Two hours later, the phone rang, and I rolled over gingerly to talk to Troy, the car lover at the import parts store. I gave him directions to the truck stop: "I'm right behind Curly's Place GIRLS GIRLS GIRLS Topless. Can't miss it."

He expected to be there in half an hour or less, so I took a cool shower, sprayed myself down again with Solarcaine, packed up, and left the bag on the bed for when I checked out. Even with the sun low in the sky, I was already hurting from the heat; it was going to be a long and particularly hard day, Tylenol notwithstanding. What I wouldn't have given for Percodan.

"Buster," I called as I arrived behind Curly's. "Yo, Buster." There was a rustling in the tall grass at the back of the lot, and Buster stood up and shook the sleep off. "We'll be going shortly," I said. "I know you'll miss that little boy, but maybe we can find you another one on down the road. This is not a stable situation, I'm afraid."

I ordered breakfast to go at the counter, and nodded at Darla, who froze me out completely. Flo had apparently passed on that I was now persona non grata. I took the bag of food back and fed Buster, and then Troy pulled around back with his auto parts van and I opened the hood of the Triumph for him.

"Oh," he said, and he just stood there for a minute shaking

his head. "Oh, my. That is one bee-yoo-tee-ful car. Where'd you get it?"

"It was my father's," I said, and then I started to take it back and couldn't figure out how to do it. Too much trouble, anyway. "He left it to me."

He walked around it, feeling the curves like it was a woman. "Man. Triumph TR3A. I haven't seen one like this in years. Nineteen sixty-one?" I nodded. "All original?"

"Body and upholstery, yeah. The top too, I guess. It's been covered up for years and years."

He put on the belt for me, whistling with joy the whole time, then pulled the van around to give me a jump. When I started the car, he leaned back against his truck like a chef who had just popped a particularly savory bite in his mouth. "Mmm," he said. "Beautiful."

"I'd let you drive it," I told him as he was unhooking the cables, "except I've got to be in New Mexico tomorrow and I'm a little pressed for time."

"Hey, this was totally worth it," he said. "Oh, I brought you an extra belt, just in case. On the house."

I was gathering up Buster and putting him in the car when a big black Mercedes came squealing into Curly's parking lot. A youngish man in dark gray pinstripes—they clashed with his dark sunglasses, I thought—jumped out to check the front door, which must have been locked. He shook his head when he climbed back in; then they flung gravel in their haste to get across to the truck stop. There were three of them, all told, two in front, one in the back, and when they got to the truck stop the two younger ones hustled inside and the older gentleman in the backseat followed in a more leisurely fashion behind them.

"Damn," Troy said as he got into his van. "What do you suppose those birds want?"

"Hungry for hotcakes," I said, yawning. I was trying to keep it calm, but something was wrong about this. I waved so long to Troy. Then I gunned the Triumph across the bridge and the wrong way down the access road to the motel. I ran into my room and grabbed up my bag, flung it into the backseat, and squealed back around to the office, where Betty damn near jumped out of her shoes when I threw the door open.

"Three men, Betty," I gasped. "In a black Mercedes. Were they just in here asking about Michael and his mother?"

"It's none of my business what a mother does to keep her family together," she said. "I told them she was at the club. I didn't know what else to tell them. They were very brusque." She was babbling; Betty would make a terrific grandmother but a lousy Green Beret.

"Betty," I said. I took her gently by the arms and turned her to me. "They were in here, weren't they?"

"I sent them to the truck stop. I said they were over there getting breakfast."

"Jesus," I said. "They found her, haven't they?" Betty's eyes were big and she nodded.

"Call her. Tell her to pack up and get out of there."

"I did. She called a cab but it isn't here yet." Betty was close to tears. "And anyway, she doesn't have any place to go."

I stood up and took a deep breath. "Jesus Christ Almighty," I said. "Call her again. Tell her I'll be in front of her door in thirty seconds."

She took a good, sharp look at me. Then she picked up the phone. "This is Betty. No. No, it's not here yet. I know. I know. Listen. There's a Clay Forester here who knows something about your problem. Clay Forester."

"Michael's friend," I prompted and she repeated it into the phone. Then she hung up.

"She's ready. One fourteen."

I took another deep breath. "What can you tell me about the men who were just here?"

"The younger ones had badges. The older gentleman asked the questions. Dressed real nice, white hair. Money. The young men had a hard look to them."

"Cops?"

"Or something like. Maybe state police. Or FBI."

Jesus. Christ. Almighty. "Is there anything else I need to

know?" I looked across the way and thought I saw them climbing back into their car.

Betty took me by the elbow. "Don't let them take that little boy back. She told me his daddy broke his arm once. I know he's a bad man, and he's got a long reach. Get them a long way from here if you can."

I hadn't checked out of the motel, but she waved off my credit card. "I never saw you. You never checked in. And ten seconds from now the computer will agree with me. You get on, now."

"Thank you," I said, and she shook her head.

"You get on."

The hotel room door opened as soon as I pulled up, and Michael's mother, arms laden with paper bags, bustled out. "They're coming," I told her, and stuffed her bags in the back with mine. It was a shameful world, I thought, if this family could pack their belongings into the back of a Triumph. "Michael, climb back there. Quick, now."

Michael squealed with delight. It was like a nest for him, nestled in there among all the bags, and with Buster for comfort to boot, he'd be just fine. Mrs. Cartwright and I slid in, and we were off. I turned onto the bridge, hoping we could make it across before we met the Mercedes, but I was wrong. We were going to pass, slowly, at the exact midpoint of the bridge.

So much for my years of CIA training.

"Put your head in my lap," I said, my first best idea. Mrs. Cartwright looked at me like I'd asked her to aspirate a worm. I guess in a way, that was exactly what she thought I'd asked her to do.

"If you think for one solitary second—"

"Christ, woman, will you listen to me?" I grabbed her head, she wrestled it upright and punched me in a very sensitive spot, and the guys in the other car got a perfect view of her offended profile as they passed. The driver's mouth opened and the Mercedes stopped momentarily. Then he recovered and the car sped to the end of the bridge to turn around.

"Well, that may be the end of our little trip," I grunted, accelerating off the bridge and onto the on-ramp, tires squealing. "We've got about fifteen seconds while they get turned around."

"Sweet Jesus preserve us," she said. She turned around to see behind us, but of course couldn't, since the back of the car was stuffed solid. I checked the side mirror. They had dropped one young man at the far side of the bridge and were now doing a U in the gravel. Then they were flying across the bridge, and that was the last I saw as we topped a rise and disappeared beyond it.

"He'll turn your hotel room upside down," I said. "Prints, all that. They'll get a positive ID for sure."

"They got your tag," she said. "They'll know who you are too."

"Well," I said, "they'll know who somebody is. I have no idea who this car is registered to." For the first time, it occurred to me to check the windshield for the inspection sticker. There wasn't one. "That's about the least of our problems right now."

I pushed the accelerator to the floor. The traffic on Interstate 40 was sparse this far out of Memphis—nothing like the morning rush going in—and I weaved back and forth in traffic from the left lane to the right, checking the side mirror. I was doing about ninety-five and could probably do more when the traffic eased up a bit. "We had half a mile on them, and I think I can open it up some more, although they can probably outrun us. That's a Mercedes CL-500, and it probably has a five-liter V-8, a monster engine. Whew. That's, like, an eighty-thousand-dollar car. You have some important people chasing you."

"My husband's Uncle Edward," she said. "He used to be the state attorney general. Now he's in private practice. You can see what he's practicing."

I passed the last semi in sight and opened it up. A hundred. A hundred and ten. Michael squealed with delight as the little car accelerated. Roadside reflectors whished by like supersonic fireflies.

"They'll get a roadblock set up," she yelled over. "They've probably already called ahead. You'll go to jail for kidnapping or something, I'd guess. It won't stick, of course. You'll be out in twenty-four hours. But he'll have us back."

Jee. Zus. Christ. "Who are you? I'm guessing your name's not really Natalie."

"My name is Kathy. But what's more important is my husband's name: Daniel Cartwright. Lieutenant governor and soon to be the next United States senator from the Great State of Tennessee."

It just gets better and better, I thought. That's why Michael's name was familiar. I remembered the newspaper headlines back in Nashville; I guess the future senator part just slipped below my radar. All the color must have rushed out of my face, because she became momentarily kind. "If you want to pull over and let us out, I'll understand," she said. "It's an awful risk."

It was certainly worth a thought. Here I was whooshing through Arkansas at somewhere around 120 miles per hour with a fugitive woman and little boy and a farting dog, with mystery men in a big Nazi car in hot pursuit and a kidnapping rap if they caught us—if, that is, I didn't roll our car and shred us doing high-speed evasion maneuvers I'd never executed in my life.

One thing was for sure: I didn't want any more vehicular manslaughter on my hands. I slowed down. Instinctively I checked the rearview; where I'd normally see daylight, I saw Michael watching me with interest.

"I won't let them take you," I said. "But we can't outrun them. And it's too dangerous to try." The needle dipped below 100. "Where would they think we're going?"

"My only family left is a sister in Oklahoma City. But they've had her house staked out off and on for weeks."

I checked the mirror, then braked hard to avoid climbing up the back of a lumbering minivan. "So they might expect us to stay on the Interstate clear to Oklahoma City."

"They might."

"If we can take an exit unseen, I think we can mess with their minds in a big way." I nodded toward the map in the dash. "Mrs. Cartwright, you're our navigator. Michael, can you and Buster help her?"

"Sure," he said. "This is fun."

"I'm glad you think so. Now here's what we need." I checked the highway ahead. Not yet. "We're looking for an exit with a short off-ramp and an underpass. Michael, have you ever played hide and seek?"

"Sure," he said again.

"Good. You're going to help us play hide and seek with your Uncle Edward. Mrs. Cartwright—"

"If we're going to be fugitives from justice, I suppose we could be on a first-name basis."

"Okay. Kathy, I'm Clay."

"I remember. Our next exit is a mile ahead."

We were descending a long, slow grade and then ascending again. The exit would be just over the top of the hill. "Okay," I said. "We'll check it out."

I sped up a little to pass a semi, and as we went up the hill I stayed in the left lane. There was a flash of light at the top of the hill and there way back behind us was the dark Mercedes.

"Shit," I said. She shot me a look. "Sorry. Sorry. We don't talk like that, Michael." I looked over at Kathy. "They're closer than I thought."

"Do your best," she said, and she held on as I accelerated again.

As we crested the hill I threw us over into the left lane and then back right into the exit, and what I could see looked good: an underpass just ahead. "Hang on, everybody," I shouted. "Hang on tight." I downshifted and stamped on the brakes. Buster hit the dash with a yelp. I downshifted again into second, stamped the brakes, and we took the corner at thirty-five, the back end skidding until I could straighten her out. We pulled through the underpass and onto the access road on the other side, pulled up far enough that we could just see through, and there we sat.

Buster looked up at me reproachfully and started licking his shoulder.

"Sorry, dude," I said. "Emergency. Kathy, can you check your watch? We had thirty seconds on them. Can you tell me at a minute?"

"Got it," she said.

And we sat, the engine idling high, my foot raised slightly on the clutch, depressed slightly on the accelerator. Both my feet hurt like hell. It was time for more Tylenol. Maybe more Solarcaine, too. Or maybe just some morphine straight into the vein.

"Time?"

"Thirty seconds left."

"We'll backtrack," I said. "Take another highway. Something."

"Check. Twenty seconds."

I was gripping the wheel and gearshift both with white-knuckle force, and I guess I was a little keyed up. I jumped when she spoke.

"This car is too conspicuous. Any small-town cop will remember an a.p.b. on an old yellow sports car."

"I like this car," Michael said, which I was starting to think myself. But what I said was, "Your mother is a smart woman, Michael." I didn't take my eyes off the underpass. "I think she's right."

"Time," she said.

A flash of movement, and just as I eased up the clutch for a fast getaway, I recognized the big grille of a Dodge truck. He emerged from the underpass, turned right, disappeared.

"Kathy, can you find the Memphis airport?"

She nodded. "But I'm not sure—"

I raised my hand. "Silence," I said. "This plan is devious and brilliant." And I started laughing; it had been a long time since I'd been brilliant or devious, but I was once a very good lawyer. "We'll ditch the Triumph in long-term parking," I said. "And I'll rent another car."

"A bigger car," Michael suggested.

"Michael," Kathy said, shushing him. "It's a fine idea. I've saved a little money—"

"Don't worry about it," I said.

Getting help from me was for some reason making her a little testy. "I have money."

"I wouldn't take it," I said, easing back onto the road and taking the on-ramp.

"But—"

"Listen. What you did to earn that money makes it precious." I shot her a look, shifted up into third, then into fourth. "Admittedly most men—Michael Martin Cartwright excepted, of course—are not worth the dirt they're made of. But I'm helping you just because I want to. Because you deserve it. Because he deserves it. That's all. No strings. End of story."

Her face was still blank, but she nodded thanks. "God will bless you for it."

I rolled my eyes. "Oh, I don't doubt that," I said.

It was at that moment that Buster chose to release another shitbomb. "Which was just about what I was expecting," I said, and I raised my eyes to heaven. "Thank you, Lord."

"Oh dear," Kathy said, and against her will she was smiling. "Michael, you and I must pray nightly for Mr. Forester. He needs God in the worst way."

"And that's usually how I get him." We came up on the 40/55 interchange.

"Take 55 south," she said, "and we're all but there."

"All right, gang," I said. "We did it. High fives all around." Michael giggled as he slapped me five, and then his mother handed back Buster, and I would have defied the pissed-off ghost of J. Edgar Hoover for one look at the smile on that little boy's face.

"Can you drive a stick?" I asked as we approached the airport and turned onto Rental Road, and again she looked at me as if I were something on the bottom of her shoe.

"Don't treat me like my husband," she said, which I guess meant yes, she could certainly drive a stick. I stopped and she took the helm just short of the rental agencies. I told her I'd find her in long-term parking; this way the clerks couldn't have any memory of a yellow sports car.

I chose Avis, mostly for that old slogan: we're number two so we try harder. I could dig it. "I'd like to rent the biggest, blackest car you've got," I said. "Something that makes me look like a Republican for two weeks."

"Ah-ha," said the guy behind the counter, a junior-executive type with shifty eyes that betrayed he really didn't belong here. (That and the tattoo I could just perceive on the top of his left hand. He was a slacker in drag.) "Do you want to impress clients or women?"

"Either," I said. "Both."

"I've got a new Cadillac Sedan de Ville," he said, checking his screen. "They don't come bigger or blacker than this one. But it's going to run you some money." He took a good, long look at my longish hair and blue T-shirt. "Fifteen-day rental will run you $747.98, plus tax, plus surcharges, plus mileage if you go over fifteen hundred. Do you think you'd go over fifteen hundred? 'Cause then it's twenty-nine cents a mile. It adds up fast."

"I'm just driving it around town," I said, giving him a don't-worry-about-it wave. "And money I've got. What I don't have is a big black car to drive." I slid across my Diners Club, filled out the forms, and walked calmly out the door like someone who didn't have to be in New Mexico in twenty-four hours and wasn't in the meantime harboring fugitives in his other car.

I trolled long-term parking for half an hour, my pulse rising by the minute. There were open spaces here and there, but no Triumph. She was right: it was not the kind of car that would be inconspicuous. I tipped an imaginary hat at a police car easing past, then at another one the next aisle over.

This was not, I suddenly realized, a great place to hide a car, something I'm sure that would not have been lost on Mrs. Cartwright, who was irritating but extremely intelligent. The airport was a hotbed of activity.

I backtracked to Avis, and sure enough I found them, around the corner, hidden from the street. I parked a good distance away—since they wouldn't know what I was driving, another big black car creeping up suddenly might be a little scary—and then walked up.

"There were police all over the lot," she said. "I don't think they saw me, but I had to get out of there—"

I raised my hand. "I know. We'll have to dump the car and get out of town. I think you'll be pleased with our new transport, though. The contrast boggles the mind. I'll pull up behind you so we can load up quick." When I climbed into the Caddy I had a brainstorm. I called Troy at the import parts store on the cell phone while Mrs. Cartwright stuck her bags in the trunk. "Except for the vitamins and enzymes," she said. "Pack them up front because they need to stay cool."

"Hey, Troy," I said, and identified myself. "How'd you like to drive that Triumph?"

"You know I'd love to," he said. "But what are you still doing in town? You should be halfway to New Mexico."

"I need a favor," I said. "I know you've got no reason to—"

"Tell me," he said.

"I need to leave the car here for awhile. People are looking for it. I swear on my dog's life that it is my car, and that I haven't done anything wrong. In fact I'm trying to help somebody. But some bad people are going to be looking for that car on the roads and I need to stash it."

"Hey anybody with a car like that is okay with me," he said. A quick thumbs-up to my fathers, Steve the Abandoner and Ray the Fixer. "You want me to pick it up somewhere?"

"That would be great. It's around back at the Avis place at the airport. Keys are under the mat."

"Done," he said. "Call me when you get back in town. Meantime I'll stick it in the yard and put a tarp over it."

"I can't thank you enough," I said.

"Done," he repeated. "Call me when you get back."

By then we had everybody in the Cadillac without being seen, and I didn't intend to stay around for that to happen. "Let's go, gang," I said. "Ready?"

"Ready!" Michael said.

"Ready," Kathy sighed.

Buster spoke not at all, and saved his other form of communication for some time when it would be most persuasive.

We rolled out of Memphis again behind tinted windows in a car so quiet I could almost hear my watch tick. Kathy put in a Raffi tape, and within twenty minutes Michael was snoozing in back with Buster, his head at one of those perverse angles that in grown people would indicate violent death.

Raffi was singing a song about going to the zoo, zoo, zoo, which I could do without, how about you, you, you? "Can you take that out please?" I asked Kathy.

"Better not," she said. "He'll wake up without some noise." She looked tired; the early morning roust didn't agree with her, either.

"You can sleep if you like," I said. "I'll wake you if anything happens."

"Listen, I'll pay you back," she said. "Or my sister can pay you when we get to Oklahoma City."

"You really don't like to be helped by men," I said, and she looked right at me and shook her head.

"I love Michael," she said. "But sometimes I wish I could just cut that little pecker off. It'll only lead him places he shouldn't go."

"As a male myself," I said, shuddering a little, "let me strongly protest. None of us would be here without the penis."

She sniffed.

"Okay," I said. "Fine and dandy. You hate your husband. But don't cut off our penises." It was a little surreal to be conversing with a member of the Moral Majority about the male member. I hoped I could remember this conversation later to tell Otis.

"I don't hate my husband," she said. "That's un-Christian."

"Sure you don't," I said. "And these last few weeks, you've seen men at their absolute most piggish. You've had contempt for all those sad or lonely or merely horny men who wanted you to dry-hump them and stick your ass in their faces. But don't hate all men because of that."

"Well, I never," she huffed, and flashed a look at the sleeping Michael to make sure he had slept though all that. Then she crossed her arms and stared angrily out the window.

After about ten minutes of driving, she looked across at me. "I'll tell you something, Mr. Forester. When I danced, I was offering it up to God. I can't help what anyone else was thinking while they watched." And she stared at me like she dared me to find anything bizarre about the idea. She was a tough nut to crack.

Well, further talk along those lines was not worth the effort. I went another direction. "You know, you don't look old enough to be the wife of the lieutenant governor and future etcetera, etcetera. I thought there were laws about things like that, even in Tennessee."

"He's eight years older than me," she said. "But you know, he's not that old. They call him the Boy Wonder of Tennessee politics. He was elected to the state senate while he was still in law school. He was lieutenant governor when he was thirty-four. He has lots of powerful friends. And except for the Gores—who he hates, I might add—he comes from the most important political family in the state."

"Not a good man to cross," I said. We'd be coming up on Little Rock in an hour or so, and I was hoping for food and a restroom break, but even with our little penis talk I didn't feel comfortable broaching the subject. "But why won't he let you divorce him? Why'd you have to run away?"

"Another divorce would be political suicide for him."

"Another?"

She sat for a while and thought about what she wanted to tell me and how. "What I'm going to say," she said at last, "is known by a few people. But nobody would ever say this anywhere that it counts. I'm Daniel's second wife. He let the first wife divorce him, and it almost killed him in the next election. And that was supposedly amicable. I can assure you that ours wouldn't be."

"Supposedly amicable?"

"She was always the villain in our house. I believed him. Until—until things started to happen. Then I tracked her down and found out the truth. He was just as mean to her. Worse. He threw her down the stairs. She lost her baby. A lot of money changed hands to keep her quiet at the divorce."

"Kathy," I said, and I shot a look in the rearview to where Michael was still slumbering. "Your husband, if you'll forgive my saying so, is a son of a bitch. If his political future is so important to him, aren't you worried that he might—you know—throw you down the stairs too?"

She shook her head. "I've thought about that. I don't think he could have anything like that done to me. And I know he couldn't do it to Michael. I believe—as well as he can understand the concept—that he loves him."

God save us from that kind of love. "We'll get you to a safe place," I said. "And then we need to put some pressure on him."

She laughed, and it was not a happy laugh. "Don't you think I thought of that? I went to our pastor. To Uncle Edward. To half a dozen other lawyers. I think they believed me. I showed some of them pictures." And here she took out half a dozen Polaroids from a larger stack in her purse and handed them to me. They were awful: Michael, his arms covered by palm-print bruises, his poor bottom beaten raw; Kathy with a shiner no sunglasses would cover, with bruises up and down her rib cage. When she spoke again, her voice was full of quiet fury. "But they said they couldn't do anything about it. Couldn't. Ha. Wouldn't, you mean." She veered right up to the edge of tears and then skated back, and the wall went back up to stay. "He's too powerful in the state of Tennessee. No one will stand up to him. No one."

I gripped the steering wheel hard and clenched my teeth. "That's not right," I said.

"No, it isn't," she said. "But this old world is full of heartaches. That's why we have to turn our eyes to heaven."

"Please stop," I said. "I can only take so much in one morning."

She turned puzzled eyes to me. "What are you talking about?"

"I'd just appreciate it if you'd keep your Jesus talk to yourself," I said. "I'm on a vacation from Jesus."

The cell phone rang. It was on the seat next to me, and I was able to pick up before it woke Michael. "Speak to me," I said.

It was Ray. "Son," he said, "I just got a call from the Tennessee attorney general—the man himself—and what I'm wondering is which one of you is crazy."

"Jesus, they move fast," I said. "I thought it'd take them longer to trace the tag."

"They ran your hotel room for prints," they said. "They also asked me if you had an aerosol habit. Can you believe that? I have not breathed a word of this to your mother," he said, and you could tell he was worked up almost into a lather, "but what in the name of all creation are you doing out there?"

"I'm helping someone," I said. "Since I haven't done that for a while, you'll just have to trust that I know what I'm doing. But I haven't kidnapped anyone, I haven't hurt anyone, and I don't think we're in any real danger."

That's all Ray needed to know; the word *help* was sacred to him. "You've got to dump that car, then," he said. "Damn yellow thing sticks out like a cat in a hen house."

"Already taken care of," I said. "Listen, talk to the woman riding shotgun for a second and then you get to work cleaning this mess up." I handed the phone over to Kathy. "Here, make my life easier and tell this gentleman why you're on the run."

And she did, in fifty words or less—she was a tight, tamped-down woman—and handed me the phone back.

"That's a shit-kettle you're roiling around in," Ray said.

"Thank you for that expert analysis, Brent Musberger," I said. "Any chance you can do something back there to get them to call off the dogs?"

"I'll do what I can," he said. "You have any ideas on your end?"

"Well, to start with, you can get me numbers for the Memphis and Knoxville papers," I said. "A few words from the kidnapped woman might be newsworthy."

"Okay," he said. "That's a start. But son, I have to confess. I did a bad thing before I thought about the implications of it. When they asked where I thought you might be headed, I told them you were headed off to your college reunion in Maine. I hope that won't spoil anything for you."

I went to Duke, of course, like my stepfather and his father before him. "Ray," I said, "you know I've never so much as set foot in Maine."

"Really?" he said, and I could tell he was grinning fit to swallow the telephone. "You didn't go to Bowdoin? Well, my memory isn't worth a damn anymore, is it?"

"No, sir, it isn't," I said. "But I love you just the same."

"Same here, son. Same here. You be real careful and I'll call you later."

I beeped off with a big smile on my face.

Kathy raised an eyebrow of inquiry. "Your father?"

"Yes, ma'am," I said. "My father." Fortified by the phone call, I took the Carlisle exit. A man's got a right to stop and drain his bladder, no matter what some woman might think about it.

9

And so, at last, fortified by a piss break, three bottles of Dr. Pepper, a handful of barbecue beef sandwiches, and a plastic-wrapped brownie that had been sitting on the shelf so long it was actually dusty—and a couple of bottles of Evian for the Cartwrights, the only thing in that joint that she would have let pass between her lips, although she told me, shaking her head, that plastic containers leach CFCs or some other such thing—we pressed on toward the prize. Michael was awake again, and his mother pressed a handful of capsules into his palm and one at a time, laboriously, he swallowed them with swigs of water.

"He's not getting enough antioxidants or essential oils," she said. "We've eaten such c-r-a-p—pardon my French—I worry for him."

"What's he taking?" It looked like a handful of horse pills.

"Oh, grapeseed oil, flaxseed oil, Omega-3, plus some red clover and bioflavonoids."

"All that came out of your plastic bag?" I looked over at her little grocery bag, now revealed as a magical thing.

"Oh, and there's more. She laid out on the seat one by one bottles and vials, calling off their names as she did it: barley grass powder, herbal cleansing powder, Super Ester Vitamin C, bee propolis, acidophilus, milk thistle, enzymes. I had to turn my attention back to my driving; it boggled the mind.

"Do you actually take all those?"

She looked across at me. "Do you actually ingest bleached white flour, processed sugar, and hydrogenated oils?"

I checked the label of my brownie. "Partially-hydrogenated," I said. "Is that better?"

"Cottonseed?" she asked with what I could have sworn was a smirk.

"Yes," I said.

"Does it have polysorbate or sorbic acid?"

"Well, yes," I admitted. "Both."

"You might as well get in the tub and drag a radio in on top of yourself," she said, putting her bottles back in the bag. "You'd kill yourself more efficiently."

"Well thank you for that update," I said. "Maybe I don't want to kill myself efficiently. Maybe I want to linger."

She packed away the bag and put it at her feet. Michael had forced down his last capsule, and was reading a VeggieTales book in the back seat. We drove in silence for a while, through North Little Rock and on into Little Rock proper, if indeed that can be said of Little Rock.

"Mr. Forester, where on earth are you going?" she said, after we'd been quiet for a good long while. I could see the red-rimmed blue diamond of the Arkansas flag flapping over the state house.

"I'm right in the middle of the lane," I said. Anna Lynn used to complain about my driving; turned out she was right to.

"No," she said, and if it looked like this topic had just occurred to her, it probably had. "I mean, where are you going? What are you doing out here? What's a guitar player from Robbinsville—is that right?—Robbinsville, North Carolina, doing heading west through Arkansas in the first place?"

"That question betrays some personal interest," I said.

"I'm waiting," she said.

I switched lanes to pass a slow-moving delivery van, then switched back into the right lane. "I'm going to a funeral," I said.

"Yes?"

"In New Mexico. Someone—someone I didn't really know."

"This is not satisfying my curiosity," she said.

"I'm not accustomed to satisfying people in any fashion."

"That's no kind of answer. What kind of male role model are you presenting to my son?"

I looked at Michael in the rearview. He was looking back at me and smiling with interest. I turned my eyes back to the road and prepared to be some species of role model.

"My father left home when I was a baby," I said. "I never knew him. He died in New Mexico a few days ago. I'm going to the funeral. And if you tell me I'm on a spiritual quest you'll find yourself standing beside the interstate so fast it'll make your head spin." I looked back at Michael, who was suddenly intrigued. "Not you, Buddy," I told him. "You're in like Flynn."

"A spiritual quest," she said, arching her eyebrow. "Far be it from me to suggest such a thing."

We were through downtown and the traffic was easing up. "I'm just going to New Mexico because I'm curious," I said. "That's all. Wouldn't you be?"

"Yes, I would," she said. "And it's certainly good for us that you are. God put you in the right place at the right time." She elevated her eyes heavenward and put her hands together stiffly in prayer.

"That's enough of that stuff," I growled, and then, wonder of wonders, she was grinning. "So you did that on purpose? Since when did you get a sense of humor?"

"Don't treat me like my husband does," she said, which was always the answer to my question, even if the answer itself was different.

"Far be it from me," I said. "What does that mean, anyway? You know, my whole life I always wondered what that meant."

She shrugged and yawned.

"Really," I said, "take a nap if you want to." I know I wanted to; it was cool and quiet, just a low hum of road noise, and the leather seats were smooth and soft as butter.

"I can't go to sleep around you," she said. "No offense."

"None taken," I said.

"It's just that, nice as you've been, I really don't know you from Adam. Sleep requires a lot of trust."

"Yes it does," I said. "I saw a man sleeping right next to the highway this week. He had a lot of trust."

"Hmm," she said.

"What's your sister's name?"

"Pam. Pam Standerfer."

"What kind of name is that?"

"God only knows," she said. "She certainly didn't ask us for permission before she married him. He's a backhoe contractor. Owns his own business." She sighed. "I guess I shouldn't talk," she said. "I married the lieutenant governor of Tennessee. At least he treats her well."

"I'm hungry," Michael said, although how he could still have room in that stomach after what he'd already ingested today was beyond me. "Can we get something to eat soon?"

"Sure," I said. "If your mom says okay." I turned to her and smiled. "No pressure."

"Okay," she said.

"Where would you like to eat?" she asked, just as we were passing a Cracker Barrel sign. Maybe my saliva was apparent, because Michael instantly sung out, "There!"

"It's in Conway," I said. "About half an hour. Can you wait?"

"I want to eat there," he said. "I want fried apples. And macaroni and cheese. And ice cream."

"It's okay with me," I said. "If your mom says okay." She gave me a stare that would have melted plastic.

"Okay," she said. "If you'll take some extra enzymes. Good Lord, the nutrition is all cooked out of that food. And when I think—"

"We'll be there in no time, Buddy," I said. "How's Buster doing back there? I haven't smelled him for a while."

Dangerous last words, like "Hand me that match, I don't think there's any gasoline in this can."

"Never mind," I said when it became possible to talk again. "He's doing just fine."

Kathy was still mad at me as we pulled off the interstate onto Highway 65 and then turned into the Cracker Barrel parking lot. Or at least I figured she was mad. We hadn't passed more than a dozen words, which was okay with me. I was feeling more reflective than talkative.

"I want fried apples. And macaroni and cheese. And ice cream," Michael told Wanda, our server.

Kathy rolled her eyes, sighed, and chose the lesser of evils. "I'll have the vegetable plate. Carrots, pinto beans, turnip greens, and the sweet potato casserole."

"What's the carcinogen special?" I asked Wanda.

"The what?"

Kathy kicked me under the table, a wicked jab like that old broad in the James Bond movie with the knives in her shoes. "Okay, I'll have a grilled pork chop with hash brown casserole and fried okra. Unless you have corn."

"We have corn."

"Bring me two sides of corn. It's my favorite vegetable." And I moved my foot so that I heard only the satisfying thud of Kathy's toe against the chair leg.

"That hurt," she said when Wanda walked off. She rubbed her foot underneath the table.

"I have a right to eat the way I want, especially if I'm going to pay for it. And I am."

"We can pay our part—" she began and I cut her off. Michael was playing with golf tees and didn't seem interested, although I knew he was probably used to tuning in even when he didn't seem to be. It was probably a survival trait with him now.

"Here it is: I have plenty of money. Until I get you to your sister, everything is my treat. If I get picked up on a Mann Act rap then you're going to need every penny you earned to defend yourself."

"The what?"

"The Mann Act. Passed in 1910. Interstate transportation of women for immoral purposes."

"You're an odd bird, Clay Forester," she said, a slow smile spreading across her face. "And how did you come to be rolling in dough on a musician's salary?" she asked.

"I'm independently wealthy," I said, figuring that would kill conversation; it usually did. People would laugh and move on to another topic. But Kathy just kept looking at me—that look she did where it wasn't clear that she would even breathe again until I told her the truth.

"No," she said. "Really."

"Really," I said, and I gave in. "My mother's family was well off. Then she married my stepfather, who was well off. And then I got a big insurance settlement and I was, well, well off. What I'm doing for you is not the widow's mite. I mean, I'm glad to do it. But I won't miss it. In fact, if you need more, I'd be happy to give it to you."

She shook her head, and I was heartened by the arrival of our biscuits. I opened two, spread butter on them, and opened up two strawberry jam packets to forestall further conversation.

"Let's call Pam," I said. I'd brought Ray's cell phone in for that express purpose. "Tell her we can be in OKC in about four hours. If somebody is still watching the house, it'd be best if you could pick a rendezvous. And tell her to watch out for a tail."

She just looked at me as I proffered the phone. "Where did this brilliant deviant mind come from? I thought you were a head-banger."

"People are surprising," I said. "For example, I didn't know that you knew the word 'head-banger.' "

"I was a teenager once," she said. "And although I'm ashamed to admit it, I once listened to AC-DC for pleasure." She beeped her sister's number. "Long ago, you understand. In my other life, as a sinner."

"Of course."

"Pammy," she said then. "It's me. Yes, I'm fine. We're both fine. No. They can't trace this. No. Listen, I want you to meet me. Yes, it'll be okay. You'll just have to trust me. Do you remember that place where we took the boys last summer? No, just us. The men weren't there. Right. Can you meet me in the parking lot at eight?" She smiled. "Good. Just in case, watch for company. If we see anything suspicious we'll call you on your cell phone. I know, baby. Thank you."

She beeped off and handed me the phone.

"She'll meet us outside the zoo at eight o'clock. No one's

staking out the house, but she'll be careful. And she says she has a place for us to hide. She's a good girl."

She was blinking back tears, which pissed her off. Whether it was because it was happening in front of Michael or in front of me, I don't know, but she grabbed that emotion and throttled it like she would a copperhead in a baby's cradle.

"You're ready for this to be over," I said gently. "Someday it will be."

"What do you know?" she said. Then, again, she mastered herself for Michael's sake. I could see her turn to wood; it spread up her body until she was sitting stiff and even her words came out formal. "Of course it will," she said. "By the time school starts, Michael will be making new friends."

"I've been making friends," he said, his mouth full of biscuit.

"Manners," she said.

"Sorry," he said, again with his mouth full.

I was half asleep as we drove the eastern half of the state. We crossed over into Oklahoma without incident and were headed through landscape that surprised me. I guess I thought Oklahoma looked like it did in *The Grapes of Wrath*: Dust Bowl and blowing tumbleweeds. But this was green, rolling hills, lots of trees. I couldn't tell when we passed over from Arkansas.

I could tell the growing pressure again on my bladder, though. Three Dr. Peppers and three glasses of iced tea at Cracker Barrel. Kathy was amazing, and she was having a similar effect on Michael: they could hold their urine better than any mother-son combo I'd ever heard of. "Mrs. Cartwright," I said, reverting to the formal for this request, "I need to stop and use the facilities again."

"You're a grown man, Mr. Forester," she said. "Stop whenever you need to. We could do the same." I took the Sallisaw exit and stopped at a Texaco station. "Anybody want anything from the store?"

"More water," she said. "If you wouldn't mind."

"Sure," I grunted. No more talk about water just at this precise juncture. We were relieved, gassed up, and back on the road within ten minutes. Michael was feeling tired himself after high-fat food and the driving, and he was asleep before we passed over Lake Eufaula twenty minutes later. The sun was low in the sky and the world was golden, that brief stretch when everything looks dashed with fairy dust.

I made the mistake of saying that out loud. I expected maybe a chuckle or a nod or an isn't that so.

I did not expect her to draw herself up straight and stare daggers at me. "Mr. Forester, if you're trying to make a pass at me, you can just let us out here," she said. "You have not purchased that right. Those men in the club didn't touch me and you're not about to."

"Whoa down there, Mrs. Cartwright," I said. "Put that horse back in the stable. I know your recent history is terrible, but I'm not putting the moves on you. Even if I wanted to I wouldn't know how."

"Men always know how. It's just one of the things women hate them for."

I shook my head sadly. "It doesn't have to be this way. Men and women do not have to be enemies."

"Only since the Garden of Eden," she said.

I shook my head again. "I don't believe that."

She snorted. "And you know so much about men and women?"

"I was married once," I said. "We were happy for a while. I don't know if that makes me an expert."

"And what happened to her?" she asked. "You haven't mentioned her before now, and you're not wearing a ring, so obviously you're not still married. What happened?" Her voice was dripping with contempt; this kid asleep in the nest behind me was going to ring up some serious therapy bills if he ever really understood all his mother felt about men. "Did you beat her? Sleep around on her?"

I felt the heat growing in my neck and my cheeks as she was talking, could feel the iced tea sloshing around in my stomach, and maybe I can be forgiven for what I said.

"No," I told her, biting off my words so as not to expand upon them. "I killed her."

Well, that'll turn your conversation in a new direction, let me tell you. She skittered next to the door, her body drawn up against the side of the car. "Let us out," she said, and to her credit, there was only a hint of fear in her voice. "Stop the car right now or I'll scream bloody murder."

"It's not what you think, Mrs. Cartwright," I said. "But thanks for the vote of confidence."

"I'm serious," she said, and her mouth was drawn into a snarl. "Stop the car now. I have a knife and I'm not afraid to use it."

"I drank in those days," I said. "Too much, maybe. It sure seems like it now." She was rooting through her purse but her eyes didn't leave my face. "My wife and son were visiting her parents in Grand Rapids, and I went out with some colleagues to celebrate a big win. We had struck a compromise so a fat-cat corporation could avoid a big legal judgment they deserved to pay. So I was celebrating this great achievement, and I was drowning my guilt, and I was looking forward to my family coming home and maybe somehow getting back to the life we used to have."

She stopped fumbling around in the bag and she was quiet. If she had a knife, she'd found it, but her hand slid empty from her purse, and she was just watching me, because she knew that we had bumped up against my own heartbreak for the first time. Maybe it intrigued her. I can't say what goes through women's minds. "What happened?"

"I went to pick them up at the airport," I said. "Like I said, I'd had a few drinks. I didn't feel drunk. But maybe I was. Like I said, I drank a lot in those days." The sun had dipped to the horizon, and now it was in my eyes. The golden moment was over; now the light just stung. I lowered the visor for what little help it could give me.

I made my voice as neutral as I could, like I was talking about something I might have heard about on TV. "On the way home from the airport, we were sitting at an intersection. A garbage truck ran the red light. I pulled out when the light turned green. I didn't see it coming."

She waited, watching, and for some reason—maybe because I didn't know her, because I'd never see her again; maybe because she too knew something about the shape of suffering in this world—I kept talking. "I heard the horn blare. I heard Anna Lynn scream, and then she turned around and she was looking at me when the thing hit us and we went rolling over and over." And all of a sudden, there were tears in my eyes and I couldn't go on and it pissed me off.

I struggled to keep talking, to choke it down like you'd hold a hated enemy under water until he drowns. "Do you know why she looked at me instead of at the truck?"

Kathy shook her head. She was watching me, her eyes wide as if she was witnessing another truck wreck.

"She looked at me because she knew we were going to die. It was horrible. Her eyes—"

I had it under control again; I'd had plenty of practice. Nobody needed to know what was in her eyes. I cleared my throat, let out a deep breath, shook my head, cleared my throat. "Only I didn't die, you see. I didn't die."

Kathy had put her bag in the floor and she leaned forward, and there was a look of concern I had never before seen on her face. "But you did, you know. On the inside. You fooled people, because you were still walking around and so they didn't know. But you were dead from that moment on."

And of course, she knew whereof she spoke. It was so true that I lost it again, and then some. I was sobbing now, my shoulders shaking. My cheeks burned, snot was pouring from my nose, and I had to pull off the road.

There's a moment in every life that you want back. Maybe more than one, but that was my moment, when I touched the gas and pulled into the intersection. It wasn't so much to ask, was it? To have that one second over? How could one second be allowed to wreck your whole life, to kill the people you loved most?

I saw her eyes, Anna Lynn's eyes in that moment. They were full of fear, full of loss, full of blame.

If only they'd been full of forgiveness. There was so much that needed to be forgiven.

And so I sat on the side of the interstate, crying and crying and I couldn't stop. I was trying to be quiet, but still I felt as if I was shaking the whole car. It was all too much.

Then I felt a tiny hand on my shoulder, a tiny voice saying gently, "It's okay. You cry if you want to."

Michael's voice was followed by his sleepy face, and I blinked my thanks because I didn't trust my words. And there was Kathy's hand on my arm, suddenly solid, tangible. I took a series of deep breaths. I closed my eyes, held them shut, opened them again.

The moment passed.

"You should blow your nose," Michael said.

"You're right," I said, and I took Kathy's proffered tissue.

After I had honked and wiped, I put on the turn signal, *click click*, pulled onto the road, and tried to act like the whole thing had never happened. I pointed out a car with Alaska license plates. I yawned and stretched and tried to act nonchalant.

I got away with about eighteen seconds of that stuff.

"How long ago did this happen?" Kathy asked.

"Oh," I said. "That? A long time ago."

"It feels fresh. Like it just happened."

I nodded solemnly. "To me too."

"Don't you ever talk about it? About them?" She could see the answer just by looking at my face, at the sudden devastation in it. "Clay, how do you ever expect to get over it?"

"I don't expect to."

She sighed, female exasperation working past the sympathy. "You mean you don't want to." I could feel, in fact, her sympathy start to evaporate, steaming like water off a street. "You made one mistake, if it was a mistake. It was tragic. But it can be forgiven."

Nothing from me. I am a rock; I am an island.

"She wouldn't want this for you, Clay. This life you've made. It's not what she'd want. It's certainly not what you'd have wanted her to do if you'd passed, is it?"

True enough, so far as it applied, but still I showed nothing. A rock.

"God," she said, addressing the ceiling, or perhaps something beyond it, "why did you let men run the world? One crisis and they all go to pieces. No man was ever worth anything in a pinch."

"I seem to recall that Jesus had a penis."

Her lower lips contracted in her strain to keep from smiling, and at last she had to turn so I couldn't see it. "I choose not to believe that. I like to think he was like my Ken doll. Kind face, cool clothes, and completely smooth below the waist."

"You're a heretic, Mrs. Cartwright," I said. "A Marcionite, if I remember my heresies."

"A what?" She arched an eyebrow.

"I was a double major at Duke: history and religion. That was a long, long time ago. Now I don't think of either of them as particularly useful. But anyway: what made Jesus Jesus, if you believe the stories, was that he had a fully functional penis and yet he chose not to be ruled by it."

"Maybe so," she said. "You're awfully theological for a rock musician."

She was smiling again, but I was of a sudden tired unto death, and I came back testy. My very skin hurt. "Mrs. Cartwright," I said, "I have a mother and two maiden aunts who make you look like a Visigoth outside the gates. I've thrown up more of the Bible that was crammed down my throat than you will probably ever digest."

And as you might expect, she got her prim, well-I-never look, her lips drawn thin.

I should have apologized, I guess. Hell, I should never have said it in the first place. But I was tired and hurting and cranky, and I was embarrassed about my public nervous breakdown, and all I could think about was that I still had at least another ten hours of driving before I got to Santa Fe.

Maybe then, after all that, I could rest.

God, I hoped so.

I had heard this Raffi tape so many times that I knew the songs. Or maybe I had known them from a long time back. Little Ray liked Raffi, or seemed to. We heard that he was supposed to, and so we played them for him and they didn't make him scream and foam at the mouth like I did when I heard Celine Dion, so we figured it was just about okay by him.

We were listening to Raffi on the way back from the airport. I hadn't thought of that. Of course, why would I? I hadn't heard a note of Raffi for ten years.

Michael and Buster could sense the sudden tension in the car. In the rearview, they looked up at me expectantly; their experience with men was not a favorable one, and long silences or tensions could go to bad places.

"Let's sing," I said, turning up Raffi. "Want to?"

"Sure," Michael said. Kathy said nothing, just looked out the window. I'm sure she couldn't wait for this ride to end, which it would shortly. The mileage sign said we were thirty miles out of OKC, and now it was starting to look like Oklahoma. As of Shawnee the trees and green hills were a thing of the past; now it was beginning to look flat and ugly.

We sang "Willoughby Wallaby Woo," a thrilling ditty about various animals sitting on us.

"That's a funny song," Michael said after the first verse.

"But full of valuable life lessons," I said, and then we sang some more. When we finished "Willoughby Wallaby Woo," Kathy said quietly, "You have a lovely voice."

"Thank you," I said in what I hoped was a conciliatory tone. "It's my father's."

"How come you haven't gotten married again?" she asked, and the peanut-butter sandwich song started without me. "You said what happened was a long time ago."

"Married?" My head rotated without my consent, and then I forced it back to look at the road. "Are you kidding me?" As if she'd asked me how come I hadn't had a prefrontal lobotomy.

She shrugged. "You're a good-looking man. You have a nice voice. I'm sure you're not totally devoid of other good points. And you said it's been a long time. How long? Years?"

I nodded.

"So why not? Haven't there been other women?"

"Not really." I was getting my irritation back on. "I've lived a pretty monastic life. I mean, there is a woman, but it's mostly platonic. Or at least I think it is."

"Are you planning to marry her?"

"Good Christ, no." Then I remembered Michael. "Sorry."

"Why not?"

"Woman, are you so hot to get married again?"

"We're not talking about me," she said. "Of course I'm

not. My first responsibility is Michael and getting him in a good home. A safe home. I'm a long way from thinking about marriage."

"I'm a long way from thinking about marriage too," I said.

"Well, I'll bet she isn't."

"She?"

"The woman. The one you're not thinking about marrying. I'll bet she's thinking about getting married."

"Maybe she is," I said. "I don't really care to talk about it."

"You should." She sighed. Men were so predictable. It was so sad. "There are lots of things you should talk about. Holding it all inside like this really isn't healthy."

"I do a lot of talking. And I have my music. I am strong. I am invincible. I am woman."

Not even a smile. "Your music isn't going to save you," she said. "I used to sing. Singing a song is like acting. You can hide behind it, and you don't have to show yourself. It just looks like you did."

"It's not like that," I said, shaking my head. "You can live through it. Like through a story. Okay, it's not real, exactly. But it can represent your real self. It can tap into something, a stripe of love or longing like a vein of ore. You couldn't do it well if you didn't feel something somewhere."

She shook her head sadly and a little primly. "It's a shame, Clay. If I wasn't full up with what's happening to me, my heart would be breaking for you."

I tried to get her to meet my gaze. Don't people ever know when to let things lie? I clenched the steering wheel, pushed against it like it was a weight machine, like it was a four-wheeled gym, and my voice was grating even to my own ears. "I said I don't care to talk about it."

"In a few minutes I'll be getting out of this car," she said. "We'll never see each other again. I feel like I owe it to you to be honest about what I see in you."

Now I was screaming, snarling. I didn't want anybody to see anything in me. Or, at least, I didn't want them to talk about it. "I don't care to talk about it." Buster and Michael cringed away against the corner of the back seat, and Michael's eyes were big and rimmed with tears. "Anyway, woman, you should talk. I don't need personal advice from a woman who's been letting waitresses raise her son. From a woman who can somehow entertain the notion that she's been lap dancing for Jesus."

She dropped her head into her hands and I could tell she was weeping, although she was doing it quietly, so as not to let Michael know.

I was a sorry excuse for a human being.

"I'm sorry," I said. "Really."

She didn't stop, didn't look over. I looked hard at the overpass ahead; if I'd been alone in the car, that bridge abutment would have been calling my name.

"She wouldn't have wanted this for you," she said finally in a voice I could barely hear, a voice that all the same was full of strength. "She doesn't want this. Who you've become since."

"She doesn't know what it's like to be the one left," I said, and if I had been tired before, now I felt like somebody could pour me under a door. "And you don't know everything, Kathy. It's not fair to say that to me. Not until you've lived it."

"Don't you think I've lived enough? I do. I've lived all I can stand to live."

And of course, who was I to talk? What was I to say to that?

We passed Tinker Air Force Base, enormous bombers from World War Two and Korea and Vietnam somehow mounted on posts outside the gates. I pointed them out to Michael, who still said nothing, just stared out the window. I couldn't blame him for not wanting to look at me. I was just another loud and angry man.

I could see skyscrapers ahead, a patch of them rising from the plains like some strange growth or infestation.

"My God, this city is ugly," I said. "No wonder Timothy McVeigh wanted to blow it up." There was no reply; I was not so angry that I wasn't a little appalled at myself.

We were driving past oilfield supply places, scraggly trees, lots and lots of vacant lots. Downtown we passed a big public building, concrete and glass, peeling and leprous, and undergoing a facelift in the same way someone administers CPR. Still nothing, so I threw out another bon mot. "Your sister must have the aesthetic constitution of an Eskimo to survive here. Or else she's a Southern Baptist."

"We're going to take I-44 north," she said. "I'm sure there's an easier way to get there, but that's how she brought me." Her voice had all the warmth of frozen cod. She looked over at me. I didn't look back. "In fact, why don't you just take this exit. I'd like for you to drop us off here."

"No," I said. "I'll take you."

"You don't understand," she said. "I don't want you to take us anywhere. I don't want to spend another minute in your company. My son has seen enough men like you to last a thousand years."

"I'll take you," I said.

Out of the corner of her eye I could see her shake her head violently. "Let us out now, you pathetic little man."

A film of anger covered my eyes, coated my brain. Without even checking behind me I whipped across three lanes of traffic to take the exit she indicated, horns blaring behind me, a Honda Accord swerving onto the shoulder to miss us. I didn't care. My stomach was boiling and steam was coming out my ears.

She didn't give me the satisfaction of screaming or even of grabbing on tight to something. She just looked across at me and matched me rage for rage, and then she shook her head and repeated her conclusion. "You are pathetic," she said.

I bounced onto the access road and braked too hard once we got there. Things fell into the floorboard. Michael and Buster fetched up against the front seat with a thump, and Michael started crying. Buster released the master fart of his career. My eyes watered and I gagged for breath.

The car hadn't even stopped moving when she was outside it, throwing the back door open, pulling the crying Michael forth, Buster in his arms like a security blanket, pulling her plastic bags out onto the asphalt, spilling the contents of her life in her haste to get away from me.

"Put the dog back, baby," she said. She reached for Buster, but he clutched tighter still.

"No," he wailed. "No." I'm not sure he even heard her. I'm not sure he knew what he was saying no to.

"This dog isn't ours," she said, louder, and Michael was wailing still louder; derelicts were looking over from the sidewalk, and I was ready to commit hara-kiri.

"Christ Almighty, keep him," I said, and nobody heard me. So I yelled again. "Keep the damn dog. He's a worthless piece of shit. I'm sure you'll be very happy together."

They looked up at me then, and the mixture of emotions I saw there—fear, anger, sadness—was a potent brew. I sobered of a sudden like a drunk who sees flashing red lights in the rearview mirror.

"Please," I said, meaning a lot of things I couldn't possibly say. "Keep him."

Kathy nodded once, a little inclination of her head, a tiny moment of grace in a world fucked beyond recognition.

It broke me.

"I'm sorry," I said, my words fumbling over themselves in their haste to be born. "Please. Get back in. I'll take you wherever you need to go. I'll—"

She closed the doors firmly, stepped away, and raised her hands, palms toward me, washing her hands of me. Grace only extends so far.

I had never taken the car out of gear. When I saw that Michael wasn't even going to look at me to say good-bye, I put on my turn signal, the blinker clicking loud in that noxious silence.

"I'm sorry," I said, but of course there was no answer.

I watched in the mirror as Kathy took Michael's free hand and turned him around. All I could see of Buster was his tail, wagging, wagging. Life must look wonderful when you have the intellectual capacity of a three-legged garbage-eating dog.

"Okay," I said. "Fine. Good on you." I bumped back onto the access road, the stench from a cattleyard somewhere downwind on Agnew competing with the remains of Buster's parting gift. I turned the air conditioner on recirculate—as if it could help any to recycle pure phosgene—and sat beneath a dingy halogen light, waiting for the signal to change. The wind picked up, pushing yellowed sheets of newspaper past me down the street, and I saw dark, towering storm clouds far off to the west in the dying light.

My god, this was an ugly city.

And at that moment, I felt right at home in it.

10

If there is a darker place than Western Oklahoma and the Texas Panhandle at night, I hope never to see it. After I left Oklahoma City behind, I passed the occasional town: Yukon, El Reno, Weatherford, Clinton, Elk City. They were not really towns so much as momentary breaks in the darkness, the garish glow of McDonald's and Texaco and Holiday Inn at least momentarily suggesting that I wasn't driving through some primeval void.

God, I needed a drink. I ran the back of my hand across my mouth. My lips felt chapped. I couldn't have driven the Triumph; I couldn't have shifted and clutched to save my life. My feet were so badly burned I could barely rest them on the floor. In fact, my whole body radiated heat and angry pain.

And I needed to hear someone else's voice. Someone besides fucking Raffi. When "Willoughby Wallaby Woo" came on again I ejected Michael's tape violently and threw it out the window. I immediately regretted being such a son of a bitch, especially while I was fiddling with the radio and finding nothing but country western. I had just driven past Yukon, where the roadside water tower announced proudly, "A Great Place to Live: Home of the 1994 State Softball Champions and Garth Brooks." Then I found KATT FM 100.5 out of Oklahoma City, a hard rock station after my own heart, and knew that maybe I was safe from the silence for a few more minutes, at least.

But it clearly wasn't enough, even after great songs from Everclear, Creed, Van Halen, and Nirvana. It was going to take someone better adjusted than Kurt Cobain to make me feel better about myself. So I did an inventory of my few remaining friends and relations. I couldn't call Otis; he was onstage just now. I couldn't possibly talk to my mother or Ray after what I'd done; I was too ashamed. I was raised to believe that the only thing worse than cruelty to a woman, if indeed there was anything worse, was betraying your country to Mother Russia, and I had certainly been cruel, more than cruel in the time just passed.

And so I called Tracy. I thought maybe I could talk to her without having to really talk to her; I wasn't ready for that, if in fact I was ever really going to talk to her about what had happened. Still, just to hear her voice would be something, a wall to keep the creatures at bay.

The gatekeeper answered, of course, Alvin York, the sergeant major of Robbinsville. Nothing could be easy anymore. "Hello, Sir," I said. "It's Clay. May I speak with Tracy?"

"I'll get her for you," he said. "How are you, Clay? Are you safe in Santa Fe yet?"

"No, sir, I'm not," I said. "But I have hopes."

"You be careful," he said. Was that concern I heard in his voice? "That little girl's been through enough."

"She has," I said. "And I will. Thank you."

"I'll get her for you." He put the phone down and then she picked it up and said hello and my heart soared like a bird over a line of trees.

"I didn't expect to hear from you," she said.

"Why not?" I asked. "Wait, don't answer that. Is it because I'm pathetic?"

"Who says so?" she said. "If anybody but me says that I'll kick their ass."

"You cannot talk like that," I said, shushing her. "You're a good girl. And your dad will think I'm a bad influence."

"He knows that you're a bad influence. He's known it for a long time. He's been telling me so since we were fourteen."

"I blame Otis."

"Otis wasn't under the bleachers with me trying to sneak his hand under my freshman cheerleader uniform, I can assure you."

"I still blame Otis. I want to put an ad in the paper—like those things about financial responsibility?—that says I will no longer be responsible for my actions. I blame Otis. And my mother. And my missing father. I could have been a decent human being."

"What are you talking about?" she said, and her voice changed. "I can't figure out what's going on from just your voice. I wish I could see your face. Are you having some kind of therapeutic breakthrough out there on the road? Or are you just having a breakdown?"

Both. Neither. Who knew or cared? There was something else I wanted to tell her. "Tracy," I said, "You really should find someone who'll treat you better. Someone who's ready to treat you the way you need to be treated."

"Okay," she said. "Now I wish you could see my face. I'm making that face where I scrunch my eyes almost shut and turn up my nose at you. The one where I think you're talking complete bullshit?" I had to laugh. "What are you babbling about? How do you think I need to be treated?"

"You want someone who'll marry you."

"Oh," she said. "That."

I was barreling through the dark, a cone of dim light just ahead of me, lightning flashing way off to the west. Nobody said anything for a long time. I thought maybe we had lost our connection and I called her name.

"I do want to get married," she said softly. "To you. Is that so wrong? I know some guys would be pleased at that kind of news. And I want to have kids with you. You'd be a terrific father."

"I was a terrific father," I said. "Once. But that's over and done with. I couldn't go through it again. If something were to happen—"

"Oh, Clay," she said, and I could almost see her shake her head. That's what women all do to me if they're around me long enough. "You just can't live your life like that. You can't live your life forever based on the fear that someday you might lose somebody."

I took a deep breath. Sometimes you know you shouldn't say something; you know full well that it's hurtful, and damned if you don't let it fly anyhow. "Well," I said, "that's how I'm planning on doing it."

"I love you," she said. "And I hope you change your mind."

"It's not going to change," I managed to force out. "Love is the most dangerous thing I know." I shook my head. "Tracy, really. You ought to find somebody else."

"Goodnight, Clay," she said, and her voice was not icy but mournful; I could hear her love and irritation all at the same time.

The phone went dead, droned in my ear for a time, then went to beeping, then to a recorded voice that encouraged me to call an operator if I had difficulty placing a call.

I considered throwing the phone out the window, but unlike Raffi, it was blameless. I was the asshole this time. So I laid it down gently and shook my head again.

Cruel to two women in one day. A personal record, best I could recollect. Not even in my fraternity days had I ever crushed more than one woman a day.

"You are a son of a bitch and a bastard," I heard myself say out loud. No one contradicted me.

The rain in my future became the torrential downpour in my present. I lost my rock-and-roll radio station. The rain pattered down, pattered down, and the wipers sloshed back and forth—a rhythm that I thought might lull me to sleep, and would that be such a bad thing?

But I was still curious about a couple of things, so I pulled over after midnight at a truck stop in Elk City to gas up, bought a couple of cassette tapes: the Stylistics, Harold Melvin and the Blue Notes, the O'Jays' greatest hits. It was Otis that first got me to listen to all those old soul groups back in the Seventies; the Chi-Lites, Blue Magic, The Delfonics, Main Ingredient, the Four Tops, the Spinners, the Jackson Five, Bloodstone. Until then I was just your ordinary redneck white boy listening to Hank Williams Jr. or something. I thought all these black soul groups dressed like pimps, but that didn't last. Otis and I in fact learned to do a mean O'Jays before we discovered there was more of a market around Robbinsville for rock and roll. Maybe this was a

wasteful purchase—I was sure I had all these tapes or something like them at home somewhere—but they were there and
this was here, and I was going to need something better than
right-wing talk shows if I was going to somehow get through
this night.

While I was in the truck stop, I wandered. I meandered. I
drifted past the coolers in back once, twice, more.

I could almost hear the foam rising off the beer in those
coolers, and the cans glinted in the fluorescents like light off a
hypnotist's watch.

I bought two roast beef-and-cheddar deli sandwiches, a big
bag of Cheetos, a package of Oreos, some beef jerky, three ar-
tificially banana-flavored Moon Pies.

I bought a twelve-pack of Original Coors in the gold can.
On sale, I noted with pleasure. I was a responsible person.

Responsible for everything.

Back on the highway, the rain pattering hard, I wolfed
down a sandwich and then I cracked open a beer one-handed.
It was cold in my hand, sweating, and the aroma was acrid
and musty and bracing.

I used to drink Coors at Georgetown. After a long, hard
morning of being law students, a bunch of us used to play
softball at the big green belt down New Jersey from
McDonough Hall, just north of the Capitol. Then we'd go
home and open the books again in the evenings, those of us
who did such things.

Someone always had a case of Coors on ice in the back of a
car. In those days it was sort of romantic, this beer brewed
from the icy waters of the Rocky Mountains, the beer of
hunters, trappers, cowboys, and mountain men. I think Billy
Rowlands, who was from Texas, was the guy who got us
started drinking Coors first year, and he met some initial resis-
tance. Most of us had been beer snobs. We drank Heineken or
Moosehead. But after a hard day of moot court and a couple
of hours of softball, nothing felt better in the warm afternoon
than to lie sprawled in the grass and laugh and talk and drink
Coors.

That's where, my last year at Georgetown, I got to know
this tall blond girl, Anna Lynn Schrader, and I probably have

the beer to thank at least for that, because we didn't run in the same circles and I don't know how I'd ever have had the guts to talk to her otherwise. Although we had taken one course together, Products Liability and Safety—and so at least knew each other to nod to—she was a Goody Two-shoes burning up the environmental law track, and I was a crank training for trial work. She was editor on the new *Georgetown International Environmental Law Review;* first time I ever heard her voice, she was telling Billy that she was editing articles on Mexican-American shared groundwater and marine plastic pollution. And me? I was devoting most of my energy and time during my last year to the Appellate Litigation Clinic, writing briefs for the Supreme Court and even arguing a case in front of the Fourth Circuit Court of Appeals. Anna Lynn was animated about her future; I was resigned. She had wings; I was going to be a flightless drone, if a well-paid one.

You get to know things about people by watching them play games. Anna, for example, did not play softball like the other girls. She played with abandon. She was tall and rangy, and she caught everything she could get to. She didn't care if the ball jumped up on her. She wasn't afraid to slide. She wasn't afraid to dive for the ball. She wasn't afraid to do anything. She was so beautiful and so earnest, this big blond Dutch girl from Michigan; that scared me too. When I finally insinuated myself into her company and she was directing remarks to me instead of Billy, she didn't talk about how much money she was going to make or about the rush you feel walking next to or on your way to being those in power, which was why I thought I was in law school.

No, she had this crazy idea she was going to make the world a better place.

In 1988 beer didn't taste like death and loathing; it tasted like new love. It tasted like spring afternoons and cherry blossoms and green grass and laughter, like the pealing chimes from the Taft Memorial calling off every quarter hour.

Those were good times. The best. Driving my rented Cadillac somewhere in western Oklahoma now, I took a long swig of Coors and it was like a rush of liquid gold. I felt alarm bells go off in my head and fireworks before my eyes. I saw

Anna, the way she stood at the plate, waggling the tip of the bat as the ball arced in; I saw her, her eyes red from weeping, the day she told me what I thought was the worst news that I could ever take in; I saw her in our final moment together which actually held the worst news I could take in and still survive in some fashion, when I would have given anything to have the time to tell her what I hadn't been able to tell her.

And they say Volvos are the safest cars in the world. Well, maybe they are. One of us, at least, did survive a crash with a speeding garbage truck.

My windshield wipers were going back and forth, still heavy with the rain, *thump thump thump thump*, and I took another long swig, *glug glug glug glug*.

I hadn't had a drink in ten years. They had been ten bad years, ten years of loss and remorse and anger, and I was due a little relief.

It felt good.

So did the next one.

And the next.

Before I knew it I had a growing heap of dead cans in the passenger floorboard. The hard rain and the alcohol blurred the last of Oklahoma pleasantly, blurred the yellow and white flashing lines of the roadway, even blurred the words of the song I had set on Repeat, "Betcha by Golly Wow."

The phone gurgled at my side and I fumbled for it, beeped it on. "Grand Central Fucking Station," I said, taking a drink before I went on. "What can we fuck up for you today?"

"Son," Ray said, "turn down that music and try talking to me again in a slightly different fashion."

"Sorry," I said. "Sorry, Ray. I've had a bad fucking day."

"Son," he said, and his voice took on an edge; it was late late at night where he was, and he was probably tired as hell. "An apology isn't worth a damn thing if it's immediately followed by another offense."

"No sir," I said. "It isn't. I'm sorry. Really." I turned down the Stylistics and slowed to take the Shamrock exit so we could talk.

"Damn," I said in wonder and amazement. "I'm in Shamrock, Texas." I pulled over off the access road.

"You're supposed to be in New Mexico, son," he said. "What the hell is going on with you?"

"When is the funeral?"

"Nine o'clock in the cathedral downtown. Eleven o'clock graveside at the national cemetery. It's a military burial."

"Military cemetery?"

"Your dad served his draft out in the Army National Guard. Maybe you didn't know that."

"No, sir, I didn't. There are a lot of things I don't know about the man."

I opened the door and got out. The rain was letting up a bit. It felt good, the drops splattering against my face and hands. I laughed.

"But did you hear me, son? You've got"—and here he paused to check the clock and do the math—"ten hours or so left to get there."

"I'll make it," I said. Rain dripped off my eyelids, my nose, into my nostrils. "Ray, am I a son of a bitch and a bastard?"

To his credit, he did not hesitate. On the other hand, nor did he ask me what made me bring it up. "No, son," he said.

"Am I?"

"No," he said again. "Clay, do you need me? I'll be on the next plane if you need me. I'll come to Shamrock or Lucky Charms or whatever it is. In a heartbeat."

"No sir," I said, although through the numb blur of my current feelings I felt warmth spreading across my chest. "I know you would. But this is my spiritual quest. Tracy said I had to face Darth Vader alone."

"I'm not sure exactly what that means," he said. "Although if Tracy said it, I'll bet it's good advice. She's a peach."

"You know who Darth Vader is," I said. "He fell for the dark side of the force."

"I know who Darth Vader is."

I saw Tracy hanging up on me, turning to go upstairs. But I couldn't see her face, couldn't see whether she was smiling or weeping or just shaking her head. "She is a peach, isn't she?"

"Tracy? She sure is."

"Whatever that means. I know it's a good thing. Oh, boy.

Ray, I have fucked up royally. Pardon my French. Everything. Ten years ago. Tonight. Everything in between."

"Maybe so, son. But it's not too late—"

I shook my head and clicked him off mid-platitude. It was too late. For Anna Lynn, for Ray, for Kathy and Michael Cartwright, and probably for Tracy and me.

I turned off the ringer. He would call back. And call back. I tossed the phone into the car and stood there on the access road. The horizon was a million miles in every direction, and away from the road it was so dark I imagined the coyotes needed flashlights. Hmph.

I let my head drop to the car door and closed my eyes, but the world seemed to be lurching like a ship at sea, and I opened my arms in alarm. I had forgotten how to be drunk, a useful skill I once possessed.

I raised my head again, my face completely wet, my hair matted with rain, and now I saw a familiar sign alongside the Caddy. I was standing on old Route 66, or at least a simulacrum of it; a lighted billboard farther down advertised a Route 66 museum in Shamrock proper.

And that's when I realized that this is how my father would have gone to California all those years ago. It would have taken forever, that old Greyhound stopping at every city and pissant town the old song mentioned: Amarillo; Gallup, New Mexico; Kingston, Barstow, San Bernardino. And Shamrock, Texas, too. I smiled.

"I'm getting my kicks, all right," I said. "Thanks, Dad. Thanks for everything." I got back in the car, pulled back onto the interstate, ejected the Stylistics, who were bringing me down, and tried out the O'Jays. Better.

And another beer. Better still.

The Texas high plains rushed by outside, ghostly and glistening, like something out of a painting instead of a photograph. I saw an occasional tree, so windblasted it looked like bonsai. Power or phone lines hung alongside the road from poles like crosses; the grain elevators were white and blocky and made me think of those sacred kachina dolls.

I was listening to those great songs from the Seventies— "Backstabbers" and "Love Train" and "For the Love of

Money"—when I got another signal through the blur of sensation. Urgent pee request.

There was a rest stop three miles ahead, and although this had sneaked up on me again, I had my doubts I could make it. I clamped my legs together, grabbed hold with my hand and squeezed, sped up to near ninety. I took the exit ramp with graceless haste, and all but squealed up to the back of an old Ford van plastered with bumper stickers, which was alone in front of the bathrooms.

I managed to remember the keys, and then I lurched up the pavement toward the john.

A figure materialized out of the darkness, tall, black, and female, and tried to take my elbow. "Hey baby," she said. "How about a date?" She tried to swipe her hand across the front of my pants, which would have been disastrous for both of us.

"No, thanks," I said and dodged out of the way.

I counted to 127 at the urinal, a new personal record for longest piss. Somebody back in a stall was whistling something Baroque and then paused for a moment to groan before an answering sploosh.

The hooker came up to me again on the way back. "Hey, baby," she said. "You want a date?"

"I just turned you down," I said. "Don't you remember?"

"I remember," she said. Then she smiled slyly and moved forward purposefully. "But I thought maybe you'd changed your mind."

"No thanks," I said again. "Don't ask me again."

"She has been doing that for hours," said a voice thick with Spanish sibilants. I looked down and saw what I must have missed in my earlier headlong flight to safety. A young young Hispanic woman—no more than a girl, really, eighteen at the most—sat at the curb next to the van nursing her baby.

"Poor woman," she said, looking at the hooker and shaking her head sadly.

I stopped, swayed a little to get my balance, and surveyed the scene. Across the grassy median were the half-lit slumbering semis, their engines idling up and down like giant sleeping cats. The van was the only other vehicle near, and it wasn't much of a vehicle: an old powder blue Ford Econoline with rusted-out back panels. Illinois plates. The hood was up, and I could see a guy with battered white Converse high-tops tinkering underneath. I could also smell burned oil, see the black crust caked on the tailpipe.

"Poor woman," I said, staggered back inside the Caddy, and started it up.

The O'Jays were singing "992 Arguments." I reached up to pull the car into gear.

The woman looked up at me, the baby at her breast.

"Shit," I said. "Fucking shit on toast." I let out a groan of anguish and exasperation. Then I shut off the engine, got out, reached for my wallet, pulled a couple of twenties.

"I'm sorry to bother you," I said, stepping carefully over to the woman on the curb. "Can I help in some way?"

"Help is never a bother," she said. The infant was asleep now, but still making tiny suckling noises. "Why don't you speak to the father?" She inclined her head to the front of the van.

"The father?"

"One of them," she said, shrugging. "The other is in there," and now she nodded to the bathrooms.

"The other," I said. I was well and truly drunk. "Okay," I said, and I shambled around to the front of the van.

The man turned at my approach, and I could see that he had on cutoffs and a black T-shirt. He was powerfully built, also Hispanic, handsome as Antonio Banderas. "Can I help you?" he asked, his accent thrilling, his attitude frankly belligerent.

"I know a little bit about cars," I said. I sniffed again. Yes, definitely burnt oil. Not good.

"Take a look, then," he said. "I can't make head or tails of it."

Yes, definitely a problem. I got up under the hood. "She won't turn over?"

"Not at all."

I stood tiptoe and put my head closer to the block.

"What do you think?" came a loud and hearty and distinctly un-Hispanic voice from very close at hand, and I clanged my head hard against the hood.

"Oh, that looked like it hurt," the voice said, and I struggled to focus. It hurt like hell. I put my hand to the back of my head and felt something wet, although whether it was rain or blood I did not know.

"Here, let me help you," the new voice said, and God help me, it sounded all but Irish. It was more the alcohol than the head injury, but in truth, I was a little wobbly, and I welcomed the strong hands at my elbows. They seated me at the curb near the girl, and the voice said, "Let me take a look at you. There's a bit of blood there, isn't there?" He got down on one knee in front of me, a shock of gray hair atop a large creature dressed all in black except for a stripe of white at his throat.

A priest.

"Here," he said. "Look me in the eyes, if you will."

I did. They were blue as a mountain lake, and deep-set above a bulbous nose you could have built a condo on.

"I know that nose," I said, before I could stop myself.

"And is that the truth," he said, arching an eyebrow. "And where have you seen a monstrous great honker like this before?"

And suddenly I knew. I placed the voice, the laughter, even the whistled Bach in the bathroom. I did know that nose, and the person who lugged it around. "Appellate Litigation Clinic," I said, thinking hard. "Georgetown Law, 1988."

The priest turned his head sideways in wonder, took a close look at me, and his puzzled mouth slowly sprouted a smile. "Clay," he said.

"Father Tom," I said.

"Clay Forester," he said, and his smile spread like sunlight across the broad prairie. "What in the name of all the saints are you doing in darkest Texas on such a night as this?"

"Giving you a ride," I said, and shrugged, for it was suddenly obvious that this was what I was here to do. "Your van is going to need new rings at the very least. Maybe a whole new block."

The other man shrugged. "He is probably right, Father. I can't do a thing with it."

"Of course he is, Jorge. He always was. Clay, Father Jorge Cárdenas. He just finished law school at Loyola. First in his class, unlike either of us. Jorge, my old friend from Georgetown, Clay Forester."

"It is a pleasure," he said and shook my hand. He had a strong grip. But *Father* Jorge? There were some disappointed girls in his hometown when he declared for the priesthood, I can tell you that. What did they use to call them at Georgetown? Father What-a-Waste. "And this is María and José," he continued, indicating the girl and her baby.

"Hola," she said, "again."

"And could you give us a lift then, Clay?" Father Tom asked. "We are in a bit of a hurry if the truth be know. Where are you headed?"

"New Mexico," I said. "Does that help at all?"

"Indeed it does. "We're headed toward Amarillo ourselves. Would you mind dropping us a wee bit north of town?"

"It'd be a pleasure," I said. And it would. Father Tom had been a Jesuit priest in my class at Georgetown, some years older than the rest of us; that made him close to sixty now. He was specializing in social justice issues from poverty to pollution, and so Anna Lynn loved him. If all priests were like Father Tom she would have left the Dutch Reformed Church in the blink of an eye. In fact, he'd been a guest in our home twice after we'd married, but then he got assigned back somewhere in the Midwest, and anyway, by then conditions were not so conducive around our house for entertaining guests.

I got up and went back to the car, unlocked it, and turned around, leaning against the door. The bumper stickers on their van said things like "God's Peace, not Man's Peace" and "No more Bombs for Peace." One had a peace sign inscribed over an ichthys sign.

I wondered if I had driven into some benighted alternate reality where the Sixties never ended.

Father Jorge loaded their few bags in the trunk—they were certainly traveling light, even with the baby—and I opened the back door for María. "Thank you," she said quietly. She got settled into the seat, groaning a little at the feel of the soft leather, and put the baby into her lap. Father Tom kicked the beer cans aside without a word and got in next to me.

"You wrote, I think," I said when we had pulled out onto the highway. There was no avoiding it, for he knew much of what had happened to us if not the whole horror. It was a beautiful letter, as I remembered it, full of his sense of Anna Lynn, of the shock of her loss. "After the accident. I never wrote you back."

"You had other things to deal with," Father Tom said. He turned to Father Jorge and explained, gently, "Clay lost his family in a car accident. It was some years back. But you know how these things are. Let us remember him tonight in our prayers," before turning back to me and continuing. "I just wanted you to know we were thinking of you. I said novenas for Anna Lynn and for your son. I prayed for you."

"Lots of people did," I said grimly. "But it didn't bring them back."

"No," he said. "It never does, does it?"

The baby in María's lap shifted. She looked down at it, smiled, closed her eyes.

"Where in Amarillo are you headed?"

"About fourteen miles out of town," he says. "The Pantex weapons plant."

"The what?"

Father Tom nodded to his cohort in the backseat, and Father Jorge leaned forward. "The Pantex weapons plant develops and fabricates chemical high-explosive components for nuclear weapons, assembles and disassembles nuclear weapons, modifies and repairs nuclear weapons, and performs surveillance testing and disposal of chemical high explosives."

"Oh. And why are you going there?" I asked, although I had a sneaking suspicion, what with Father Tom and the obviously even more militant Father Matinee Idol that some more Sixties tomfoolery was afoot.

Father Tom smiled and confirmed my fears. "I thought maybe you were going there for the same reason we are. That maybe you read about it on the Internet. The demonstration,

I mean. People are coming from all across the country to shut the plant down." He spread his hands. "Symbolically, of course. The business of war cannot be shut down for good."

"What is the demonstration for?"

Father Jorge spoke again. "The plant is an environmental hazard, for one thing. It's contaminated the groundwater across a four-state area."

"But that's a small thing, lad. Pantex is a site where nuclear materials are burned, where bombs are manufactured. It's a vital cog in the machinery of war. It's a prime spot to make a symbolic gesture."

"Okay," I said. "What does that mean, exactly?"

Father Tom spoke casually, as though the events he was describing had already occurred. "We'll join the other protestors. At dawn, we will commit acts of civil disobedience. María and her baby are going to join others in front of the gates. Jorge is going to join others in chaining himself to the railroad tracks so the trains carrying nuclear materials can't get in or out. And I'm going to give loud, angry Irish speeches and make people in uniforms angry and probably get the bejesus knocked out of me again. We'll all be arrested and thrown into the Potter County jail. It's a nice old jail, I'm told. You want to come with us?"

I laughed, flashing on Anna Lynn, who would have raised a fist of solidarity. There was a part of me that was tempted. But only a little. She would have done it to prove a point; I would have done it to piss people off. It was one of the differences between us—one of the stumbling blocks, it turned out. I just didn't care about anything that passionately, and she was ever a passionate woman.

I shook my head. "You know, Tom, I hate to say this after you've traveled this far and all, but I don't see the point. You'll be a momentary annoyance. It's ultimately more trouble to you than to them."

"What's the point of doing anything, then, Mr. Forester?" Father Jorge asked, clutching the headrest in front of him as if he wanted to choke it. "Don't you believe some wrongs require action, even if it is a symbol alone?"

"Now, now," Father Tom said, turning to calm him down.

"Not everyone has the activist blood in their veins. So, lad, you don't care to add this to your list of experiences, then?"

I shook my head again, a little chastened now. "I've got to be somewhere. As much as I'd enjoy getting the bejesus beaten out of me."

He laughed. "Where is it you're headed, lad?"

So I told him the story. I had it down to its component parts now and could relate it dispassionately and without feeling much of anything. I left out the people I'd met on the way, of course, and that I'd fallen off the wagon in a major way just a few hours ago. It would have been apparent to him, although I was proud at least to be driving in a straight line. Sometimes you have to pride yourself on small accomplishments.

"That's quite a story," he said when I'd finished with it. "I remembered the bit about your father. You made a joke about it first time you told me about him going off to embrace his destiny. But it's a different thing when you're saying goodbye, I suppose."

"It does put a new complexion on things," I admitted. We passed the exit for Groom, Texas, where on the north access road a huge red-and-white water tower loomed precariously over what apparently had once been a truck stop on Route 66 and was now simply an empty parking lot. I was in a suggestible state where everything seemed to have some relation to me; I was at the same time the falling tower and the ramshackle asphalt.

"I've wondered about you sometimes," Father Tom said. "You dropped completely out of sight, Clay. I asked the alumni office. You dropped your membership. The bar association couldn't find you. Where've you been, lad?"

I laughed and shook my head. "I moved home with my mother. I thought in a little while maybe I could get myself together." I raised my hands from the wheel for a moment in a sort of shrug. "That was ten years ago."

"Lord, now, has it been that long? It seems like only yesterday."

"It has. And it does."

On the south side of the interstate, a huge white monolith

came into view. THE LARGEST CROSS IN THE WESTERN HEMI-SPHERE, a sign proclaimed, and then we saw it in its fullness, lit like a pyre in the middle of the night, this enormous white metal cross looming hundreds of feet above us like some pagan idol.

"That's what it feels like to live in my mother's house," I said. He laughed, although I was serious as hell.

"I remember you talking about your family," he said. "Your mother and her sisters. Is your stepfather still alive?"

"He sure is," I said. "Alive and kicking."

"Retired?"

"No, he still practices. You remember him?" He nodded. "He still does lots of pro bono work. I think his favorite thing is representing poor black sharecroppers against landlords and scam artists."

"Still a man after my own heart," he said. "Have you thought of doing some work with him?"

I shook my head. "I can honestly say that I haven't given the law any thought in ten years." And even though I hadn't, I had been one of the most promising associates in one of D.C.'s largest firms. I had represented General Electric as co-lead counsel in front of the United States Supreme Court, and that wasn't even my biggest case. It would have been a jarring transition from that to, say, defending a black mother accused of food stamp fraud. "I went back to playing music. That's all."

"Still playing the devil's music?"

"Yes, sir."

"Good for you. I like a little rock and roll now and then." He creased his forehead for a moment, trying to remember something. "I think your stepfather went to Boston University, didn't he?"

"Yes, he did. He never met Martin Luther King, but he was in the law school while King was there at the Divinity School. And Barbara Jordan was one of his classmates. I think they were friends. He sure talks about her a lot."

"Ah, that was a fine woman."

"Ray calls her 'The Great Woman.' He'll say, 'as a Great Woman once said.' As far as I know, he always means her. I

think he misses her." I laughed. "She was always used for object lessons around our house. Whenever I was feeling down
on myself, which was pretty often—"

"Past tense, of course," Father Tom said.

"Of course. Anyway, whenever I was upset about the way
the world was treating me, Ray used to remind me that
Barbara Jordan didn't make law review when she was at BU.
I didn't know then what he meant. Maybe not even when I
was in law school. Now I think I do. Something about how
people can't always know your true worth."

Father Tom nodded. "That's one to remember."

We passed another sign for the Big Texan restaurant ahead
in Amarillo: 72-OUNCE STEAK DINNER FREE IF EATEN IN ONE SIT-
TING. I tried to do the math. If it hadn't been the middle of the
night, I was drunk enough to try it.

"Four and a half pounds," Father Jorge mumbled. He too
seemed stunned at the idea. He was probably thinking it
would feed a whole village or something, about how many
pounds of grain or soybeans or whatever went to raise that
cow for some glutton's table.

"That's a tremendous waste of cow," I said, catching his
eyes in the rearview and getting at least a little nod in return.
María was asleep, her hands cradled protectively over and
under her baby. I laughed. "You know, María threw me for a
loop earlier. When I asked if she needed help, she told me to
talk to one of the fathers. The *fathers*. Like there was more
than one."

Father Tom smiled, but his lips grew slender. "She's a good
girl," he said quietly. "Jorge brought her home to stay with us
in Chicago."

"María came to us from Chiapas," Father Jorge said quietly. "You know Chiapas, Mr. Forester?"

"I know it's in Mexico," I said. "The band buys organic
coffee from Chiapas."

"María's father was a Zapatista there, fighting for the
rights of the indigenous people. He was assassinated by a
paramilitary group backed by the Mexican government."
Father Jorge dropped his head, and his voice was quiet, so as

not to wake her. "She was raped. Many times, by many men. Bastards." He dry-spat to his right, toward the door. "They left her for dead." He raised his head and I looked in his eyes; I would not have wanted to be one of the men who did it. "She was fifteen years old. Quince años. The good Mexican bishop don Samuel Ruiz García, of the diócesis de San Cristóbal de las Casas, he asked us to bring her to America. Father Tom arranged her adoption by members of our church. She became a citizen last year, before the child was born. So he is an American too." He nodded to himself. "An American."

I watched the mother and child, the mother herself little more than a child, the child the end product of violence and evil and lust. Her hand gently cradled his head; even in sleep she would let no harm come to him.

"How could she—" I stopped, swallowed. It was too much, opened too many doors I wanted to keep closed, locked, barricaded forever.

"Love the child of her affliction?" Father Tom asked.

"Yes," I said. "What they did to her—"

"What they did to her was terrible. Horrible. Almost beyond reckoning. But what God made of what they did . . . Well, that was beautiful. It"—and his voice softened with the deep-held conviction—"was purest grace, lad. The very essence of God."

I shook my head. "I don't believe it works that way. I'd like to. But I don't."

"Oh," he said, "but it does. Not always. Or not right away. But it does."

"Because all works for good to them that love the Lord," I said, and my sarcastic appropriation of the Apostle Paul was painful and piercing in the enclosure of the car. I snorted. "How can you drag her into what you're doing? Hasn't she been through enough?"

"She believes in what we're doing," Father Jorge said. "Anyone with eyes to see knows that the United States is the greatest weapons exporter in the world. We love our country, but we are angry about this thing. She thinks, maybe she can save some other little brown girl somewhere. Maybe she cannot. But the gesture itself is something against such a past as hers."

"So some other little brown girl will be raped by people carrying AK-47s or Uzis or spears instead of M-16s," I said. "Jesus. I can't see that it makes a bit of difference in the end. Nothing does."

Father Tom shifted in his seat, and there was the clank of empties beneath his feet. "Clay," he said, "there is a tall wooden crucifix in the church in Corte Madera, the arms blown away in some war sometime or other. Under it someone with eyes to see wrote, 'Jesus has no arms but ours to do his work and to show his love.' That is what I believe. What we believe. We must act as we think he would have us act if we are to be his arms in the world."

I laughed at him, and it was not a pretty sound.

"Clay," Father Tom said gently, "have you ever talked to a psychiatrist about your depression?"

"What depression?" I said, which I guess was a little like Captain Ahab asking, "What whale?" I laughed at him again and shook my head, but had to stop because it was making me sick to my stomach. I needed another beer, or no more. "No. I haven't seen a psychiatrist, Father, and I haven't dealt with my grief, and I haven't medicated myself so I won't feel it anymore. I don't want to lose it. I like it, in a way. The pain. It lets me know I'm alive."

"You like it because you think you deserve it," Father Tom said, and he laid his hand on my shoulder. "If you were wise enough to be a Catholic and I could get you in the confessional, I'd give you a rosary and a swift kick in the ass, and that would be the end of it. I can see that you've long ago done your penance for whatever it is that you think you did."

I certainly didn't believe it, but it was a kindness of him to say so. Although we were still some ways out from the lights of Amarillo, I took the exit Jorge indicated, and we headed off into the dark, flat plains. The road was paved but narrow, and fence posts flashed by to either side of us on the other side of deep culverts.

"I'd stick to law," I told Father Tom. "You shouldn't lecture people about their neuroses. About their suffering."

"Suffering?" Father Jorge said. I had felt him back there for a while, itching to give me the swift kick in the ass Father Tom wanted to prescribe. "What we inflict on ourselves is not suffering, Mr. Forester. This is suffering." He indicated María with his outstretched hand. "And even so, she has forgiven them. She has overcome her suffering. Transformed it into love."

And maybe she had. I admired her, for sure. "One little tragedy and men fall to pieces," I murmured.

Father Tom turned his head sideways and regarded me with an arched eyebrow.

"Just something that a wise woman told me yesterday. I think it was yesterday. I've been awake a long, long time now." I wondered where Kathy and Michael were now. Safe as this refugee, I hoped. "Maybe she was right, that woman. I couldn't have done what Maria did."

Now we saw bright lights across the plains—could see them from miles away, in fact, like the aftermath of a prison break: the tall halogen lights supplemented by spotlights playing across the fences.

Father Tom put his hand gently on my arm. "Forgiveness is easier than hatred in the long run. Something to think on, lad."

"Who do I hate? Who do I need to forgive? You've got it all wrong, Father. It won't work."

I don't think he planned to tell me any more, but in any case we were all distracted now by the flashing lights of cop cars ahead, dozens of them. Texas Highway Patrol, Amarillo police, sheriffs—maybe FBI, CIA, and NSA for all I knew. The road was blocked off well short of the gate, and we could see a milling crowd moving forward and then being pushed back by men in uniforms and riot gear.

"Well, lad," Father Tom said as we reached the outskirts of the crowd, well lit by the spotlights and TV crews, "I suppose you'd best let us out here."

It seemed so wrong, somehow. "But you're not even going

to get to the gate, Tom. You're all going to get thrown in jail for nothing."

"It's not for nothing," he said. María stirred as we pulled to a stop at the side of the road.

"Don't throw her to those wolves."

"We are doing the work of our Father, Mr. Forester. That is enough for us." Father Jorge shook his head, as though I couldn't be expected to understand.

But I understood all right, or thought I did. "Fuck you and your armless Christ, Jorge," I said, and my laughter was louder and harsher even than before. Both María and José woke up whimpering. "Christ with his arms blown off. Seems just about right to me. He belongs right up there with his blind father. God with cataracts and a white cane, tap-tapping across the earth, splattering the innocent."

The baby was crying; here was my secret identity blown again: just another loud angry man. Father Jorge looked as though he wanted to ask me to step outside, and I guess I would have gotten my ass kicked by a priest on national television—something I had never imagined might happen to me. But Father Tom waved him ahead, and he and María slid out of the car without another word to me.

Father Tom opened his door, turned to get out himself, then turned back, took my hand, and held it meditatively for a moment—strongly, although at first I tried to pull it back. His face was red with anger, but he didn't want to leave it like this. "Nothing is an accident, Clay," he said, and he squeezed my hand, hard, like you might squeeze a kid to reinforce your message, like kinetic punctuation. "I've been sent to tell you something. I don't know what it is. What's at the heart of your anguish is something no one else knows. But I think you know." He looked me right in the eyes, and his face took on a gentler cast as he saw my pain. "I'll be praying for you."

It hit me in the chest like a car door. I could barely muster a good-bye, barely register the car doors closing. I was trembling, could barely breathe.

This was exactly what it felt like when Anna first told me, like the life had been knocked almost all the way out of me and was just hanging on in my tingling fingertips and toes. This was the feeling I had been trying to avoid feeling for ten years. Somehow I fumbled the car into reverse, managed to jockey back and forth to turn around without losing my car in a culvert or sideswipe a media van, and managed to find my way back to the interstate.

Once there I checked the clock: 2:20.

I dialed the phone as I was passing into Amarillo, where construction made for some scary twisting back and forth beneath the pale halogen lights. I slowed down to keep from pinballing from one concrete wall to the other; I did not have the greatest control over my motor skills at this time.

"Otis," was the answer at the other end.

"This is the strangest trip I ever heard tell of," I began, because that was all I could say with absolute surety.

"Dude. Hey! We played nothing but penis songs tonight. 'Lick It Up,' 'Slide It In,' 'Big Balls,' 'Rock you Like A Hurricane.' First it was fun, then it got to feeling a little lame. Maybe you're right about that whole thing. And that chick—that Denise that thought you were such hot stuff?—she came in, saw you weren't here, and left like someone had tried to set her ass on fire." He stopped for a second, maybe to catch his breath. "What is that shit you're listening to?"

"Dude, this is fly. This is the O'Jays." And it was good stuff, "Put Your Hands Together," and I sang it loud for him.

There was a moment of silence on the other end. "Dude, are you drunk?"

Up ahead was a flickering flame that lit up the whole horizon. Like the burning bush, I thought. Then I figured it must be New Mexico, like maybe the whole state was on fire like Otis said, but it was too early to see that, even if it was true. Then I saw it was the burn-off for a gas well or some such thing, but it was still pretty amazing, such a big, bright flame on such a dark night in the middle of so much nothing. "Drunk? Oh-ho, Nelly. You don't know the half of it, man. First, I haven't slept in, like, three days. And let's see: today alone I've terrified two sets of already-traumatized mothers and children, pissed off two priests, had a high-speed chase with the FBI after me, delivered protesters to a top-security government weapons installation, cursed God, and made fun of Jesus. Only then may you add in that I'm drunk."

"Clay, what the fuck are you—" He stopped, got a hold of himself, then proceeded in a faux-Mr. Rogers calm. "Clay, I thought I was the one needed looking after."

"It has not been a beautiful day in the neighborhood," I said. "This trip makes *The Wizard of Oz* look like the video from somebody's grandparents' vacation to fucking Yellowstone National Park."

"Sounds like."

"Before I pissed everybody off or disappointed them, which is what I always do—" I began and then my nose wrinkled up like a brussels sprout as I passed another set of stockyards, this at the Wilderado exit. "Whew!" I said, and I was gagging. The stench made the Oklahoma City Stockyards seem like a cherry orchard; I thought for a second that maybe good old olfactory menace Buster had found his way back into the car, like one of those tabloid stories of dogs tracking their masters down a thousand miles away. I thought I was going to ralph on the Corinthian leather.

While I was buckled over, my hand brushed against something loose in the floorboard, and I brought up some of the pictures Kathy Cartwright had showed me and that got me real serious real fast.

"Otis," I said. "You still there?"

"I'm here."

"What was I saying?"

"Damned if I know. Clay, where are you, man? Pull off the road and let's talk. You're scaring the shit out of me."

"Can't do it," I said. "I've got to get to this funeral if it kills me." In the photo on top, I caught a glimpse of Michael, his shirt pulled up to show the blackened bruises across his back and arms. "But listen: I did help a little boy and his momma get away from a bad man. Ask Ray. He'll tell you."

"Good work, son," he said. "This is like *Mission: Impossible 2*. 'Difficult should be a walk in the park for you.' "

"I mean it. They were in some serious shit. They needed

help. And I helped them. That counts for something, doesn't it?"

"Who is the man who would risk his neck for his brother man?"

"Shaft," I said.

"Right on. Who's the cat who won't cop out when there's danger all about?"

"Shaft," was again the right answer.

"Can you dig it? You know, this cat Shaft, I hear he's a bad motherf—"

"Shut your mouth."

"I'm just talkin' 'bout Shaft."

"Well, we can dig him." I opened another beer. It had gone warm; I'd have to pick up some more cold ones directly. "Man, what I wouldn't give to play that scritchy-scratchy guitar. You know, that wocka-wocka sound?"

"You be the wrong color to be so righteous."

"Do not be playing homeboy with me, Otis Miller. I distinctly remember you listening to my Bee Gees album during the Saturday Nite Fever craze."

"Do not let that get out, man," he said. "I be ruined among the brothers. Hey, have you pulled over yet?"

"I have not," I said. "I'm rocketing through the black Texas night in a rented Caddy, and I'm feeling no pain. None whatsoever."

"Uh-huh."

"Oh, I forgot something. I broke Tracy's heart. I told her I didn't want to marry her, I didn't want to have kids. I told her she ought to settle down with somebody more reliable and down-to-earth. I suggested you."

"I know you were drunk when you said that."

"Flying." I ejected the tape and hit "search." "Blind." The radio rounded up a rock station crackling out of Amarillo still. Tommy Tutone. "Listen," I said, upping the volume again. "We used to do this song."

"Clay, do you need me to come after you?"

"Why does everybody keep asking me that? Shut up, man. You're making me miss the song."

"Clarence Shepherd died," he said. "I read it in your Aunt Sister's column. He was a nice old guy."

"Well," I said, "we're all going to the same place eventually." I saw the lights of a distant truck stop. "I'm at least going to have some more cold beer before I go." Some part of me recognized that I was at the place where I could go down into hard, head-banging, hungover sobriety or push on past the stupor to another buzz, and I chose buzz, hands down, pedal to the metal.

"Dude, I'm worried about you. I mean it."

I took the exit fast, with a whoop, and my head bounced off the ceiling as I said hello to part of the curb. "You should be," I said, and I hung up. Then I pulled into the lot, parked—slowly, with exaggerated drunken care—got out of the car, stretched, and turned a complete circle, my arms up high in the air. The night was dark and warm and deep, just right for swallowing me whole.

11

RIDE THE SANDIA TRAMWAY
WORLD'S LONGEST!

My eyes stung like someone had rubbed them with sand, my eyelids stuck when I tried to blink, and my throat was so dry, even with all the drinking I'd done over the past hundred hours or so, that I couldn't much more than croak along with the stereo. My back and butt and legs hurt from driving, and all of me throbbed with sunburn. Sometimes I closed my eyes, but I knew that if I did that for even a few seconds I would be asleep, and I really did want to find out what was going to happen to me.

What was left of my life was lived between highway lines and bounded by the darkness. There were flashes of light—green mile markers and exit signs, the white highway reflectors on the road, yellow on the shoulder—but they were simply reflecting what little light I put out. So I was grateful that, now and then, out of the night, came a sign, a light in the darkness, a carrier of meaning.

It was a long way I had come to get to where I was now.

I remembered the time Ray stood up at our Georgetown graduation party to give a toast. I knew he was going to, and I was proud to see him, this handsome and elegant man, standing in front of our professors, our new employers, our friends and family, to frame our accomplishment. He had a glass of champagne in his hand, although he did not yet raise it. I had a glass of champagne in my hand and five more in my stomach. Maybe that accounted for this strange tingling as he looked around and then began to speak.

"A friend of mine at Boston University, a Great Woman, once wrote, 'The law is supposed to be the configuration of rules and regulations which, if implemented, will lead to justice. The question is not if the law will win, but will justice be served?' " He looked down for a moment, and then out at the assembly, suddenly quiet, and repeated, "Will justice be served?" I don't know that they all—or even many—recognized the source. I did; Barbara Jordan's words always had an incredible beauty and balance. But the words themselves captured the attention, and it was now that Ray raised his glass of champagne and everyone stood and followed suit. Even my mother, even my aunts, giggling like they'd been caught browsing through dirty magazines at a 7-Eleven.

"Today we celebrate. Not, mind you, because two lawyers have been added to the roll of lawyers. If anything, that would be a matter for condolence, if still, mind you, an appropriate occasion for drinking.

"But no, instead we celebrate because of who these lawyers are, and who they will be. We celebrate because these two will be servants of the law, not lawyers who will try to make the law serve them. They will be lawyers who will seek justice. Here's to my son Clay and his future bride Anna Lynn. God bless them."

*Hear, hear*s around the room, *salud*s, and heads nodding.

That champagne didn't taste any different from the stuff that preceded, that followed. I got drunker than Peter O'Toole at a film premiere. And somehow, in the years that followed, I forgot everything he said. I became everything he despised. Everything she hated.

And driving across the high plains of the Texas Panhandle, I took another drink.

Tucumcari Tonite
Scenic Public Golf Course
1200 Hotel Rooms
Next Five Exits

The moon was full and huge; it ran in front of me like a little boy playing tag. At the beginning of the night, I had been

Charles in charge and it had been trying to catch me, but since I dropped the martyrs off at the massacre in Amarillo it had crept ahead, and now I feared it was going to get away from me entirely.

The moon was so bright that for a stretch of highway I turned off my headlights and drove dark, but then I saw headlights behind me and figured it would louse up my trip even more to have some Texas Ranger wearing mirrored sunglasses at night saunter up to my window and inform me that the Great State of Texas had some few traffic rules I had not violated but he was hard-pressed at the moment to recall what they were.

I flipped the lights back on, for all the good they did me.

Anna Lynn and I married in her home church in Grand Rapids in front of a pastor with an unpronounceable German name and a group of relatives who looked dour even in their joy. It was a plain church, almost cold, a church built by Puritans on downers. And there sat her teary-eyed parents, solid, stolid, and rich, steeped in all the Calvinistic virtues and vices, and depressing as hell to be around.

Although they were happy enough at the moment, I knew they feared Anna Lynn was making a mistake, and they were right, although they were right for the wrong reasons. They thought Anna Lynn should marry someone more like them: industrious, deeply Christian, conservative, and family-centered. They didn't know her well enough to know how miserable she would have been with someone like that. But she was also plenty miserable with me before it was all over and done.

But not at first. We honeymooned in Grenada, one of the southernmost and most unspoiled of the Caribbean islands, and a place we Americans had bombed and occupied back in 1983. It was surreal, an island paradise that had supposedly been a hotbed of Cuban Marxism before Reagan sent in the troops to protect a bunch of American medical students who couldn't get admitted into a real school.

Pardon my cynicism; I guess med school rejects have a right to feel secure too.

We landed on the one runway that made up the airport—

Anna Lynn read from her guidebook that Castro's advisers had built the runway before we booted them out—walked out of the plane onto a movable stair like something out of *Casablanca,* and then across the concrete, the world sparkling with light under a blue sky.

The airport was open-air, with huge ceiling fans instead of air conditioning. We stood in an enormous line for our bags and customs, then made our way out to the curb. Minivans booming reggae were filling up with passengers, but we got into a little Nissan Sunny, threw our bags in the trunk, and headed for our hotel on the beach.

All along the road in from the airport, goats and cows were tied so that they couldn't quite wander into the street. Bunston, our driver, said they used to roam free but cars and buses kept hitting them.

"Crunch," he said, bringing both his hands up from the wheel and clapping them together to illustrate. "Jus' like dat. I remember one t'ing—"

"Would you mind putting at least one hand on the wheel?" I said, my voice climbing into a higher register.

He laughed. "Hey, no worries, man. No worries." But he did drop a hand down to steer, and so I sat back and watched out the window.

The island was green and primitive—houses like cinderblock buildings, dazzling white laundry draped across dark green bushes, and the palm trees fifty or sixty feet tall, the tallest things on the island by official decree.

I carried Anna Lynn over the threshold of the hotel room because we couldn't remember when I was supposed to do that, and, frankly, because we thought it would be funny. She was a strapping girl every bit as tall as me, and I staggered in as far as the bed, which was where we remained until time for dinner.

"I read somewhere," Anna Lynn told me the next morning as one of those ominous minibuses careened on two wheels around a blind corner toward St. George's, the capital city, "that there were more medals awarded to American soldiers in Grenada than there were actual American soldiers in Grenada."

"Maybe it was hazardous duty," I said. "Maybe they were forced to ride this bus." Deafening reggae was booming out from under the seat, and eleven people of various ages and blacknesses were stuffed into the van with us. The seats were a zebra-skin pattern, and over the driver's head was a sticker that said "Sexy Senior Citizen."

She took my shaking hand in hers and raised it to her lips. "Nothing is going to happen to us," she said, as the beep of the horn announced our speeding approach around another corner. "We're going to lead a charmed life."

"From your lips to God's ear," I said. If another bus was coming around the corner from the other direction, we were all food for the seagulls.

But we survived that moment and plenty of others like it, and we spent an entire week doing nothing—the first time in years we'd had even a few hours of that luxury. At first, I will confess, I thought I was going to go insane without something to do, some deadline to meet, and Anna Lynn had to give me that look—you better get yourself under control, mister—and then turn her glower into a smile. And wonder of wonders, I chilled out. I kicked back.

I remembered what life was like before law school.

We strolled the tiny cobbled streets of St. George's, bought mangoes and oranges in the market place, lay for hours on the white sand beach at Grand Anse. We played volleyball with Canadians and Germans, and I cheered as Anna Lynn's team invariably won. She was, as ever, the best player out there, diving for balls no one else would aspire to, and her serve was a chilling thing to behold, like a lightning bolt from the hammer of Thor. Only I knew that she was a ringer, that she had been all-Michigan in volleyball as a girl, and I kept that info to myself—that and my joy.

We snorkled one afternoon, and since Anna Lynn had had the foresight to get her scuba certification before we left, she was able to go down scuba diving the day before we left. I stood sweating at the side of the boat and watched her, her shape recognizable but indistinct through the cool, clear water, and felt a strange chill. It seemed to be prophetic somehow, but of what?

"Oh Clay," she gushed when she came up, "I wish you could see it. It's beautiful! So much life! So much . . . everything!" She took my hand and swung it back and forth in her excitement.

"I'll bet," I said, like the wet blanket I feared I was going to become; then I feigned some excitement of my own. "I'm glad you had a good time."

At night we danced in the hotel nightclub to bad Caribbean ballads or steel bands, went for moonlight walks along the beach carrying our shoes in our hands, swam in the ocean, and made love, over and over again.

"Let's stay here," she said the night before we left, both of us about half drunk on rum punch, a Grenadan fruit punch with fresh nutmeg grated on top. "Let's practice law here. We can be barristers, you know? We can wear those funny wigs. We can eat lambi and drink rum punch and make love every night and wear our hair any way we like."

"Can't do it," I said, and the hurt look that flitted across her face told me that I could at least have said, "Wouldn't that be fun?" To my credit, I hadn't said something about how we had to get back to the real world, which was my first inclination. That would have been deadly.

But that's what I was thinking. Strange as it seemed to me then and now, I was ready to get back into that world where my life was circumscribed by others and my relationships were suspect and superficial.

It was safer, somehow, I thought, and truer to life than the idyll we shared on Grenada.

MISSION POSSIBLE: ABSTINENCE
SAY NO TO TEEN SEX

I had passed over into the state of New Mexico. I could tell by the sign, for one thing, and by the New Mexico weigh station for trucks, ablaze with light and fully staffed with highway patrol. Nothing else about the landscape looked different, but the moon was going, going, gone, and there was a strange gray fuzz across the horizon slowly becoming visible behind me.

I drove off the road once, and only running over the dark remains of a semi's blowout startled me back onto the straight and narrow. It felt like I had hit a deer or a small child. I shook my head hard, as if I could slosh around the froth passing for my brains in some meaningful way. Nothing. My eyes were so dry I moistened them with spit, thought about propping them open with toothpicks, and drove on.

My office at Welsh, Abernathy, Phelan, and Klein was on the seventh floor. It faced the Capitol, and I could just see the Washington Monument if I put my face to the glass, which I didn't do for fear of looking like someone who cared to see the Washington Monument. My desk was the size of some New England states, cherry, dark, shiny, and desolate. I had a legal pad atop the blotter, a pen holder, Anna Lynn's photo, and nothing else.

My mentor, Carroll Abernathy, told me when he checked in on my unpacking, "Clay, a cluttered desk suggests a cluttered mind. Make them think your mind is focused only on their problem and they will eat out of your hand." Carroll was the Abernathy of Welsh, Abernathy, Phelan, and Klein, and in the grand scheme of corporate law, he didn't even have to note my existence. There were dozens of partners to supervise new associates, but he'd taken a special interest in me because of my trial work. When they made the offer, in fact, he told me he thought I could be one of the best trial lawyers in the country and he wanted to work with me personally.

I took the job; maybe it proved I was desperate for praise from the rich and powerful. Maybe it just proved that I wanted to be the best at what I did.

Maybe it doesn't prove anything.

I worked long hours, not because I liked it, but because it was expected of us. New associates worked at least seventy-hour weeks. "Billable hours," Carroll said at our weekly meetings. "Bill, bill, bill." My days were marked out in increments of a quarter of an hour. Even if I made only a thirty-second phone call, we billed for fifteen minutes. It was strange, looking at my billing statements. I found five times as many hours in the day as there were supposed to be. It made me feel as though I was aging at a faster than normal rate. I had trouble sleeping, even when I got home after midnight. Sometimes I slept on the couch in my office, shaved and showered at the health club across the street, and showed up at my desk bright and early and ready to get back to work.

I told myself that Anna was working hard too, that her work was satisfying to her, that maybe she didn't miss me so much, although I missed her terribly, like rain or sunshine. I had to keep a close watch on myself, or I would catch myself mooning over her picture, losing three or four fifteen-minute billing periods to the inertia of love.

Of course, it wasn't all phone calls. I did background. I did research, looked up precedents, wrote briefs. A couple of times I took interrogatories alongside a senior litigator.

I didn't so much as walk near a courtroom.

But I would, Carroll told me during our monthly lunches. He was hearing good things about my work. I was thorough and methodical. I saw connections. I was a hard worker.

The places he took me for lunch served aged beef and martinis. He smoked cigars after, offered one to me. I puffed away at it, thinking it was like putting my head inside a smokestack. When I got home after lunching with Carroll, my scent made Anna Lynn sneeze. So I took up cigar holding, rather than smoking, which seemed to help at least a little.

Anna Lynn and I had lunch together too, sometimes as often as twice a week, and I tried to block out Friday nights to spend with her. We would go out to dinner, maybe see a movie. We made love when we got home, sometimes twice, and for a few minutes I remembered the sheer joy of love, thought it couldn't be possible to feel anything better or more meaningful. Then we fell asleep, and in a few hours, I left for the office.

She called once or twice a day. Sometimes I didn't take her calls. Sometimes I said I had to call her back. I rarely did. I didn't get to write down a .25 next to her number on my phone log.

We went to parties for clients, because Carroll wanted to show me off, and I wanted to show Anna Lynn off. We went to a reception at Kennedy Center where we met Pavarotti.

The firm rented the National Gallery of Art for an evening party, and we kissed, holding each other tightly, desperately, our bodies twined and elongated like the figures in the El Grecos.

I thought that maybe it would be enough, that she was seeing the importance of what I did, that the glitter of money was making me sparkle a little bit, too.

Then all of a sudden I knew that it wouldn't be enough and that bad things were in store for us, bad times like icebergs dead ahead.

"I feel like I'm losing myself," I told her that night after the gallery reception when we were in bed. "Like I'm losing you. Like saying one is the same thing as saying the other."

"Quit," she said. "You can be my kept man." And we both laughed and laughed. Anna Lynn's salary from her environmental nonprofit would barely cover my BMW payment.

"Can't do it," I said, although I had learned enough about marriage to say, "But wouldn't that be fun?"

"Sure you can do it," she said.

"We need the money," I said, although that was the least of my reasons for what I was doing.

"We need other things more," she said. "I just don't think you remember that. Except maybe one night a week."

"Someday I'll make partner," I said, pulling her close. "I'll be able to ruin someone else's life."

"Some consolation," she said, nipping my ear. "I hope I'm still around to see it."

She wasn't, of course. We laughed again, and then we made love, and I thought maybe I was just being paranoid. Things couldn't go on this way much longer. Someday this mad rush for partner would all be over. We'd be able to give each other more time and attention. We'd treat each other the way we had in Grenada, the way our wedding vows had said we would.

We'd actually written our vows, which made the congregation in that prim church in Grand Rapids a little nervous. Very earnest, very loving. We would always put each other first, support each other in every endeavor, love each other no matter what. They would have been impossible to follow in any case; they cancelled each other out. How can both of you always put the other first? And anyway, lawyers know how to look at vows and say, "That doesn't apply in this particular case."

Just a year after our marriage, it felt like we were complete strangers. Worse, really; complete strangers might hope to get to know each other some day.

VISIT LOS ALAMOS, BIRTHPLACE OF THE ATOMIC AGE

The Eastern sky behind me was starting to look like some kind of Georgia O'Keefe picture or something: tendrils of pink, orange, red, and purple layered up from the edge of the world. Then the sun, a big orange nuclear reactor, slipped over the horizon.

The interstate was empty. All along the highway, trucks were pulled onto the shoulders of access roads and picnic areas, their yellow running lights glowing. It was like I was the only person awake on the face of the earth.

In the summer of 1990, Carroll Abernathy took me off everything else I was doing and assigned me to the firm's highest-profile litigation: a little something having to do with a client's tanker losing eleven million gallons of crude oil in Prince William Sound the year before. Maybe you heard about it.

At first I had to shake my head. I was caught up in history, and it was too much. The previous March, Anna Lynn and I had sat in front of CNN watching the oil on the shore, two and three inches deep, the dead birds dripping with slime.

Seeing rescuers trying to help a dying bird, she squeezed my hand so hard I could feel my knuckles crack. "It's only going to get worse," she said. "There are something like seventy thousand birds migrating up there at this very moment. They don't know any better. They don't have CNN. They haven't heard that the rookeries are fouled by the biggest oil spill in history. And thousands of sea lions, too. It's a disaster of biblical proportions for the wildlife. Biblical." She squeezed

again. I feared I would never be able to sign a check again.
"The Federal Refuse Act and Clean Water Acts both cover
this kind of thing," she said, and she spoke with the voice of
an Old Testament prophet, grim as hell. "A year from now,
Exxon is going to be out of business."

What was true, though, was that if Exxon had to choose
between spending a tanker full of money on lawyers and stay-
ing in business, or paying plaintiffs and going out of business,
it was going to do the former, and Carroll called me into his
office on the one-year anniversary to say that Welsh,
Abernathy, long on retainer to Exxon for other matters, was
going to step up to lead-counsel status in state and federal
courts out in Alaska. Already over a hundred suits had been
filed, with more to follow, and he told me three things: consult with the people on the ground to find out what their strategy was; brainstorm with the defense team on ways to use the
law to save our client's ass; and plan to give up my personal
life for the duration.

I stood there for a moment. I had a strange pulsing sensation in my hands.

"Do we understand each other?" Carroll said. He was used
to issuing orders and having people flee to carry them out. "Is
there a question?"

"Wouldn't it be better from a public relations standpoint—
not to mention a moral one—for our client to pay for what
they did?"

He laughed, a quick hard bark that showed it had never occurred to him, and then the laugh was gone from his face and
he shook his head. "Not for them. And certainly not for us.
This oil spill is going to make us rich, rich men." He looked
up. I considered what he said.

"The Refuse Act and Clean Water Acts are on point," I
said. "I'll find a way to make them work for us."

He smiled, he turned back to his work, and I walked back
to my office.

I didn't tell Anna Lynn for almost a week. I told myself it
was because there wasn't an appropriate time. On the few
nights I managed to come home at all, she'd been asleep for

hours, and the last thing she would want was to have a conversation.

When I took off my clothes and snuggled in next to her, I ran my hand up her leg and under her nightshirt until it rested on her hip, solid and real, and I remembered that she loved me. She had married me, hadn't she? Everything was going to be all right. I was going to make partner. I was going to be home with her more often in just a little while. We only had to get through this.

The Friday morning she called me early, I was sitting looking over the motions filed by the local attorneys in Seattle and Anchorage, smart guys who had gotten off to a good start. Some of their ideas were audacious to the point of being ridiculous: for example, their contention that claims for lost earnings by fishermen or cannery workers should be offset by the money that other workers earned by participating in the spill cleanup. But other things were based on more solid ground, and could actually work: Tort reform measures passed by the state legislature could limit Exxon's payments, even for a monumentally damaging fuck-up like this. And maybe most important, if the courts bought it, they argued that a punitive damages award in one case should bar similar awards in others. Exxon would only have to pay out a big sum one time and it would be protected from having to do so again.

I was underlining something in the Clean Water Act when the phone rang. I checked my watch: 5:46. Someone who knew my direct-dial, since the switchboard wouldn't be open for hours.

"Clay Forester," I said in my best professional lawyer voice.

"Anna Lynn Forester," she said dreamily.

"Hey, baby," I said absently. I underlined something else.

"Did you come home last night?"

"No, I didn't make it," I said. "I grabbed a couple of hours on the couch."

"Well," she said, "you must have been home some time recently."

"Hmm?"

"Because you and I are going to have a baby."

I put down my pen, sat up straight in my chair, and let out a hoot. "No. Really? When did you find out?"

"About forty seconds ago."

"Did you do one of those home tests?" I slapped myself on the forehead and went on. "Of course you did. But that means you must have suspected something. Why didn't you tell me?"

"When would I have told you? Anyway, I wanted to surprise you."

"Well, you did surprise me."

"Good surprise or bad surprise?"

"Good," I said, and it sounded true; I felt good. Through my exhaustion I could feel a warmth spreading through my chest like someone had switched on an EZ-Bake Oven in there. "Very good surprise. The best."

"What are you doing?" she said. "Can we have breakfast?"

"Can't do it," I said. "I'm working on the Valdez thing."

A silence fell over the other end of the phone like she'd been sucked into space. Someone took a sledgehammer to that EZ-Bake Oven until it lay in cold plastic pieces.

"I can have dinner with you," I said brightly.

"What did you say?" she asked, and her voice was a cold breeze blowing off an ice floe.

"I can have dinner with you."

"Before that," she said. "What are you working on?"

I gulped, momentarily pondered jumping out the window, decided truth was the best strategy. "Welsh, Abernathy is representing Exxon," I said. "Carroll has me looking over some things."

You might have thought I'd told her I favored ripping newly conceived fetuses out of their mother's wombs with pruning shears. "I want you to get up from your desk and come home right now," she said, her voice level and slow, as though she was keeping control of it only by incredible effort. "And then I want us to talk about where you can send your résumé. I want you out of there."

"Can't do it," I said, and my voice too was level and slow,

although what I wanted to do was start screaming at her. "Exxon has a right to legal counsel, just like murderers and rapists and people who wear black socks with sandals. Somebody is going to represent them. It might as well be us."

"Oh, Clay," she said, and that was all she said. I put the phone back on the cradle. At eight o'clock, I had my secretary send flowers to Anna Lynn's work and arranged to pick up two dozen roses to take home. I told Carroll that I was taking Anna Lynn out to celebrate, and he slapped my back, smoked a cigar with me, and mentioned that he thought of me as his own son and he'd be proud to stand godfather for us. I felt like Michael Corleone.

So this was how you lost your soul.

DANGEROUS CROSSWINDS AHEAD

I was passed by a car with Tennessee plates, and against my will I took my mind off this strange dawn-lit lunar landscape I had wandered into for just a moment to wonder about Michael and Kathy Cartwright. I had done them wrong, I decided. What they needed was patience and quiet, and I had given them testosterone and psychosis.

And what kind of world had I driven myself into? The hills—mesas, I guess they'd be called—were layered like flavors of sherbet, red and yellow and white and dotted with dark green evergreen trees like cedars. The buildings I saw all looked like shacks. Adobe, plywood, beat-up trailers—it didn't look to me like anyone in New Mexico could raise the price of a Bomb Pop if the ice-cream man came by.

Then somewhere east of Santa Rosa, the hills disappeared. We must have been up on top of a plateau, because the land spread out flat in all directions, and there was so much sky it started to make me feel as if I was dissolving. Too much space. Too much nothing. And we all know that Nature abhors a vacuum.

The day I arrived in Anchorage, I saw a lone eagle circling over Cook Inlet. Maybe he just smelled fish, but it still felt like an omen. Alaska in the dead of winter was no place for a

Southerner to be, even if his wife wasn't great with child and so angry at him that she'd probably put a pitchfork through him if it wouldn't leave her baby fatherless.

Which my wife was.

I called every day and left messages, but it was over a week after I got to Anchorage before I got to talk to her, and even then it was no more than "I feel fine" and "Take care of yourself."

"Don't tell me about your work," she said. "I don't want to hear about it." And there wasn't much else to tell her other than what I'd been watching on HBO there in the Hotel Captain Cook, so that was that. It was cold and dark outside, and I was starting to feel that way inside as well.

As I was showing Anna Lynn's picture around to a bunch of other lawyers in Railway Brewing Co., this microbrewery in an old railroad depot on 1st Avenue, one of them—a pretty little girl from California named Becky Clausen—came over and took it from my hand. We were like a Hollywood film community out on location, and it didn't matter much if we were plaintiff lawyers or defense lawyers; when the day's work was over, it was us against Alaska.

"You must miss her," she said. She was such a tiny little thing, her hand could barely hold the picture.

"You don't know the half of it."

"How long have you been here?"

I checked my watch. "About thirty minutes." In front of me were my empty plate, the remains of a cheeseburger, and a couple of empty beer glasses.

"No, I mean in Alaska. Less than a week, right?"

I finished up another beer and nodded. "Is it that obvious?"

She shook her head and smiled. "No. It gets easier for some. I hardly think about home. I've been here for months."

"Months, huh?" I raised my finger and asked for another beer.

"Some of us were getting ready to go to a karaoke bar," she said. "Tim, Jerry, maybe a couple of other folks." Those guys nodded back. "You should come with us, Clay."

My beer arrived and I took a big swig. "I don't know." I

took another swig. "I used to sing a little bit. But I'm feeling kind of down."

"Then sing about it," she said. "Finish up and come on." She dragged me from the table, and a mob of lawyers went over to Rumrunner's, where a short, smiling, heavy-set Aleut named Karaoke Joe was serving as KJ, karaoke master of ceremonies.

"He'll get up later and do Elvis," Tom said as we took a table in the corner. "You can't tell the difference. Except for he's an Eskimo." He was a young guy going very bald, and he had passed drunk about an hour previous.

"How does this work?" I asked. "If one were disposed to do this thing."

"Write down your request and take it up to Karaoke Joe," Jerry said. He was an older guy, single, local, representing some of the fisheries. He was sober, funny, and nice as hell. "He'll find the disk if he has it, and then when he calls off your name, you go up and sing."

"I don't know," I said. Even with another drink, I was feeling about as low as the pavement. "I might just go back to the hotel—"

Becky punched me in the arm, hard; she had obviously evolved some ways to compensate for her lack of stature, unexpected violence being one of them.

"Ow," I said. I rubbed my arm. Then I took the pen she was holding and wrote down my request, and shortly before closing that night, I went up to the stage, sat on a stool, and sang Sinatra's "One for My Baby," a song about this guy who's drunk and missing his girl. There were about a dozen people left in the club besides the lawyers, who all were cheering anything that kept them from going back to their briefs, but all of them got up and gave me a standing ovation.

I mean, it wasn't junior-high girls chasing me to the bathroom or anything, but it was clear that I still had it, for whatever that was worth.

And that's how I spent most of Anna Lynn's pregnancy: in my Anchorage office writing briefs during the day, drunk and singing sad Sinatra tunes at night. Gradually Karaoke Joe started moving me up in the rotation, and finally he started jumping me to the top of the list when we came in and even letting me sing a couple of tunes, which made the tourists mad, at least until I started to sing.

"You really ought to be a singer," said Becky after the third time, when "Guess I'll Hang My Tears Out to Dry" left her in tears. She had a brassy little cheerleader's voice, and when she got up to sing—always Streisand show tunes for some reason—she switched keys a couple of times in the middle of the song.

"Coming from you," I said, tipping my imaginary fedora, "that is really career advice to savor." And then she hit me.

"You want to know why your boyfriend never calls you?" I asked.

"Why?" said gullible she.

"Because he's probably lost the use of both of his arms and can't dial the phone."

Everybody laughed, including her, although she waggled her tiny finger at me. "You're going to lose the use of something much more vital if you sass me."

"I don't have anything vital," I said, and it was the truth.

The first time I got to come home, in July, I had so much stored up to tell Anna Lynn that I tried to talk to her back as we lay in bed together on Saturday night. I didn't know if she was asleep or not, but I thought it was worth a try. We had barely spoken all day, and she had not so much as smiled at me once.

"It's not what you think," I said to her. "I'm not what you think I am. I'm still that guy you married because he sang trashy Air Supply songs to you."

She didn't laugh, and I knew she was asleep. I put a hand on her hip, on the bulge of her pregnancy, grown while I was away from her.

"I'm still in here somewhere," I said. "I haven't forgotten about justice. I'm doing my best to find it. Just wait and see."

She groaned in her sleep and then stretched like a cat. She was so beautiful I thought I was going to cry. But I was exhausted, so what I did instead was put my head back on the pillow and go to sleep myself.

The second time I came home was in August, and it wasn't

good between us then either. She was working on the environmental accords with Mexico that would have to be ironed out if there was ever to be a free trade agreement between us, and she was about to leave for a three-week fact-finding junket with some of her colleagues from the Environmental Defense Initiative, mostly to see the maquiladoras—the cheap, smoky Mexican factories along the Texas border that were replacing foundries and textile mills in the States. Her files on our dining room table were labeled "Matamoros," "Juarez," "Nuevo Laredo."

My files read "Exxon Valdez: Federal Court." And I didn't leave them out on the dining room table; they never left my locked briefcase.

Her suitcase was full of warm-weather clothes, shorts with elastic, and big T-shirts. I hovered around her while she packed, trying to be helpful, asking her about the water down there, about food, about medicines. My taxi was due to take me to Dulles in fifteen minutes, and I was looking for some place of connection, some place to anchor a bridge between us. Finally, with just five minutes left and feeling I'd already left for Alaska, I asked if I could put my head on her stomach. We thought it was a boy, and if it was, we had agreed to call him Ray. (It was not going to be Raylene or Rayann if it was a girl; we'd just have to start from scratch.)

"Hey, little Ray," I said, laying my hand gently on the bulge of her stomach and fighting the urge to cry. "How you doing in there? You take care of your momma, you hear? I'll miss you."

The taxi honked outside the town house, and I picked up my bag and stood up.

"I'll miss you," I said again.

"Safe trip," she said. "I won't wish you luck."

"Well, I will," I said. I looked at her to see if she wanted to be kissed—or was willing to be kissed. It was as if she had left the room already. "Luck," I said softly, and raised a hand in forlorn good-bye.

I tried to call her from the airport, but no one answered. Just my own voice, telling me to leave a message, which I already had.

I got so drunk on the plane that I thought they would throw me out somewhere over Montana.

Carroll came up for several days a week after that, and we had dinner at the Crow's Nest, high atop the Captain Cook. He had pheasant, I had venison, and after we'd placed our orders he just looked at the mountains and trees and then back at me and shook his head.

"We sent you a long way from home, son," he said. "What in the name of God do you find to do up here?"

"I work," I said. "At night I drink with the other stranded lawyers. We tell each other trade secrets in hopes that we can all go home sooner." I didn't tell him about karaoke. It did not seem to be a shortcut to making partner.

"So what's the news?" he asked as our salads arrived.

"All bad," I said. "Forget about your smoking gun. We have a leaking oil tanker, captured on TV. Everybody in the world knows our guy did it. There are Bushmen in the Kalahari, you walk up to them and say 'Exxon,' they say 'Valdez.' "

He laughed. "I know, I know. So what do we do to minimize our clients' exposure. Show me what you've learned."

I took a deep breath, finished chewing a bite of lettuce, and turned off my conscience. "Drag it out. Keep it out of the courts as long as possible and just drag it out."

"Why?"

"Things change. People die; people forget; plaintiffs get desperate for some, any money. You can settle for ten cents on the dollar five years from now versus going into court now."

His smile was so broad I feared for my life. "Exactly."

"I've been thinking about the settlement," I said. "It's got to be big enough to quiet people and actually make up for what they did. But there must be a way to structure it to make it palatable to Exxon too."

"Of course there is. But later, my boy. Later. For now, let's eat."

Anna Lynn called me that night after I got back to my room—the first time she had done that since we each left on our separate missions—and my heart was pounding when I heard her voice. But she sounded strange, as though she hadn't really wanted to call but for some reason she'd done it anyway. I asked how she was feeling, if the baby was moving, and her answers were short and came after a pause. "Well," I said at some point, "not much going on here if you don't want me to talk about work. Although I think I may be able—"

"Don't talk about work," she said.

"Okay," I said. "Okay. Are you all right? Is everything—"

"Well, I hope you're keeping warm," she said suddenly, her voice breaking just a bit, and then she just as quickly said, "I've gotta go," and the phone went dead.

I sat there on the hotel bed for a long time, because it was one of the strangest conversations we had ever had, and because I had the strangest feeling after it, one I'd never thought I'd connect with Anna Lynn, the most trustworthy, the most honest, truly, the best person I'd ever met.

Anna Lynn was ashamed of something.

12

The federal graveyard in Santa Fe was at the far north end of town, almost out of town, in fact, and I was there before even the funeral was set to start, so I drove around for a while. The sun was full up, and the sun beaming golden in through my side windows was penetrating me like I imagined it did Dracula at the end of all those old movies. My eyes were burning, my flesh felt like it could sizzle off my bones, and I was just grateful I'd stopped at a Love's Country Store for more beer before I'd headed north toward Santa Fe.

Dracula would not, even with the fortification of beer, have survived all those crosses on the white marble monuments arrayed perfectly in rows like those at Arlington. I passed a middle-aged woman on her knees, bent over a grave marker she had just decorated. Someone she loved was dead.

"Well, get in line, sister," I heard myself saying.

There were a lot of dead people here, so many that the cemetery had its own radio station, where, when I tuned in, I heard that my father's burial was still set for 11:00.

By then it was 10:30, so I drove up into the cemetery until I found the open gravesite where they were putting the fake green grass down—it looked positively plastic in this dusty city where turf was an anomaly—and figured it was my father. They were putting a picture up on an easel which I guess was supposed to be him, but he wasn't in a space suit so of course I couldn't be sure, and anyway, my vision wasn't so good anymore. From the car, I could see that he had short hair and his skin was dark, as if he'd spent a lot of time in the sun. I couldn't tell much else. He didn't look like a spaceman.

I drove up above it so I could look down and drink and decide if I wanted to come out at all. I was listening to 100.3, The Peak, alternative rock out of Albuquerque, and occasionally flipping over to classic rock stations 101.3 and 102.5 when something like Madonna came on. I do not find Madonna alternative, although I must always find an alternative to Madonna.

It was an effort to reach out and touch the radio buttons, an effort to screw the tops off the beer bottles. I had to do it consciously, with real concentration, and when I wasn't doing this, the world seemed to be contracting almost to a tunnel around the edges of my senses, leaving a drone of music, a bitter fizzing in my mouth, a straight line of sight to my father's grave.

I had gotten here just in time; I couldn't have driven another minute without piling into parked vehicles or taking out an acre of our nation's finest.

Cars began to pull up beneath me; people began to get out, dressed in black, slowly, reverentially. The hearse and other cars in the motorcade—a lot of them—had arrived and filled the lane beneath me.

The driver of the funeral home limo came around to give his hand to a woman in a black hat and veil, and that's when I got really interested. Although there were two chairs, she took the lone position of honor under the arcade; about a hundred more people gathered around her.

It took a while, and they had already started the service before I realized that the other chair was meant for me.

So I opened the door and fell to the ground in a clank of beer cans. It hurt; my poor sunburned knees felt like they'd been flayed open. I pulled myself up on the car door and succeeded only in slamming it against my left shin.

"Son of a bitch, Dad," I groaned. "I got here, didn't I?"

Then I made my careening way down the hill, moving from gravestone to gravestone like a one-year-old cruising from couch to coffee table to chair. I think I may have fallen; I don't remember. Neither do I know how long it took me to get down, but I remember looking up and seeing her, the veil lady, the lone family member, standing in front of me, her hand extended.

The graveside service was over; behind her, I could see that they were taking apart the sling mechanism they must have used to lower the coffin.

"You're a very beautiful woman," I told her, and although it was true, I instantly covered my mouth with my hands like I could stop the words physically. She was maybe in her forties, but her dark skin was flawless, her black hair shone under her hat, and she was perfectly made up—lips, eyes, rouge—like a Spanish movie star.

"You must be Clay," she said.

"You must be the potter," I said. I giggled. "Sorry. Sorry. Nobody ever laughs at that."

"I'm Rosalena Fischer," she said. "I was your father's friend."

I swayed and took another look at her, given this new information. "Way to go, Dad," I said.

"You're very tired," she said gently.

People never got everything right. Wasn't it obvious I was a little more than tired? "I'm exhausted to the point of death," I said. "And I'm so drunk. And I think I'm chemically depressed. I didn't think so before, but lately everyone has been telling me so." I put out a hand to steady myself on a tombstone and looked down at my feet. I had left my shoes in the car or taken them off in my odyssey down the hill; I was standing in my socks. The loss of my shoes made me want to cry. "I don't know what I'm doing here."

"You're here because I called," she said. She held her hand out to me. "Come on," she said. "My car is right over there." She indicated the funeral home limo, still waiting.

"I can drive," I said. "I have a license. I've only ever killed two people in my whole life."

"It'd be better if you rode with me," she said. "Santa Fe traffic is a little trickier than you'd find in Robbinsville, North Carolina. Your father used to complain about it."

"You knew my father?" I asked, forgetting what she'd already told me. She found my shoes a few grave markers up, came back and took my arm, and we made our leisurely way toward the limo.

"I knew your father, Clay. Better than just about anyone, I guess. As well as anyone could, anyway. He put up a high wall to keep out intruders."

"Did you love him?"

She nodded. "As well as I could. I can't claim that he returned it. He—" She blinked away some tears and I watched fascinated; someone was crying over my father. My dead father. "That's all over and done with, I guess. I loved him and I admired him, and toward the end, I took care of him as well as he'd permit. That's something, I suppose."

We had reached the car, and the driver opened the back door for us. The two of them eased me into the seat. "Why?" I asked.

"Because he was a good man," she said. "And a great artist. He made me a very wealthy woman, and even if I hadn't loved him I would have taken care of him." She held her arms out, turned her hands over so that her palms were up and out. "All of this is because of him."

"All of what?"

She buckled me into the car and they closed the door. She got in and we drove out of the cemetery. The woman was still there crying over the white gravestone.

"She's sad," I said.

"Yes she is," she said. We turned left on something called Paseo de Peralta.

"Where are we going?"

"I'm taking you to your father's house," she said. "You can rest there. And I have many things to show you."

" 'In my father's house are many mansions,' " I said. " 'If it were not so, I would have told you. I go to prepare a place for you.' John 14:2." My head nodded over with some violence as we turned a corner and whacked against the window. I jerked back erect.

"Impressive," she said. "Your father knew the Bible as well."

"But could he name the books of the Bible? I can. I can do it backwards. Revelation, Jude, Third, Second, First John,

Second Peter, First Peter, Hebrews. Oh hell. I get all the Epistles mixed up. Corinthians, Ephesians, Colossians, Galoshes. It doesn't matter anyway. That fat bastard Paul. So full of himself. I wish I'd been on the road to Damascus. While he was flailing around blind I'd have run him over with my chariot."

We turned left at some huge hot-pink building, then right, up a long, long hill. It was so steep I was pressed back into my seat, and my head lolled back. "Houston, I'm pulling five G's," I said.

"Hyde Park Drive," she said as we passed rocks, dirt, scrub trees. "Hyde Park. Your father always thought it was funny. A strange juxtaposition, I guess."

"Did my father love you?"

"I think he did." She smiled. "You know, Clay, my mother was scandalized, but I asked him to marry me once."

"I asked somebody to marry me once. Did he know my mom divorced him? That it would have been okay if he'd wanted to?"

"Sure. He got the Robbinsville paper. Or I did, rather, down at the gallery."

"What gallery?"

"My gallery."

"Cool," I said. "You own a shooting gallery?" I cocked my thumb and forefinger and began shooting. "Ka-ping. Ka-pow. What do I win?"

"It's an art gallery," she said.

"Well, that's nice too," I said. "So he said no? Why?"

"He said no. There was the religious thing. I'm Jewish. And he said he wanted to remain celibate."

"Sex just ruins things anyway," I said. We were rising high enough that if I looked out her window I could see out over Santa Fe and some purple mountains majesty off to the west.

She raised a hand, brushed it aside. "I told him it didn't matter. Sex. No sex. He wouldn't listen. He said he couldn't marry me. I tell you, the past was still weighing on him like a ton of bricks."

I nodded sagely. "It's like that for some people. Somebody said that the past isn't . . . something. It's not even past. Damn, how did that go?" I'd lost control of my brain, my mouth, and apparently my neck muscles. I just stopped myself from flopping over again as we took a turn.

"Sometimes I think he would have given up on everything if not for his painting."

From somewhere I dredged up one of my songs, rolled it around in my mouth, and took it out for a spin:

> *There's a lovely light in the sky tonight.*
> *A lovely light in the sky.*
> *Makes me wish for wings to mount up high*
> *But I don't know where I would fly.*
> *I don't know where I would fly.*

"More Saint John?" she said, smiling tenderly.

"No. Saint Clay of the Everflowing Bottle," I said.

"Your father always wanted to see you play," she said. "Are you any good?"

"I can sing the hell out of a song," I said. "As you can plainly see. Or hear. And I'm decent on guitar. That's about it. I just took it up to get girls."

"Did it work?"

"Only too well," I said.

"Your dad played some guitar too. And he had a fine voice."

"What kind of music did he like?"

"You'll laugh," she said.

"Possibly."

"Jimmy Buffet."

I shook my head. "Too much," I said. "My dad was an artist and a Parrothead."

"A what?"

"A Parrothead. A rabid follower of Jimmy Buffet."

"He was also an oblate."

"An old plate?"

"It means that as much as possible he tried to live a holy life, follow the Benedictine Rule. He was ordained through the monastery at Pecos."

I tried to get my head to stop rolling around on top of my

neck, because this was of some interest to me. "My father was a Catholic?"

"He was very serious about it. He went to Mass almost every day until the end."

"I'm not a Parrothead," I said. "I play classic rock. Do you think big-hair bands will ever come back?"

"Big hair?"

"You know. Eighties rock and roll. Crimp perms, spandex pants."

"Like Bon Jovi?"

"Yeah, sure. Bon Jovi, Ratt, Cinderella, Poison. I guess Motley Crüe never left, but is that because of the Tommy and Pamela videos or the music? And Def Leppard is still around. But I think they cut their hair." We took another turn and I hit my head on the window again. "Jesus Christ, who taught him to drive? Wonder Woman?"

"Wonder Woman." She smiled. "She was my role model. A JAP superhero."

"She's a stupid superhero," I said. "She has those stupid bracelets. Superheroes should not wear jewelry. Fighting crime is not about accessorizing." We were climbing again, a road so steep that my head rolled all the way back to the top of the seat and I was staring at the ceiling. "Okay, now I'm pulling like six G's here."

"Those bracelets are functional. They block bullets."

"They're silly."

"And she has boots."

"Boots do not make you tough," I said. "My father wears boots. It doesn't make him a cowboy."

She was laughing, and I think the limo driver was chuckling up past his little barrier. I was dimly aware that I was still talking, saying something like "You dudes stop laughing at me," and then I was aware of nothing.

The bright New Mexico sun was gone, and I was someplace dark and cool and safe.

I slept.

There were flashes of light, like those signs along the highway, or like acts revealed in the splash of lightning. I saw myself yelling at Anna Lynn, saw her face streaked with tears; I

saw myself putting a fist through the wall, heard her screaming high and unintelligible. I felt myself slide down the wall,
bump to the floor, cover my eyes with my bloody hand.

I saw the blood drip.

I saw the blood drip.

I was in the car. I had hit my head against the side window
as we rolled, and now that the window was gone I lay with
my cheek against the pavement, tangled in the webbing of my
seatbelt. I could hear little Ray breathe raggedly from his
child seat, could see a drop of blood plop onto the glass next
to my face, feel it spatter.

I looked up and saw Anna Lynn tangled in the right side of
our car, her face bloody, the white of her skull glowing in a
nakedness more obscene than nudity. Her eyes were open and
unblinking and fixed on me.

I screamed and screamed, high and unintelligible.

I covered my face with my hand.

I felt a wisp of breeze across my cheek. I lowered my hand.

I was watching the funeral, their funeral—watching myself
at their funeral. The graveside service on the hill at the cemetery at Robbinsville. I stood uphill from the grave, Ray to one
side, Momma to the other. They were weeping. I was dry-
eyed.

As they lowered Anna Lynn into the ground, I could see
myself begin to melt, turn to goo like the Wicked Witch, I'm
melting, I'm melting, could see myself ooze into the hole after
them.

Nobody seemed to notice.

Everyone walked away talking about what a nice service it
had been. A bulldozer covered us up. All that was left of me
was a pair of shoes—nice ones, black Italian leather polished
to a fine gloss.

"Sorry I'm late," my father, Steve Forester, said from behind me. He put his hand on my shoulder.

"You missed everything," I said, and I was pissed. I didn't
so much as turn to look at him.

"You better pick up your shoes."

"They're not mine," I said. "Anyway, you're not the boss
of me."

He took my arm and I let him lead me away. "My car is right over there," he said. We drove out of the cemetery, through the wrought-iron arch, and into driving snow.

"I just wanted you to know that I did make it big," he said. "I wanted to show you."

"I know," I said.

He pulled up in front of Rumrunner's, the karaoke bar in Anchorage. We walked inside and Karaoke Joe waved him on.

He got up and sang "Margaritaville."

The crowd went wild. He smiled at me from the stage.

I needed a drink, desperately.

When I woke, the room was dimly lit with sunshine coming from somewhere, and I was aware of a sharp ache in my head and a taste in my mouth like burning tires. I looked around. I was in a slender monastic room. I lay in the small bed, could see a dresser with a mirror just across the way, and one wall was nothing but bookcases full of books. The other wall was wall, with a single door, and behind me there must have been a small shuttered window, because that's where the light was coming from.

Above me on the ceiling were posts as thick as telephone poles, and the ceiling above them was wide planks of wood. The wall behind me was cool and felt of cement or sandpaper.

I got up to look at the dresser. I could just make out the raised square of a light switch next to the door, so I turned the light on. There was a picture of me from *The Graham Star*, a laminated picture of Tracy and me at the Fourth of July picnic a few years past.

But that was uninteresting. What I had thought from the bed was a mirror was something other: it was a landscape painting, about three by four, and it really stopped me in my tracks. I could tell it was New Mexico—there was the textured red and yellow and green of the desert floor, the blues and purples of distant mountains, and above it all the roiling blue and gray and white of storm clouds. A burst of sunlight crossed the canvas from the clouds in the upper left to the ground on the far lower right.

There was his name—our name—in the lower left corner,

scratched into the paint, Forester. The paint itself was thick, as if it had been laid on with a trowel instead of a brush. The landscape glowed, like it was lit from within. And I got the strangest feeling from it. The scene was foreboding, ominous, sad even, and yet there was such beauty to it that it almost gave me hope.

Almost. It would take a lot more than a painting to do that.

I opened the top drawer. Inside I found boxers, mostly blue and white. I found one pair of dress socks, dark. A lot of T-shirts. And here was a piece of newsprint, handled until it had become almost translucent. I took a look at it, too late tried to drop it.

It has been a sad week along the river. Our family is so grateful to all of you for your outpouring of sympathy and support following the horrible accident—

Sister's column from 1991.

I put it back in the drawer, closed it securely. Poking around in my father's drawers was not going to teach me anything about him. It was just going to hurt me.

I opened the door and called out into the hallway. "Hello?" It echoed. This was a long hallway or a long house. "Hello?"

"Ah," a male voice said, not too far away, and it called back, "Hello. Señor Forester, I come." And indeed he hurried toward me in something just short of a trot, a Hispanic guy in his forties, dressed in a nice pair of black slacks and a gray silk shirt. "I am Ramón Gonzales. I served your father. My wife has your breakfast ready."

"Breakfast?" I yawned, which hurt. "What time is it?"

"You have slept around the clock. It is Saturday morning."

I shook my head to get the cobwebs out. Not a good idea, the shaking. "Where is—" I didn't remember her name. "Where is the woman who brought me here?"

He nodded and smiled and revealed two gold teeth. "Rosalena," he said. "Sí. I called her when I heard you stirring. She will be here shortly. After you eat, perhaps you will want to clean up? She would like to take you for a drive."

"Great," I said. It was not great. "Ramón, I'm not feeling hungry just now." Actually, the thought of food was making my stomach contract violently. "But if perhaps there are some medicinal spirits in the house . . ."

He was already on his way, his head inclined respectfully. "This is a sad time for all of us," he said. He disappeared down the hallway, and I followed, down a set of stone stairs and into a living room with a breathtaking view over mountains, forests, valleys in three directions.

There was a clanking from the bar behind me, and I turned to Ramón. "Where are we?"

"This is your father's house. My family works for him." He sighed. "For eight years, we work for him," he corrected.

"This is my father's house?" He nodded and handed me a drink, something brandyish. I took the drink, tossed it off, handed it back, and stepped out onto one of the verandas. The house itself was enormous, of adobe construction, thick walls, lots of windows.

Below—far below, past scraggly evergreens I had never seen even in the third- and fourth-growth scrub of North Carolina, past other enormous houses built onto the sides and tops of lower mountains—was what I supposed must be Santa Fe, and then beyond it the multicolored desert, and then, on the far side of the valley, mountains looming purple.

I followed the porch on around . . . and around, and around. It went around the entire house, with stunning views in every direction. My father's enormous house was built on top of a mountain.

"Ramón," I said, upon returning to the living room, "some more medicinal spirits, please."

"Of course," he said.

I had washed my face, run my wet fingers through my tangled hair, and was sipping at my third restorative glass when the huge wooden front doors opened and Rosalena let herself in. She crossed to me, extended her hand, and smiled at me sadly. "Hello, Clay. Remember me?"

"Vaguely," I said. "I keep getting you mixed up with Wonder Woman."

"Must be the boots," she said. She was wearing them, calf-high black leather with her pants legs tucked in like riding pants.

"Where are we going?"

"I've got a full day planned for you," she said. "Your father asked me to take you to some of the places he loved and to let you talk to people who knew him. So that you'd have some sense of who he was." She shrugged, smiled sadly. "I guess maybe he hoped you wouldn't be so angry at him."

"I'm not angry," I said. "Or at least, I won't be after another glass of this very good brandy."

"Let's get going," she said. "I knew you were exhausted, but I didn't think you'd sleep for an entire day. There are a lot of things we need to do."

"Need to?" I said.

She took my hand. "Come on. Have you seen the house?"

"I think I'd need to be in orbit to see the entire thing."

"I know. It's huge. Your father wanted a lean-to. But I said, you have all these friends who will be coming to see you, these are your last days, and someday your son will come and this will be his home."

"Whoa," I said. "I don't want anything. I don't want this house. I—"

She raised her hand to shush me. "Let's talk in the car. I always think better in the car."

The car was a red Mercedes two-seat convertible, a sweet car, and she knew how to drive, downshifting expertly to run us down the mountain and down Hyde Park Drive.

"My father must have been rich," I finally said, after we'd driven a long time listening to the wind and her Joni Mitchell CD. "I mean, that house—"

"Your father was one of the great painters of the century," she said, "and he was very prolific—driven, I'd call it—and he made a lot of people rich, including yours truly."

It was a little too much to take, even on three brandies and twenty-four hours of sleep. I just lay back in the seat and watched as she drove.

We had headed out of town on 285 North, then turned off toward Nambe Pueblo. The desert landscape was strange and beautiful, like the surface of the moon. We came up over one hill and the Sangre de Cristos loomed straight ahead, green and towering, and above them jet contrails made some sort of giant ideogram miles across.

"Was he rich?"

She nodded. "But he wouldn't spend it, at least until I talked him into building the house. He lived in the back of my studio for years." She raised her hand: As God is my witness. "After he started making money, he always gave a lot to the church, to civic causes, set aside a lot of it for you. But it was important to him that he give his money away. He used to talk about what a terrible wrong it was to be rich in the poorest state in the union, in a place with so much despair and so many needs."

She took the curves fast, and when I turned to watch her driving, she just smiled and said, "I'll watch the road. You watch the country."

We sped down into a green valley, twisting and turning around blind curves as bad as in Grenada, a tiny village of adobe buildings crowding the road.

"He left you everything," she said as we climbed up out of the valley. "I'm executor, so I know. I have eighteen paintings at the gallery he said I could sell, plus there are another fifty unsold at your house, some of which he didn't want to sell. And there's the house itself. If you're not going to keep it, I could put it on the market for you tomorrow and get you two million. Maybe three."

"I don't want it. Any of it. Was he crazy? He didn't even know me."

"But he did, Clay. He knew everything that happened to you for twenty years, or at least everything in your aunt's column."

"He doesn't know me at all. And he certainly doesn't know what happened to me."

She sighed. "I guess I hoped you'd be more forgiving. You've been through a lot, I know. But lots of people have. Besides losing your father, I've lost both my parents in the last three years."

"I lost him first," I said, like a six-year-old.

"Everybody loses people they love. Have you lost so much more?" Her eyes flashed, and somewhere deep down in my cotton-candy-cushioned world I could tell I was stepping on a nerve, for all the good that awareness did.

"Did they all know they were going to die?"

"Yes. My parents both had Alzheimer's. It was a long, lingering thing. And your father was diagnosed two years ago."

"So you got to say good-bye, at least."

She nodded. "I did. And more."

I looked straight ahead. "You got to tell them that you loved them, that you forgave them, that you were sorry as hell for not making them happier when you had the chance, that you'd marry her again in a second if she'd only have you."

She looked across at me and nodded again, and the flash of fire was gone. "Something like that," she said.

"Then you've got nothing to be unhappy about," I said.

We were descending again into a valley, following a harrowing narrow road down, and all of a sudden she pulled off onto an overlook, and the view was stunning: past the village below, multicolored hills on the far side of the valley; mountains to the east with great thunderheads looming over them; and over the mesa ahead, one patch of tall clouds. Otherwise the skies ahead of us were blue and almost luminous.

"This is the painting in his room," I said, and she nodded.

"This was one of his favorite spots to paint," she said. "I brought him up here last about four months ago. After that he had to paint at the house, or he was too weak to do anything at all."

I got out of the car and stepped over to the edge of the drop-off. Tenacious sagebrush grabbed onto the slope below me.

"I need to tell you that I've got a vested interest. I want to represent the rest of the paintings he left you."

"Sure," I said. I waved my hand imperiously, like an emperor. It made me feel a little unsteady next to the edge, and she must have seen it, because she took my arm and pulled me back to the car. We drove on down into the valley through the village of Cordova, then hesitated for a moment as we pulled up onto State Highway 76.

"What's that way?" I said, indicating right and the mountains.

"Truchas," she said. "Where Robert Redford shot *The Milagro Beanfield War.*" She threw it into gear, pulled up onto the highway, and headed left, back toward Santa Fe. "He owns three of your father's paintings. Paul Newman has two."

We stopped at a little restaurant off the highway in Chimayo, a big old adobe house with lots of cars outside. We went through the restaurant and were seated in back on the patio, and I took a look over the menu, decided on the combination plate—"Combinación," the waitress repeated as I handed the menu back to her—and a beer.

"I used to eat here with your father sometimes," she said, waving flies away from her face. "But he ate here much more often alone. Every time he was out painting he would stop for the day and eat here on the way back to Santa Fe." She tapped our table. "This was his favorite spot."

My Dos Equis came, cold, the bottle beaded with sweat. I was becoming a beer connoisseur after a long layoff—that, or a drunk. Then the food followed shortly after, although it didn't look like any Mexican food I'd ever eaten. Where were the mounds of cheese? What was this strange red sauce dolloped over everything?

"It's Northern New Mexican," Rosalena said. "Not Mexican. And you should be careful. Those chunks of meat there, carne adovada? They'll be hot."

"Sure," I said. I took a bite. The chile ate a hole in the side of my mouth. I drank my entire beer and didn't make a dent in the burning. Then my water.

Rosalena was laughing. "Beer or water won't cool it off. Milk does."

I put down my glass, half empty. "Jeezus Chrish," I said.

She crossed her hands and put on a demure smile. "So," she said.

"So," I said, still trying to shoo the pepper from my mouth.

"You came."

"Against my better judgement, I have to say." I ate about twelve chips and began to feel that perhaps my mouth wouldn't be permanently disfigured.

"Why did you come?"

"Curious, I guess. Plus it began to seem preordained. And anyway, how many times in your life will your missing father die? Not more than three or four, I guess."

"Well, if you're curious, why don't you ask me some questions."

"Okay," I said. "What was my father like?"

She took a big bite of her blue-corn enchiladas—stacked instead of rolled—chewed slowly and reflectively, and swallowed. "Oh my," she said. "That is good."

I nodded my head, the cranial equivalent of impatient toe-tapping, and she smiled her acknowledgment. "I know," she said. "This was the part he tried to prepare me for, and I'm just not prepared."

"Give me something," I said, draining my beer and signaling for another. "Anything. The last time I saw him he was wearing a fucking space suit. Begging your pardon, of course."

"Mission to Mercury?"

I nodded.

"That was a terrible movie," she said.

"We're in agreement on that," I said.

She took another bite, chased it with some posole—what looked like hominy but was in a stew with pork and red chile. "He was a lot like you," she said. "Good heart, sad spirit."

"I am sick unto death of people talking about my spirit," I said. "Next they'll be telling me they're seeing a black aura around me. Or a black cloud, like that character in *Li'l Abner*."

"Your father had a great gift. I suspect you did, or do. Like him, I sense that you've been broken. But like him, it comes out as self-hatred, not as viciousness." She took another bite, saw my skepticism, swallowed, and said, "Listen, kid. I'm not a Gypsy fortune-teller or something. I'm just a Jewish girl from Long Island transplanted to the desert. But I'll tell you once and for all, you have a beautiful spirit. I'll bet people in North Carolina love you. Your friends stick with you. And you make a good impression. Or I'm guessing you normally would, under different circumstances."

"Hey, I'm on my best behavior," I said. "If you don't consider the drunkenness and body odor and such." There was a rumble of what sounded like thunder and I looked up. The sky was growing dark.

She shook her head. "Don't even talk to me about behavior. Behavior is the clothes we put on everyday. I'm talking about the soul."

I snorted. The beer simply could not reach the table fast enough to suit me. "Why does everyone say things like that to me?"

She laughed. "If I were to tell you bad things about yourself, you would listen to me."

It was not a question. "Yes," I said, at last. "I would."

She nodded. "Your father," she said. "Your father all over."

"I do have a question for you," I said at length. We had been eating in silence, and I was watching dark clouds crawl over the Sangre de Cristos, where they were probably dumping rain by the bucketloads. "You said my father knew everything about me?"

"He kept up with you as well as he could through the paper. Your Aunt Sister became a very real person to me. I think I could probably recognize her by voice alone."

"I was looking through his dresser," I began, and I fidgeted a little with my napkin, moved it to my lips, back to my lap. "He knew about what happened to Anna Lynn and little Ray?"

She nodded and bit her lower lip. "Yes," she said. "He knew. He was so torn up over it I thought it was going to drive him crazy."

"A thing like that could do it to a man," I said. "But if he was so upset, why didn't he say anything? Call? Write?"

"He sent flowers to the graveside service. He wanted to come. But he thought it would be too much."

I crumpled up my napkin and threw it onto my plate. I had lost my appetite. "Too much? For who? For me? Or for him?"

She didn't say anything. I pushed my chair back and got ready to get up.

"Please don't judge him for that," she whispered. "He was afraid."

"Afraid?" I said. People from other tables looked over. I stood up. "Afraid? I needed a father. That was the most terrible moment of my life. And he wasn't there. I could have traded all the other moments he wasn't there just to have him for that."

There were tears in her eyes and she nodded. "I know. But Clay, you had a father. Ray Fontenot. And he was a good one, from everything we understood. Another father would have just . . . complicated things then."

I stood frozen; she was right, of course. "But still," I began, and then I sat down, put my head in my hands.

"He was scared," she said. "You must know what that is like. He was afraid of what you'd do or say. As sad as his life was in that respect, at least he didn't have to deal with your hatred and rejection."

"I could have forgiven him," I said, looking up.

"But would you have?" She put her napkin on the table. "He was scared. Broken. And in some ways, he never got unbroken. Some people never get over the bad things they do. The bad things that happen to them. Can you understand that?"

Those dark clouds that had been looming overhead for a while began to express themselves then, first as splatters of that long-sought rain, and then as hail, pea- and marble-sized. Before I could answer, we fled the patio—she threw down a handful of bills, which were probably swept away by the floodwaters—and ran for the car.

"Yeowtch," I said, as she raised the roof on the convertible and I stood outside doing a hail dance, arms over my head, feet flapping. Cold, hard things were bouncing off my forearms and scalp, so my dance wasn't helping in any real sense.

"Get in," she yelled, and I did, dripping, smarting, covered with welts. "My poor upholstery."

"My poor upholstery, my ass," I said. "Look at my arms. And I'm soaked to the bone. "

"And you smell all the better for it," she said. "How long were you on the road without stopping?"

"I don't know," I said. "A long time. I got sidetracked. There were . . . incidents."

We were driving back to Santa Fe in a new way, a narrow road through Chimayo, which seemed to be mostly this one road and some arroyos. Ahead of us traffic was slow because of the rain; our windshield wipers were working fast and still not doing much for visibility.

"Incidents?" she said. "That sounds . . . interesting." She got a wicked look in her eyes. "Tell me about these incidents."

"It wasn't like that," I said. "I haven't had an incident with a woman—or a man, mind you—for, I don't know, ten years, maybe. Those kinds of incidents just cause trouble. They complicate things. Not that the ones I just had didn't." I peered ahead; the rain was letting up the tiniest bit and I could see several cars ahead to a big truck holding us all back.

"Clay, you're not making the slightest bit of sense," she said. "Although I should be growing used to that. Still, you were a lawyer once, right? How did you manage that? I can only assume that at some point, stone-cold sober, you could communicate in some fashion."

"Hardee har har har," I said.

"Listen," she said, turning serious. "I'd like for you to go see your dad's best friend this evening," she said. "Take a shower first. A real one."

"I'm not up to it," I said. "Nope. No more adventures for this boy. Let alone incidents."

"Oh, I think you will be up for it, that is, when I tell you that this friend of your father's is a priest who plays on Saturday nights in a salsa band."

I inclined my head a little in response. "Okay. A priest who plays salsa. That is intriguing."

"His name is Father Nieto," she said. "I'll give you directions to Club Alegría. He plays with his band every Saturday night. If you get there before seven you can have a good talk with him before he goes on."

"Are you coming with me?"

She shook her head. "You'll talk more if I'm not there taking up so much space." She smiled. "I know I talk a lot. Plus, I don't get treated so well there. There are too many guys there trying to pick somebody up, too many fights. It's a very macho scene. Like Manhattan in the Seventies, except Hispanic. No, I'll give you directions. You can take your dad's car."

"What dad's car?" I asked, and she laughed out loud. This was going to be a nice surprise.

When we got home, she took me out to the garage and showed me. Next to a white panel van sat a cherry red 1967 Mustang convertible with a white ragtop. "It didn't look like this, exactly, when he first got here," she said. "But he fixed it up over the years. He drove a van when he went out to paint, but he drove this car for pleasure."

"He always did love convertibles," I said without thinking. "But I can't take this."

She showed me the keys. "Suit yourself. But you already know I'm a devious one. I had the rental car picked up. Your things are in the trunk."

"I don't want it," I said.

"Suit yourself," she said again, and smiled. "At least you can drive it to see Father Nieto, provided you think you can drive."

"I can drive," I said, wobbling only slightly as I grabbed the keys from her hand.

"All right, then," she said. "I'll leave the directions with Ramón. Get cleaned up, for God's sake. Then go talk to Father Nieto. Maybe I'll see you later."

She turned to go, but I threw something out after her. "Hey," I said.

"Hey," she said.

"Rosalena," I said.

"Hey," she said again.

"You're a pretty hip Jewish woman," I said.

"Thanks."

My voice softened without my realizing it. "I wish he'd married you."

She blinked wetly once or twice, surprised, before she got her smile back. "You and me both, kid," she said. "You and me both. So long."

Rosalena climbed into her Mercedes. The gravel of the driveway crackled under the tires. She backed down the mountain and out of sight. And I went in to get the hot shower and shave I'd needed for days. It felt good.

13

The car was a monument to Detroit engineering, back in the days when that phrase still signified something. The stick shift was precise and an easy throw from point to point. The clutch caught just right. The engine purr-rumbled through glass packs. "He had an eye for cars," I muttered as I downshifted to take the incline down Hyde Park Road. "I will give him that."

I drew more than my share of looks as I drove through town, more for the car than anything else, but still, everyone likes to be noticed. I checked my directions and turned onto Agua Fria headed out from town.

Way out, as it turned out. It didn't look like much of a happy place, this Club Alegría out Agua Fria Road. For that matter, I hadn't seen any cold water along the road, so I was having some serious truth-in-advertising questions before I even got in the door, although who am I kidding? I've been having truth-in-advertising issues for years and years.

"Is the Salsa Priest here?" I asked the bouncer, a big, mustachioed Hispanic guy who looked at me like I was the type of troublemaker who required some thought before admitting.

"His name is Father Nieto, hombre," he said, at last. "And he's getting set up. Are you a friend of his?"

"No, hombre. But my father was."

He straightened up and took another look at me. I tried to straighten up in response. It was futile.

He nodded. "Your father was Steve. Padre said to keep an eye for you, send you right in if you showed. Yeah, Steve was a good guy. When he and the padre got together, man, they used to make people laugh their asses off."

I swayed a little bit at this news. "Really?"

"Oh, no doubt, man. But you go in and talk to the padre. He'll tell you a lot more than I could about your dad."

And he stood aside so I could go inside. It was a multilevel place, the bar on one side, the bandstand down two tiers and against the far wall. I could see the band setting up: guitars, drums, keyboards, horns, and one priest.

I had a sudden desire to pull the cell phone out of my pocket and dial.

"Hello," Otis said.

"Uhuru, I've just beamed down to the surface of the planet."

"Clay, I am so beyond angry at you, man—"

"I'm going to approach the inhabitants. They don't seem threatening. Wish me luck."

"Listen—" he was saying as I hung up. I turned my head this way and that and listened. Nothing.

When I looked back toward the bandstand, the priest was right in front of me. He was big, balding, clothed all in black except for the white of his collar.

"Friar Tuck," I said.

He laughed, a jolly Santa Claus kind of laugh, which was the only kind of laugh he had. I could tell already that everything was large about this guy.

Including his hand, which swallowed up mine, reluctantly extended once I got a gander at his. "Clay," he said. "Rosalena told me you were on your way."

"Well," I said. "And here I am."

He pulled me over to one of the tables near the stage, seated me, took the chair across from me. "Can I get you anything?"

"Sangria would be fine," I said. I was thirsty. New Mexico was drying me out like a goddamn food dehydrator. My skin was starting to peel—partly from my hellish and still tender sunburn, I have to admit—and my poor nose was clogged with snot pralines that had gotten freeze-dried there.

"Sangria it is," he said. "Ernesto," he called in his big, hearty voice to the guy wiping down the bar. "Dos sangrías, por favor."

Ernesto nodded and went to work. There was a long uncomfortable silence. Father Nieto sat leaned across the table toward me, his elbows on the table, his face open and expectant.

When it became clear that he was going to get me to speak first, I gave him the bare minimum. "You understand that this is not the normal circumstance where boy gets together with his father's best friend for a drink?"

"Oh, I think I understand that," he said.

"Since I guess you know I didn't realize he was still alive until a week ago. Less. And then he wasn't, actually."

"I understand," he nodded, and he settled in to wait for more.

"You must be a killer in the confessional."

He laughed. "I get everything out of them," he said. "And then I help them make it right."

Now it was my turn to laugh.

He leaned forward. "Do you believe confession is a sacrament?"

I stopped laughing and leaned back, away from him. "I'm sorry, Father. But you and I don't know each other well enough to have this talk."

"Do you believe confession is a sacrament?" he repeated, and if possible, he leaned even closer. I felt like I was caught in a priestly avalanche.

"What do you mean? Do I think it's sacred or something?" Our sangria arrived, and like everything else about Father Nieto, it was big. When he ordered two sangrias, what came was two pitchers of sangria, sweating in the dry air. I poured a glassful from the pitcher set in front of me, grateful for the opportunity to pay attention to something other than Father Nieto for a moment.

He did the same, and then he took a sip, set his glass down, and continued, "No, Clay. Does it work? Not, is it sacred. It doesn't matter if it's sacred, unless it works."

"I don't understand," I said, thinking that I didn't or didn't want to, either of which was fine with me.

"Here is my question," he said, "boiled down to its essence. Does confession restore you to yourself? You confess your wrongs, you express repentance, you are reconciled with God and man. Do you believe that?"

Two pitchers began to seem just about right. I finished off that first glass and bought myself some more time pouring another. "I don't know," I said. "Maybe. Or maybe for some people. I don't know that there's anything that could reconcile me with God and man."

He laughed. "Are your sins so great? Are you, how do they say, the Guinness World Book record holder of sins? Do you carry such guilt?"

I looked him in the eye and clenched my jaw to keep from saying something I should not. What at last came out was this: "Father, I carry guilt that doesn't even belong to me."

He got to his feet. "Let's play a song," he said, leading me to the stage. "Do you know 'Margaritaville'?"

I shook my head. "Do you know any Roy Orbison?"

"Surely," he said. He introduced me to the musicians, a handful of Pacos and Rubéns. One handed me his guitar, a big acoustic that made me feel pregnant, and they looked at me expectantly.

" 'Only the Lonely,' " I said. "In A." I played the verse through, letting them see the chord progressions, then the chorus, then the bridge, and they were nodding and noodling away before I'd even finished. The horn players put their heads together and were putting some Latin flavor to the shoo-be-doos. I shrugged. "Okay." I counted off and we started.

And it wasn't half bad, me and the band playing another of the saddest songs I know to a salsa beat. Father Nieto played maracas next to me and took a harmony part. When we finished, he slapped me on the back, but it was restrained, as though through the music he had seen something about me that had not been clear to him before.

"Do you want to play that with us tonight?" he said as we walked back to our table.

"Maybe," I said. "I may be under the table before then."

"Tell me about it," he said.

"About what? Being under the table? I've just returned to alcohol in a big way. I find it very comforting. I can't believe I ever stopped."

"I know a little about alcohol. Tell me about why you are drunk."

I took another drink and acted like I didn't hear him. "Tell me about celibacy," I said. "You, me, my father. What the fuck is up with that?"

"For me, it is the state ordained by God," he said, shrugging that huge head a little to one side. "It has freed me to love more completely, because the body is no longer a part of it." He shrugged again. "For your father, it was a chosen state. He believed it was ordained to him. Perhaps it was, although I have my doubts. For you, however"—and here he shook a huge, admonishing finger at me—"it is not healthy. You are a man, out in the world. You need the love of a woman."

"I had that once," I said. "It didn't work out so well for me. Tell me something, Salsa Priest. Why was my father such a good painter? He must have been, right?"

"I am not such a judge of these things," he said. "But I will tell you what I know. He looked for more than what was there."

I didn't understand, and he saw that. "What do the paintings say to you?"

"I've only seen a couple," I said. "And I'm not much of an expert on this either. But there's . . . a light, I guess. A life. It's not just rocks and sky."

Father Nieto nodded. "Exactly. He was painting the two worlds, the seen and the unseen."

"The two worlds," I repeated, as if he'd said my dad was painting Martians.

"He was a very great artist. Anyone who can paint the face of God has to be."

"Okay," I said. "Maybe so." And although I was having a hard time holding my head straight, I poured a third glass of sangria. I only spilled a little.

He leaned forward when I set the pitcher down, and placed

his paw on my arm in a gentle yet alarming way. "Tell me, Clay," he said. "Tell me about the guilt you carry."

I looked down at his hand, then up at his face, and shook my head.

"Tell me. I am a priest, after all. Nothing of what passes between us will ever leave my lips."

I shook my head again. "I can't. I've never talked about it. Not to anyone. Everyone thinks they know the truth. But it's only the tiniest portion of it. Of the truth, I mean." I shook my head again. "I wouldn't even know where to start."

"So," he said, removing his hand from my arm and sitting back in his chair, "it has been a long time since your last confession, my son?" He smiled wryly.

"I guess you'd have to describe it that way."

He nodded, as much to himself as to me. I could see he was thinking, and he took a deep breath before he spoke again.

"There is much of your father in you."

"Isn't that from *Star Wars?*"

He smiled again and poured himself another glass of sangria. "Clay," he said, "I knew your father for twenty years. I baptized him. I sponsored his work at the monastery. I heard his confessions. I said his last rites." He took a drink, lowered the glass, looked into it. I saw a couple of orange slices floating in red liquid, but he seemed to be seeing something else. When he looked up, his face was solemn. "I loved your father. He was a good soul. More, he was my best friend, el amigo de mi corazón. I would like to help you. I would like to see the son walk a different road than the father."

I shook my head for the third and decisive time. "It's too late for that, Father. It's such a fucked-up mess—begging your pardon; I shouldn't say *fuck* in front of you." He raised a dismissive hand and I went on. "It's just that God has just screwed me over like a sailor, and nothing in the world could ever fix it. There's no point in talking about it. You see what I'm saying?"

He nodded. "So you see God's hand engineering your distress?"

I sighed and shrugged. "It doesn't matter," I said. "None of that Job shit, all right? I don't need to gather my friends and listen to them argue about it. He made it happen, He let it happen, He laughs his ass off because it happened. None of that shit matters. Just shades of gray."

He leaned forward. "Isn't it also possible to imagine God weeping at your distress? At your despair?"

I blinked away the momentary surprise and pulled my cynicism back over me like a blanket. "Maybe for someone else that would be possible. Not for me. I just can't see it."

"It can be true. If you will wish it to be."

"It doesn't matter," I said again. "There's no point in talking, even if I knew where to start."

He waved this away as well. "Look back at your life. Start at the moment when you knew that your heart was broken. That is always the best place to start confessing."

I looked at him, this huge priest who played salsa in a nightclub on Saturdays and said Mass on Sunday. There was music coming in over the speakers, some Spanish Latin thing. There was probably a name for it. Merengue. Samba. Mamba. No, that was a poisonous snake. It'd make a great dance, though, the Black Mamba.

He was watching me waiting, as he waited. He would not speak next if a black mamba slithered across his feet.

I thought of Tracy, talking about putting things behind me, of Kathy Cartwright asking, "How do you ever expect to get over it?"

I thought of Anna Lynn in the car on the way back from the airport, the silence between us so thick you could have swum it, the crash so loud after that nothingness that the noise alone could have killed.

I thought of her eyes on me.

I picked up my sangria and drained it in one long motion. I set it down on the table before us, carefully, tentatively, as though the table's apparent solidity might be an illusion.

Then I opened my mouth, and the words began to come.

His name was Ambrose. At first I didn't know if that was a first or last name. To be honest, I didn't pay much attention to him. Maybe it was his only name, like Madonna. I do know that it's a saint's name, although he didn't act like any saint I ever heard of. Well, maybe Saint Augustine in his younger, wilder days.

Oh, I knew things were bad between us. I guess you just always think that things are going to get better. I was working on the *Exxon Valdez* case, on the side of the bad guys, Father, I have to confess that as well, although I thought I could do some good. I was going to show her. I was going to show Ray. That's my stepdad. I was going to show them that I was a good person, not some corporate drone content to take it up the ass for money. Sorry, Padre.

"I have to tell you something," she told me when I got home from Alaska. She met me at the door, red-eyed from crying. That was in June of '90. That's never a good thing, is it, Padre? Always a bad sign, that look, that phrase. Especially when she follows it with, "I just want you to know that it's over now." Also always a bad sign. "It's over now."

My breath started coming fast and shallow, like I was hyperventilating, and my heart was pounding in my chest—I could actually hear it pounding—and my hands were shaking so bad that my keys fell out of my fingers and onto the kitchen floor. Then they were tingling, like I was holding onto some kind of electric wire. She had taken a seat, although she looked like she was getting ready to get up if she had to—at least, as fast as a woman that pregnant could get up.

"No," I told her. That's what I said. Just "no." I don't know if I didn't want her to say it, or if I wanted not to have heard her.

"I want you to know that I didn't do this to hurt you," she said. "Or at least, not mostly."

"Oh," I said. That's what I said next. "Oh." I sat down. I put my hands on the table so that she couldn't see them shaking. People always said I was unfeeling. What did they mean? I felt everything. I tried my voice again and heard only the slightest tremor, so I went ahead. "Oh," I said.

It started when they were on a trip to Mexico together. She told me the story like it was a history lesson, like she was telling me a story about other people, like it was just something that sort of happened, whoops, and then it just sort of

kept happening, and then a couple of days ago, it had somehow stopped happening.

I kept saying "Oh," which I thought was communicating
pretty well. I thought it meant "This breaks my heart," and
"I'm sorry you thought you needed someone else," and "I've
never been so angry in my life," and "Please tell me this is just
a really bad joke." But finally she stopped pacing and reciting
and crossed her arms and said, "Clay, is that all you have to
say?" so maybe she was not understanding me so good after
all, Padre.

I swallowed once or twice. I honestly thought that I was
going to die—like that old show Sanford and Son: "Lamont,
this is the big one"—that my heart was just going to explode
in my chest and then finally people would know that yes, I did
feel sadness and passion and rage. "He died of a broken
heart," everyone would say. "Who'd a thunk it?" But it didn't
happen, and I got my breath back, and finally I just asked the
scariest question I could ever bring myself to ask, which was,
"Do you love him?"

"No," she said. "I don't think so. I'm just so confused. I'm
a pregnant raging bundle of hormones, you know."

"Apparently," I said.

She shook her head. This was no time for jokes.

"So what happens now?" I mean I know what happens in
the movies. You know, either the guy goes for his gun and
shoots them dead and gets the chair, or he walks away and
never sees her again and she collapses in grief. Those were
both appealing images, I have to say. But I didn't do either. I
just sat there, my head down. I could feel the tears coming
and I did not want to cry in front of her, did not want to give
her that satisfaction of knowing that she had broken me, of
knowing that the thought of her with another man was like a
knife in my gut. So I turned away and swallowed again, and
when I did, it was like I had swallowed it all, the pain and
hurt, and I looked up at her, calm as could be, and just said,
"It's going to be okay." Like I could just say it and make it so,
like I hadn't just swallowed a bottle full of poison.

But I thought maybe it could be okay. Little Ray was born

on October fifth. I got to fly back for that, then a couple of days later, I had to be at the press conference in Alaska where the governor announced the settlement I'd brokered between Exxon and the plaintiffs. A billion dollars. Lots of money for environmental work. I didn't tell you that was Anna Lynn's field, environmental law. I thought Anna Lynn would think of me differently.

But when I got home, she was still pissed off. "It's not enough," she said, and ultimately, she was right. The settlement was rejected, Exxon went to court, and they're still ducking the five-billion-dollar award that jury gave out.

And sometime that next spring, maybe while little Ray was napping, maybe, there were more of these little accidental happenings, whoops, first one, then tearful remorse, than another, then a whole stream of them. I didn't know about it. She didn't tell me anything, not even when I came home. I guess I might not ever have found out about it except that our town house was broken into one Saturday night while we were all at dinner and they turned everything upside down: furniture, drawers pulled out and flung. I don't know what they were looking for. But in the middle of the dining room floor was a pile of letters that had been in the china hutch. I saw them. She saw them. She had Ray in her arms and I bent down first and she just said "Don't," like I was doing something wrong, or maybe like she knew the world was about to change.

Because they were from him, of course. A couple of them were just a few days old. The standard stuff. I love you. I can't live without you. I want to be with you always. I don't want to settle for hours when we can have years.

Well, Padre, I was angry. I tore them up, tore them into tiny little pieces and flung them in her face. I was screaming, Ray was screaming, Anna Lynn was screaming. None of us made a lick of sense. I put my fist through the wall, turned the china hutch over. Her grandmother's china, from Dresden. Boom. Crash. Then I sat down on the floor, with all the chips of china and shreds of paper. I said one thing: "We are the stuffed men." I know, it doesn't make sense. It's from a book

I read. Let it go. And I got up and packed my bag to fly back to Alaska.

A couple of days later I called home. I got the message that Anna Lynn and Little Ray were in Michigan at her folks', that she had a lot to think about, that if I ever came home again maybe we could sort through them.

Well, that's not the kind of thing a grieving guy alone in Alaska wants to hear, you know what I mean, Padre? I'm sure you get the gist of it.

There was this girl there, Padre. Becky Klausen. She had it all over for me. And I was lonely, but I was never that lonely, if you know what I mean. But when I got that message from my dark empty house, I called Becky and we went to this karaoke bar, and I sang "I Get Along Without You," which you probably know is this sad Sinatra song, and I thought I was doing okay, and then we went back to my room and I told her everything that had happened, and she petted me like a poor beat-up puppy, and before I knew it, we were having sex. And it wasn't even over before I rolled off her and sat on the side of the bed and told her, "This isn't what I want."

"What do you want?" she said. "Do you want to pretend I'm her?"

"I didn't realize plaintiff work warped people so completely," I told her. "I don't want you to pretend to be her. I want you to be her."

"Even after what she did to you?"

And I had to say yeah. Yeah. "It was my fault as much as hers," I told her, putting my clothes back on. "I can't blame her. I mean, look how easy it is for two unhappy people to come together looking for something."

"You must love her," she said, and then she started to cry. "Of course you do. I've heard you sing. No one's ever going to sing that way about me."

And I just shook my head and said as gently as I could manage, because Father, she really was a good girl, "Jesus, you're a mess."

She left. I sat. Somehow I got through the days. I went home for a weekend, and I was supposed to pick them up at the airport. We were all going to try to go home and live together. You know this story? Good. I don't want to tell it.

And so that's where things were. Where they are. No one knows that anything happened to us except for the end part. Nobody except for Ambrose, I guess. I still see him sometimes on Sunday morning talk shows, doing his bit for the environment. Anna Lynn said I shouldn't blame him, that he was a symptom or something. But I did. I do. Whenever I see him on TV I experience a momentary wavering in my support of handgun control.

Turns out the garbage truck had bad brakes, though. Did you know that part of the story? Ray and Carroll Abernathy took the sanitation company to court and won a multimillion-dollar settlement. Like I cared. I put it in a trust for environmental causes. I should have given it to Ambrose for his work. Anna Lynn probably would have wanted that. But the only way I will ever give him money is if I can put it in crates and drop it on him from a great height.

So that's my story. Nobody knows it. They think I just blame myself for the wreck. Like that wouldn't be enough. But it's only the end of it. What's worst is that we left so much unfinished. I didn't tell her that I forgave her. I don't even know if I had forgiven her. I'm still mad at her. Do you know how much it hurts to be angry at someone you love? I don't know if she was going to stay or if she was going to leave me. And I just think I deserved the chance to find out. That's all, Father. Would that have been so much to ask?

No.

All of that is bad, but it's not the worst.

What's worst is the way she looked at me right there at the end. Like she knew I was going to kill us all.

Like I had done it on purpose.

Maybe I did. I don't know. I don't think I did. Really, Father, I don't think I did. But I don't know. I've never even talked about it before. Honestly, I don't know anything. Outside of a few songs and how to fix a car, I don't know anything at all.

*   *   *

The bar had begun to get busy around us while I was holding forth. Father Nieto had listened, nodded, his eyes had filled toward the end, and now his huge hand was on my head as I sat bent double with the force of my tears.

"And so," he said, his voice gentle and strong at once, "now you hold yourself apart from everyone and everything?"

I raised my head, my eyes raw and wet and burning, and indicated with one hand my self, my sad sorry sodden self. "Thou hast said."

"Your father said that you moved back home with your mother and her—how did he say it?—her horrifying sisters."

I couldn't help but laugh, even in my extremity. "They can be horrifying. But they all love me, in their own twisted ways. It's a curse and a comfort to be home." More sangria had arrived, a compelling argument for the existence of a God. I poured and drank, parched from relating my story.

"Do you know where you are at fault in what you have told me?"

"I think I do."

"Do you confess your responsibility for the distance which grew between you?"

"I do."

"Do you confess your responsibility for placing other things ahead of your family's joy, ahead of their happiness?"

I nodded. "I do."

"Do you confess that you dishonored the gifts you were given by God?"

"I do," I croaked. It felt as though a bubble had risen from my nether depths and popped open somewhere in my chest.

"And do you accept that it is your wife who bears responsibility for her decisions, for her actions, but that she has been forgiven, and that she and your innocent child are with God?"

"I'd like to believe that, Padre," I said. "It's a better story than *Mission to Mars*. And surely it would have better special effects."

"Then will you accept this penance from one who has

known you and loved you through one he loved? Who loves you through Christ who loves us all?"

"No," I whispered. "I can't,"

"Go home," he said, as though I had not spoken. "Live. Love." He raised a hand in benediction, touched it to my forehead as though he were anointing me. "You are forgiven."

"Hey," I said, pushing his hand away. "You can't do that. I'm not even Catholic. I'm not even a Christian."

He checked his watch. It was time for him to go on, to become the Salsa Priest, because he just smiled sadly and stood. "You are many things you do not know you are," he said. "And you are not many things you believe you are."

And he left me sitting there to try and digest that Zen koan. I blinked. I swilled the last of my sangria straight out of the pitcher. I called out to him, "Hey, Father Yoda. What the hell does that mean?"

He turned in the middle of the dance floor, a graceful move from such a large man. "It means what it means," he said. "It means what it means. Go with God."

Oh, I would all right. Go, that is. I drained the rest of his pitcher, then I wobbled out into the parking lot.

"Hey," the bouncer said. "You okay, man? You look like a truck ran over you."

"The priest ran over me," I said. "I'm going to get some air."

"I wouldn't do it, man," he said. "Let me get you a cab. This is not such a good neighborhood to stumble around in."

"Just want to get away," I mumbled. I weaved into the parking lot, bouncing from car to car, and then on down Agua Fria toward the bright-lighted sign of a bar that made the Club Alegría look like the Waldorf Astoria. It smelled strongly of sweat and spilled beer, a real working guy's hangout. I bought a round for the house, got drunker and drunker as the people around me chattered in español, and somewhere after midnight, I staggered out into the scraggly cedars around back to throw up. I thought my guts were going to come up. It went on for what seemed like hours: retching, my eyes rimmed with tears, thick strands of something repulsive dangling from my lips. Then I heard gravel shift and looked up from my red-tinged puddle to find four dark figures standing over me.

"Hey, pendejo," one behind me hissed. "You shouldn't wave money around like that unless you want to share it."

"You can have it," I said. "It won't make you happy. Voice of experience." I reached for my wallet, realized I'd left all but a roll of cash in the car somewhere, and then took a shot to the back of the head that brought me down hard on my side. Somebody said, "Hey, fuck you, man." Then they were kicking me in the ribs and in the back, blows were raining down on me, somebody was saying, "Bust his head open," and I welcomed the pain, deserved the pain, tried to explain that to them, and then somebody pulled the cash from my pocket and they walked off and I was lying in a puddle of my own juices.

When I woke up, the sun was coming up. It was Sunday morning, quiet as the grave. I groaned, rolled over, slowly pushed myself to my hands and knees, then with some effort, to my feet. I looked down at myself; I was caked with blood and vomit, and so I turned on a garden hose on the back wall and hosed myself down until at least I wasn't sticky and crackling when I walked.

I limped back down the street to the Club Alegría parking lot and found my father's car, still there and unharmed. The keys were in my front right pocket, jammed deep, and I guess none of my welcome wagon from the night before had thought to take them because nobody saw me drive up.

I started the car, gunned it, groaned again, and headed back toward St. Francis Drive. The Sangre de Cristos were dark blue with the sun behind them; the clouds above them floated orange and fluorescent. I turned on St. Francis, found a Texaco station open, and sloshed inside.

It hurt so much to move that I thought I had been pelted with bricks. St. Stephen if he'd lived, I thought, would have felt like this the morning after.

I got a breakfast burrito, two Dr. Peppers, and a Hostess honey bun. Kathy Cartwright, God bless her, would have done a war dance around me all the way to the checkout.

In her honor, I put the honey bun back.

When I got out to the car and managed to ease myself back in gingerly, I cracked open the first Dr. Pepper, ice cold, threw back my head, and let it glug down. It felt so good, I was so thirsty and my throat was so raw, that I drank it, the whole bottle, then started the next one. Finished it, too.

Then I just sat there for a moment, in the momentary but monumental clarity of that sugar rush, and watched the sun climb into the sky, watched the mountains turn green beneath it, watched the Sunday streets come to life.

Then I burped.

I had a full tank of gas, which struck me as significant, somehow, and so at last, I started the car, stuck it in reverse, and headed down St. Francis, south, out of Santa Fe. The mountains stayed in my rearview for some time—after I got on I-25 headed south toward Albuquerque, even—until at last I came to a long descent where I came off the black volcanic plateau and plunged down toward the Rio Grande Valley.

I was listening to 100.3, The Peak, and the music was good. The Sandia Mountains loomed to my left as I approached Albuquerque, and as I drove closer to town, at last I faced a major decision. The interchange between I-40 and I-25 could do many things: it could send me winging back east toward home; it could send me west out to California, site of my father's adventures; it could carry me south toward El Paso, maybe Mexico, maybe all the way to Chiapas if I wanted; it could whip me around and send me back to Santa Fe.

I couldn't decide. My moment of clarity had fled. Maybe I needed something stronger than Dr. Pepper, although a large part of me already doubted that.

So I decided not to decide. I would go wherever the car took me.

My lane turned into a right-hand exit onto I-40 West. "So let it be written," I said. "So let it be done."

I took the turn fast, headed west now, away from my family and friends, away from all the lives I'd lived up until then. People said my father and I were alike; maybe they were right after all.

I headed past the exits for what they called Old Town, past a Sheraton tower looming a few blocks south of the highway.

The multiple lanes became only four, two on each side, as I got outside the city and passed through the desolate plains: red sand soil, and mesas with bands of red rock around their bases like retaining walls.

That's when I saw him. Like before, I was already past him before I took him in, such a singular sight was he, but on the right shoulder, inches from the traffic on Interstate Highway 40, sat the Cross Man.

I'd already forgotten his name—Matthew something—and maybe I would have whooshed past him, since I was not the same man who stopped to pick him up before. But one other thing registered on me as I passed him: he was weeping.

The cross was lying flat, and he was sitting next to the interstate, weeping.

Common sense says keep on going; keep right on going, partner. "I stick my neck out for nobody," I said experimentally, but it didn't sound right. I sighed, pulled over, backed up on the shoulder to within about fifty feet of him. He didn't look up.

I got out, approached him obliquely—I didn't fancy him as the most stable guy under ordinary circumstances, and apparently these weren't them.

"Hey," I said, kneeling down beside him. "Hey, old-timer." I gave him a little nudge with my hand, and again the most brilliant blue eyes I've ever seen, now red-rimmed from crying and exhaustion, opened and seemed to take me in with a single glance. His face was crusted with sunburn far past the worst of my own recent experience—burns that had blistered and opened and been left untended. His lips were bloody. And although he was weeping, his cheeks were dry. His body had no moisture left for such trivial things as tears.

He looked as though he had been sitting in that one spot for a long time.

"Happy Father's Day," he said when he looked up at me, his voice shot through with bitterness as sharp as mine on my very worst days, and I recoiled like he'd bitten me.

"What?" I said. "What did you say?"

"Happy Father's Day. It is Father's Day, you know."

And it was, although I'd forgotten, being away from home

and having a dead child and all. "It's me," I said. "Clay Forester. I gave you a ride in Tennessee. I thought you were on your way to Sacramento," I said.

"This is as far as I'm going to get, son," he said. "Too tired to get up again. No reason to get up again." He turned his head up to me. "He lied to me."

"He?" I asked.

He gestured heavenward with a nod of his head. "She died before I got there. Found out three days ago. My daughter on the phone. Peggy, the youngest one. 'Don't come,' she told me. 'You got no right to come here. You left us years ago. You're not my father.' I been walking since then. Wouldn't nobody stop for me. And wouldn't matter if they had." He covered his face with his hands. "He said—He told me . . ." and he couldn't go on.

"Maybe you didn't hear right," I said gently. "Maybe he meant something else." He looked like hell—like I felt.

"You go on, son," he said, rubbing his eyes fiercely. "Go on. Leave me be."

"I'm not going to leave you here," I said. "I'm going to take you back into town. Come on, old timer." I put my arm underneath him and brought him to his feet with surprising ease. He seemed to weigh nothing at all—so little that I lifted him and carried him, bruised or broken as I was.

I buckled him into the passenger seat. "Now I'll get your cross on here somehow," I said.

"Leave it," he said. "Leave it be."

"You might feel differently later on," I said. "You might want to have it. Familiar things can be a comfort."

"I'm through with it," he said. "I'll find a new one."

I shrugged. "Okay," I said. I put the top up to protect him from the sun, got in, started the car, and headed for the next exit so I could turn around and come back into town.

"Where's that little dog you had?" he murmured, his eyes closed. "That little stinker?"

"Buster," I said. "I think he's in a good home. Or as good a home as a three-legged farting dog could expect."

"My God, but he smelled things up," he said, and I laughed.

"That was his sole gift," I said, knowing as I said it that it wasn't true.

I brought him to the Presbyterian Hospital emergency room in Albuquerque and checked him in.

"Are you his son?" they asked of course, and I shook my head. "But I'll be responsible for him." My father's money could be helpful in that much, at least. I filled out the forms as they got ready to take him into the treatment room, him so delirious with sun and dehydration and exhaustion that he barely knew me to say good-bye to.

"I'll call and check on you," I told him after they put him up on a gurney and were preparing to wheel him off. They already had IVs in him, and the young resident, one Dr. Purima, told me, "I think he's going to be just fine."

I leaned over Matthew Simons. "Everything will work out. Your girls will come around. You'll see."

He didn't seem to hear any of this, but his hand, drifting, found mine, squeezed hard. "Thank you, son. The Lord'll bless you for it." It was rote memory, maybe, or maybe, just maybe, he was finding his way back, too.

"You're welcome, Matthew," I said softly. "I hope you're right."

I turned away as they took him. The swinging doors closed behind him. It reminded me of something I had heard Ray say: "To love is to make a swinging door of your heart." Maybe he was quoting Barbara Jordan, the Great Woman. Maybe not. Anyway, I liked it.

The cell phone was lying out in the back floorboard, but I had spotted some pay phones on the way in, and I walked back through the waiting room with a real sense of purpose. Sugar or no, I seemed to be having another moment of clarity.

"Hello, Ray," I whispered when I got him on the phone. "Happy Father's Day."

"Happy Father's Day, Son," he said. "I love you."

That was as far as he could get. And then we both started to cry, and it was good.

It was good.

14

There were other calls to make, of course, but I waited until after I'd had the most incredible lunch at a place called the Route 66 Diner, a heavenly chocolate malt, a burger and onion rings to die for, until after I'd reversed my course eastward down Central Avenue—what used to be Route 66, the axis along which Albuquerque built itself—until I was back on the highway, headed toward home.

I woke up Otis—it was about one in the afternoon where he was—and started singing some Billy Paul for him, "Me and Mrs. Jones," dragging out the lyric like I was afflicted with palsy.

"Kill me now," he said. Then he woke up a little. "Clay? That you?"

"Wall to wall and treetop tall," I said.

"I am so beyond pissed at you," he said. Then he did his tight-assed George Bush voice. "You are out of the will, mister."

"I'm sorry," I said. "Really."

There was a short pause before he rejoined the conversation. "You, uh, you okay, there, pardner?"

I was hurtling around the south edge of the Sandias, and the Mustang was purring perfectly as I took a long upward grade. "I'm beginning to think that I'm gonna be," I said. "Listen, I just called to tell you I'm okay, and to apologize."

"For what," he said, and then the crunching noise of Froot Loops emanated from the phone. "Friendship means never having to say you're sorry."

"It's love," I corrected.

"Same thing," he said. "I'm going to get the whole story, right?"

"The whole story," I promised. "Small-town boy makes good. King falls from grace. The little tailor. The little engine that could."

"Are you still drinking?"

"Only the sunshine, my friend," I said. "Only the blue skies."

"I'm not awake enough for this," he said. "Call me later."

"Later," I said, and hung up. I waited until I'd finished climbing, until I was up on the high plains of Eastern New Mexico reversing my tracks, before I called Tracy. I stopped and got gas, drank more Dr. Pepper, and consumed an entire bag of Cheetos and a jumbo Butterfinger despite the remonstrating ghost of Kathy Cartwright, because, frankly, I was nervous as hell. Of course, putting all this stuff in my stomach could have accounted for the sudden feelings of nervous diarrhea that began to afflict me, the guts-in-a-coil thing that hadn't hit me much in recent years because I hadn't cared much about much of anything.

I misdialed her number twice and was getting ready to put it off for a long time, but the third time it went through, and wonder of wonders, she herself picked up the phone.

"Hello," she said, and the sound of her voice filled me with such wonder that it was all I could do not to drive into a ditch.

"Hello?" she said, and I knew from experience that she was a hair-trigger hanger-upper, so I somehow found my voice.

"Trace," I said, and then there was silence from her end of the phone. "Trace? It's me. Clay."

"Clay," she said. It was neutral, no corresponding wonder, but also no instant disconnect. I took that as a positive.

"Clay," I said. "Can you talk?"

"I have all the equipment," she said. "And don't say 'I'll say.' You're not anywhere near out of the doghouse yet, mister."

"I have so much to tell you, and maybe I can't say it all

right now," I said. "Some of it I want to say face to face. But I want you to know that I'm sorry for taking you for granted. Truly sorry."

"Are you drunk?" she asked. Maybe everyone was going to.

"No," I said. "Do you remember dancing at the prom?"

"Vaguely," she said. Nothing was going to be easy, and maybe that was okay. Maybe nothing worthwhile ever was.

"You remember we slow-danced to that song 'Always and Forever'?"

"Vaguely," she repeated, although her voice had lost its edge and I knew I had her.

"Do you remember I said that I wanted to sing that at our wedding?"

"Vaguely," she said for the third time, her voice tender as the darling buds of May.

"I still do," I said.

There was a long pause. My heart pounded, and I wiped my palms, suddenly slick with sweat.

"Talk to me," she said, and I did, all the way across New Mexico and well into Texas. I told her everything that had happened on the trip. I told her about my father, and how I thought I could finally forgive him. I told her about the ways the trip had changed me. I told her everything I had told Father Nieto, and although she was crying with me when she finished, she said something that surprised me.

"Clay, that's so sad, but it's also so good. Don't you see?"

"I don't," I admitted. "Not yet."

"I've wondered all these years how I could ever compete with Anna Lynn," she admitted. "I never told you. But you left me to think that things had been so perfect between you. Made me think of her as a martyred saint. To know that she was just like me, that you had things to work on, just like we do—oh, Clay. I can't tell you how this gives me hope."

"There's another thing," I said. "Another lie, I guess. I'm sorry. But you see, I wasn't a good father. I mean, I think I could be. Will be. But I was never there for Ray. He hardly knew me. I used to go in and see him at night, when he was asleep. I loved him. I know that. I used to sing to him, and hold my hand on his little stomach while he slept. Just to feel, you know, the life in him. His little heartbeat."

"Oh, Clay," she said.

"I miss him," I said. "I miss him a lot. I wish I had more memories."

"Oh, Clay," she said. "I'm so sorry. But we'll make new ones."

"Like Job's new children?"

"No," she said. "Like ours."

And what is a man to say to that? "Here's Amarillo," I said.

"What does that mean, exactly?"

"It means I'm going to have to hang up shortly and drive two-handed through some construction," I said.

"Is that all it means?"

"No," I said. "It means I love you very much. That I'm so grateful for you, for all you've put up with."

"Oh, that," she said, and I shushed her.

"I am," I said. "It means that even though I still think love is the most dangerous thing I know, I'm not going to be afraid. Or I'll try not to be."

"I'll help you," she said. "You know I will. We'll help each other. When will I see you?"

"Look for me Tuesday night."

"Not before then?"

"I've got some things I want to do on the way back. They'll take a little time. But I'll be there, don't you worry. Just tell your father I'm coming, and if it's after dark, let him know not to shoot me as a prowler. I know there have been times he's been tempted to."

"What kind of things?"

"Huh?"

"That you have to do?"

"Just a step in the right direction," I said. "I'll tell you all about it when I see you. Right after we make wild, passionate love."

"Well," she said, and suddenly she seemed nigh on speechless, as if someone had hit her in the face with a fish. "It sounds like I have a lot of things to look forward to."

She hung up. I had one more phone call I had to make then, part of those things I needed to do. I had to think for a second, but not much more than that, about a truck stop napkin written on with red crayon: an address. I pulled over so the road noise wouldn't obscure anything I had to say, and then I dialed.

"Operator," I said, "Nashville, Tennessee. Connect me with Daniel Cartwright, 1128 Fifth Avenue."

He answered on the third ring. "Hello," he said.

"Good morning, you son of a bitch," I said. "This is your wife's attorney speaking. I just want you to know that your days are numbered. 'And they shall know my name is the Lord when I lay my vengeance upon them.' That's Ezekiel 25:17, if you're wondering. Happy Father's Day."

Spluttering noises had started erupting from the phone after "son of a bitch," but it wasn't until I finished that he started saying "Who is this? Who the hell is this? Do you know who I am?"

I let him do that a couple of times, and then I answered him as though they weren't rhetorical questions.

"Yes, sir, I do. You, sir, are a bad man. A bad husband. A bad father. And for all I know, a bad lieutenant governor. But I'm betting you'll be a model prisoner."

And I hung up, laughing my ass off. That was enough to prime the pump.

Devious. And brilliant.

I stopped at the Potter County jail in downtown Amarillo and posted bail for a certain set of protestors still in custody. The jailer let me leave a message for Father Tom with his belongings, although it was so cryptic they asked me to repeat it twice.

"Jesus has no arms but ours," I said patiently as they wrote it down. "See that he gets that."

I drove on past the Big Texan restaurant with its free gargantuan steak, raising a middle finger on behalf of Father Jorge and tight-assed do-gooders everywhere. I stopped for the night just outside Oklahoma City, slept hard, got up, showered and shaved. Then I checked the phone book for two addresses.

The first was a men's clothing store. I didn't want just to buy off the rack, but I didn't have much choice. I walked in, gave them my stats, and went out wearing a dark-gray suit, button-down oxford shirt, Repp tie, and some great loafers. Italian leather, like the shoes in my dream.

There were already cars in front of the house when I pulled up, which was how I'd expected things to go; if you prime the pump, you get water. I walked up to the door, rang the bell, and was greeted by a flustered woman who bore some obvious family resemblance to Kathy Cartwright.

"Yes," she said, in the voice of someone who had already been put-upon to her limits.

"I'm Kathy's attorney," I said. "I had a feeling I needed to be here this morning."

She let me in, but didn't say much else beyond "She didn't say anything about an attorney. I was just telling these gentlemen that Kathy's not here. That she hasn't been here. That I don't know where she is."

They were in the living room: two OKC plainclothes cops sitting stiffly together on the couch, and in the wingback chair, rising at my approach, was the older man from the Mercedes chase.

"Gentlemen," I nodded to the cops. "Uncle Edward," I said to him.

He recognized me right away, of course; a suit is no disguise. "I don't believe I got your name," he said.

"My name, surprisingly, is immaterial. It's what I have to say that's important."

Kathy's sister—her name was Pam Standerfer, I suddenly remembered—went into her panicked spiel again. "I was just telling these gentlemen that Kathy's not here. That she hasn't been here. That I don't know where she is."

A stench like falling ker-plunk into the sewers suddenly meandered through the room; the plainclothes cops looked at each other with accusing faces, although I knew that no human being was capable of producing that odor.

"Of course you don't, Mrs. Standerfer," I said. "Although I very much doubt that these gentleman had a warrant to enter these premises, or a court order forcing Mrs. Cartwright to remand her son into the custody of Uncle Edward in the event they found her here."

"A mere formality," Uncle Edward said. "I can get one."

"Can you, now?" I said in a good Irish brogue. "You pin-striped pencil dick," I said. I stood up over him and reached for my inside pocket. One of the plainclothes guys made a surreptitious move toward his shoulder holster, so I made my movements light and clear, reaching with only two fingers while I talked. "I don't think your client wants to go to court to get his son back. In fact, I think you and he are probably so used to scaring people shitless that you've forgotten that the law is supposed to be about justice. It's easy to forget. I know. But your client doesn't deserve to get his son back." I pulled the pictures out, fanned them in front of his eyes. "He deserves justice for what he's done."

He looked up at them, his eyes opened a little wider, and he looked away. He hadn't known, or had suspected but tried not to admit it to himself. "There are lots more where these come from," I said.

Then I pivoted and showed the abuse photos to the cops, whose eyes hardened, and then they looked across at Uncle Edward with something very close to hatred. "I want it clearly understood, Uncle Edward, that these pictures, and more like them, are going to be introduced as evidence in a criminal trial that my firm and I will work toward night and day unless your client calls off his dogs and does right by his family. I mean no more harassment. I mean a divorce for my client, with no opposition from yours. And I mean a fair settlement, because you and I both know what she was driven to do to protect her child, don't we?"

He nodded, and it was with sadness. The plainclothes guys got up to leave, tipping imaginary hats to Pam as they went. "I didn't know," Uncle Edward said softly. "About the pictures. Any of that." He produced his wallet and pulled out a big roll of bills. "Please tell her I'm sorry. And to consider this an advance on that divorce settlement." I took his money, and

Uncle Edward shook his head, let out a sigh. "He's my nephew," he said at last, by way of explanation.

"I know," I said. "You can't choose your family. But you sure as hell can choose your clients."

He nodded. "Do you have a card?" he asked, opening his day planner to receive it. "I know this sounds strange under the circumstances, but I'd like to think we might do business together in the future."

"Thank you for asking," I said. "But I have a feeling that my clients from now on couldn't afford you. Oh, and sorry about the 'pin-striped pencil-dick' remark. It was just too good to pass up. Alliteration or something."

"Internal rhyme, I think," he said, closing his day planner, extending his hand, and administering a crisp shake. "But no matter. I'll convey your words to my client," he said, "and I'll see to it that things go smoothly."

"Thank you," I said.

"Thank you," he said, and inclining his head to me and to Pam, he made his way to the door.

"Tell them they can come out now," I said, handing over the wad of money. "Uncle Edward won't be back." And I too turned to go. "Tell her I'll be in touch."

"But I never got your name," she said.

"It doesn't matter," I said again. I felt like the Lone Ranger. "She'll know. Tell her it was the guy who insisted that Jesus had a penis. And that everything will be all right. For all of us. Tell her that."

"Okay," she said. "I will tell her."

And off I went. I could feel their eyes on me from the windows, so I raised a hand in a wave, or a salute—God knows Kathy Cartwright deserved both. Then I jumped in the car and off I went, into the climbing sun of Monday morning, through a city that seemed a lot less ugly today. Off I went, toward a family, friends, a woman I loved. Off I went, back toward a life that might finally be worth living.

Epilogue

"Ramblings around the River," by Sister Euless
—From *The Graham Star*, September 20, 2000

My nephew Clay Forester and his bride, the former Tracy York, were married Saturday in a service at the Grace Tabernacle. Otis Miller was best man, and Glennis McDowell was matron of honor. Brother Carl Robinson officiated at the service. The groom and my sisters Ellen and Evelyn and I played and sang. A reception followed in the fellowship hall before Clay and Tracy departed for their honeymoon, a two week drive in their Mustang convertible. The happy couple will conclude their drive and make their home in Santa Fe, New Mexico, where Clay says he intends to bone up on environmental law, take up indigents and immigrants—whatever that means—and populate a large house with children. "Oh, maybe I'll play a little salsa," he said.

We are joyful beyond expressing, although it will be awfully quiet around the house without him. Children grow up so quickly these days.

The leaves are turning in the mountains, green to golds and reds and oranges, beautiful as a painting. It's just another sign of God's love for us in every season. Think of that as you see the leaves change, and give thanks.

Author's Note

No one writes a book without help, and moreover, no one publishes a book after years and years of striving to do just that without having a list of people to acknowledge—a list of which admittedly, this accounting can only scratch the surface. While such lists are usually of no interest except to people who think they might be on them—or to curious folks who wonder if the writer knows famous people or is going to acknowledge heretofore unmentioned sexual liasions—they truly serve a vital function: to recognize the people behind the artist who helped him or her achieve something of worth. So here goes:

The *Anchorage Daily News* was an invaluable source of information on the *Exxon Valdez* disaster and the subsequent legal wrangling. Jonathan Kwitny's *Endless Enemies: The Making of an Unfriendly World* first taught me about American-sponsored terrorism, and Renny Golden and Michael McConnell's *Sanctuary: The New Underground Railroad* gave me vital background about the Sanctuary movement and the Catholic Church in Latin America. Donna Jean Garrett taught me years ago about the importance of being a committed activist, and not a little of her spirit informs some of these characters. A Spring 2000 article in the *Houston Chronicle* gave me specifics on groundwater pollution caused by the Pantex atomic weapons plant, and the *Santa Fe Reporter* covered the Los Alamos wildfires and the allegations of radioactive contamination from the Los Alamos research facilities in the summer of 2000 with its usual excellence. The work of New Mexico landscape artist Louisa

McElwain was an inspiration and a model for the art described in this book. Tennessee State Senator and good friend Roy Herron refreshed my memory on Interstate 40 as it runs through his beautiful state and also answered some useful legal and governmental questions. Kathleen Norris's *The Cloister Walk* satisfied my curiosity about the vocation of oblate. The story of the armless Christ comes from Annie Lamott's *Operating Instructions*. Thanks to all of these.

I want to thank my friends and family for supporting this dream. My parents, grandparents, brothers and sisters, Tina Marie, Jake, and Chandler all share in this accomplishment. Good friends—Tom Hanks, Trisha Lindholm, Scott Walker, Chris Seay, Bob Darden, Blake Burleson, Rachel and Andy Moore, Martha Serpas, Vicki Marsh Kabat, Frank Leavell, John Ballenger, Michael Beaty, Ray Burchette, Rick Barton, Sandy Pearce, and too many others to mention—encouraged me day in and day out. Donna Jean Garrett always believed this day would come. I hope she welcomes it now and knows my appreciation. Dozens of editors of magazines, journals, and newspapers published my work over the past twenty years as I learned my craft, for which much thanks. And my agent, Jill Grosjean, loved my words and gave me unsparingly of her time, expertise, and affection. She is a true gift. May God bless you all.

I have been fortunate enough to learn from and to be inspired by many people. These have been my teachers: Robert Olen Butler, Annie Lamott, Lee Smith, the late Andre Dubus, Richard Ford, Mary Rohrberger, the late Hansford Martin, T. R. Pearson, Leonard Leff, W. P. Kinsella, Gordon Weaver, Dennis and Vicki Covington, Bret Lott, Elinor Lipman, Jack Butler, Carol Dawson, Will Campbell, Michael Curtis, Elizabeth Cox, Marc Ellis, Gregory Wolfe, Stewart O'Nan, Rodger Kamenetz, and four others I will never have the opportunity to meet but who have taught me much nonetheless about life and art: William Faulkner, Walker Percy, Thomas Merton, and Flannery O'Connor.

The Pirate's Alley Faulkner Society of New Orleans recognized me some years ago with their prize medal, and cofounders Joe DeSalvo and Rosemary James have been my champions and friends ever since. The Society's efforts in recognizing and promoting great writing are unmatched in America, and I hope they will be able to continue their good work for years to come.

I must also thank my colleagues, my students, and the administration of Baylor University, where I have written and taught for a dozen happy years now. Dean Wallace Daniel, former dean Bill Cooper, Provost Don Schmeltekopf, and English department chairs James Barcus and Maurice Hunt have supported my work with course reductions, sabbaticals, and encouragement. I'm particularly pleased to note that *Free Bird* was written during the summer sabbatical from teaching that I was given in 2000.

Matt and Julie Chase-Daniel entrusted us with their house in Santa Fe, New Mexico, during that summer of 2000, and I believe the book could not have been written nearly as well or as quickly without their generosity. Santa Fe's spirit permeates these pages.

And the music I played in the basement of the Chase-Daniels' house while I wrote was instrumental in inspiring me to write: Bruce Hornsby's *Spirit Trail* and *Hot House*, Shawn Colvin's *A Few Small Repairs*, the Goo Goo Dolls' *Dizzy Up the Girl*, Bruce Springsteen's *Darkness on the Edge of Town*, *Lucky Town*, and *Human Touch*, Bob Schneider's *Lonelyland*, Roy Orbison's *Black and White Night*, and Stevie Ray Vaughn's entire body of work. I consider these artists to be almost cocreators of this book, although of course I will take the blame for the boring parts.

No endorsements were paid this author by Cracker Barrel restaurants, the Dr. Pepper Bottling Company, nor any of the other products, companies, institutions, places, or objects mentioned in this book. I consider myself a literary realist, and part of being a realist is creating a recognizable world. But it should go without saying that all of these real-world elements are used fictionally and should not be associated with their fictional treatments here.

Well . . . except that Exxon really was responsible for spilling millions of gallons of crude oil in a pristine Alaskan sound, but I think we all know that.

Greg Garrett plays Yamaha guitars, Fender amplifiers, and Martin strings.

And finally, I thank God, the First and Foremost, for giving me this story. I've never written so well or so quickly, and even though it almost killed me, I believe God is helping me, like Clay, to come through the darkness and into the light.

Thomas Merton closes his autobiography, *The Seven Storey Mountain*, in this fashion: *"Sit finis libri, non finis quaerendi,"* or, "Let this be the ending of the book, but by no means the end of the searching."

Amen and amen, brother.

Greg Garrett
Austin, Texas
May 2001